DEATH
BY CUDDLE
Club

DEATH BY CUDDLE Club

A Dix Dodd Mystery

N.L. WILSON

(the writing team of Norah Wilson and Heather Doherty)

PUBLISHED BY:

SOMETHING SHINY
PRESS
Norah Wilson / Something Shiny Press
P.O. Box 30046, Fredericton, NB, E3B 0H8

Edited by TheAuthorsRedRoom.com
Cover by The Killion Group, Inc.
Book Design by Hale Author Services

Chapter 1

AS A THANK you gift, my mother sent me pastries. Isn't that sweet? Oh, wait, did I say *pastries*? No. Not pastries. That's what a normal 70-year-old woman might do. Yep, a normal mother would send her culinarily challenged PI daughter yummy treats as a thank you for getting her out of trouble in Florida. For saving the diamond my father gave her (AKA, the family jewels). And — let us not forget — keeping her 70-year-old butt out of jail on a trumped-up murder rap. But Katt Dodd will never be accused of being normal. What she sent me were *pasties*. Yep, stick-'em-on, twirl-'em-round pasties. (Well, I couldn't get my twirl on, but I could get a pretty good sway thing going.) Bless her skinny-dipping little … heart.

Yes, so, post-Florida, I was now the not-so-proud owner of be-tasseled hot pink pasties. Ah, a wardrobe fit for a queen. A *drag* queen. Not quite so appropriate for a professional, 40-ish, amazing-yet-modest private detective. Possibly the most amazing private detective in all of Marport City, Ontario.

Okay, so I'm not so modest.

And yeah, maybe not everyone saw it that way, especially not the guys back at Jones and Associates — the good ol' boys club where I used to work. But, hey, they'd bet — openly — that I'd never make it on my own. That I would be out of business within a very few months, and would come back crying on their doorstep when I landed on my ass. Well, I've shed a few tears in these past months, but none over them, and sure as hell none on their cruddy doorstep. I guess they don't know how well-padded that ass of mine is!

Wait, that didn't come out right.

I did mention I'm 40, right? I've got my fair share of padding there.

But what the hell — isn't 40 the new … 40? I wouldn't exactly call me a cougar, though some would. Actually, some do. How I love them all the more for it!

This would probably be a good time to mention Dylan Foreman, PI in training. Smart, sexy as sin — and OMG, so handsome! Tall and lean, but plenty wide at the shoulders and narrow at the hips, just like I like them. (Or high, wide and handsome, as my mother would say.) Thick, dark brown hair, chocolate brown eyes. And all of 28 years old. He'd been my apprentice since shortly after I hung up my shingle in the dilapidated rental office building on the outskirts of town. My friend since day one. And lately, dangerously close to a friend with benefits.

Yes, Dylan had joined me back when I was in that tiny, grungy suite, which was all my budget would stretch to. You know the kind of office building I'm talking about. Worst part of the city, motley characters hanging around the alleys out back. And inside, that faint, what-the-heck-is-that? odor in the stairwell (though you really don't want to know). And the tiny, dusty office itself with the dead aloe vera plant on the window ledge . . .

And here we were, home again.

Yes, we'd moved back. Go figure. The very same office we'd left behind when the success of the Case of the Flashing Fashion Queen allowed us to move into better digs.

Why were we shuffling back into the old place? Economics, of course.

I'd bought Mother's condo from her. Now that she was living full-time in Florida, I couldn't continue to live there rent-free under the pretext of looking after the place. No more use of the BMW, either, since we'd returned it to her in Florida. All of which meant I was no longer able to afford the cushy office with the thick-piled carpet that seemed to bury your feet up to your ankles when you walked through it. (I have calf muscles of steel now.) I even had to return that tweeting, all-in-one copier/printer/fax machine I so loved (I just nipped in under the grace period to rescind the contract). And the voice-changer? It went back, too. I kept the high-tech coffee pot, however. I mean, c'mon — it ground the coffee beans and delivered frothed milk.

The move back to our old digs couldn't have been better timed, though. Business had been dropping off as of late, no doubt due to the dismal economy. Amazing how blind an eye people could turn to phi-landering spouses during hard times. Divorce was costly for everyone, and not just emotionally. So we didn't mind the decrease in rent that went with the lower class of accommodation. Maybe in this part of town, people who could afford a divorce might be more comfortable consulting a PI whose offices were a little further removed from their usual spheres. One could only hope.

So yes, Dix Dodd, PI, and Dylan Foreman, PI apprentice, were busy unpacking on this fine, quiet Saturday in October. Unpacking boxes, arranging furniture, blowing up Blow-Up Betty and tucking her into the corner. Amazingly — or perhaps not so amazingly — no other tenant had occupied the office since we'd moved out. I uprighted the aloe vera plant and discovered it was plastic. Huh. It still looked half dead. Now that was realism for you.

We had a couple of mini-bottles of sparkling wine chilling in the mini-fridge (hey, I'm all about class). That had been Dylan's contribution (the fridge, not the wine). I'd bought the bubbly, intending it as a reward for us when we finished the unpacking. Dylan's dark eyes had seemed to grow just a tad darker when he'd seen those little bottles. Probably for the same reason my whole body had flushed hot standing in the liquor store four hours ago when I'd bought them. We'd been dancing around each other since Florida. My logical brain still thought it was a bad idea, but my libido disagreed. So far, Dylan had seemed to be content to let the two Dix's duke it out, but he wasn't above stacking the deck in favor of Lust-Crazed Dix. And he damned well knew which Dix had bought the sparkling wine.

So, as we unpacked that fine Saturday, all was quiet. Even with the sharpened edge of awareness between us, it was fun. All seemed good and right, just as it should be.

When will I ever learn?

Quiet didn't last out the afternoon. Fun escaped out the window (and probably got beat up; I tell you, it's a tough neighborhood). And good and right? Ah, that didn't last out the afternoon either.

Because there came a knock at the door. One that made my intuition tinkle like those little bells they put on the end of pasties tassels — Whoops, sorry. TMI. Let's just say the hair on the back of my neck stood up against my collar.

And then the door opened.

Damn.

I regarded the tall, slightly rumpled man standing in my doorway with astonishment. I rubbed my eyes and looked again. Still there. "Oh, crap."

He strode into my office, letting the door fall closed behind him. "Nice to see you, too, Dixieland."

You guessed it. It was my nemesis, the very last man I expected to see at my door. Well, minus an arrest warrant and handcuffs. Yep, it was none other than Detective Richard Head, of the Marport City PD, known by the unkind, uncouth, and just plain immature as Dickhead.

"*Dickhead?*" I said. "What are *you* doing here?"

He mumbled something unintelligible as he walked through to my office.

Dylan and I followed him into the room. I shot a glance at my desk. Five minutes ago, I'd dumped a box of my personals on my blotter, ready to fire them into the various drawers. I gave a quick scan of the items. No, no tampons. No neatly wrapped maxi pads. What a shame. Dickhead tended to go green around the gills around that kind of stuff.

I turned back to him. "Sorry, I didn't catch what you mumbled. Could you repeat that?"

His jaw worked a minute. Finally, he said, "I need your help." The words were grating, reluctant, and he turned toward my desk, no doubt so he wouldn't have to see the glee in my eyes at his admission.

A quick look at Dylan revealed he was just as astonished as I was. Understandable, considering that it wasn't that long ago that the good detective had been hot and horny to land me in jail for the murder of one of Marport City's rich and famous. I had ultimately solved that case (naturally), saving my ass in the process and causing Detective Head much gnashing of teeth.

Dylan came to stand by me. Was it my imagination, or did he stand a little closer than normal? And was he trying to make himself even taller than his 6' 4"?

"Detective," Dylan said.

"Foreman," Dickhead acknowledged, but he gave Dylan just the briefest of glances before turning his attention away again.

The masculine pissing contest barely registered. I was too busy savoring Dickhead's earlier words. *I need your help.*

"What are you grinning for, Dixieshit?"

I let my smile widen. "Ah, the memories."

With a barely suppressed growl, Detective Head sat. Well, sort of sat. We hadn't gotten around yet to bringing the chairs up from the moving van, so he half leaned/half sat on the edge of my desk. He looked down at the assortment of pens, pencils, odds and ends of makeup …

"Wow. Why do you have so many pairs of tweezers?" He turned to me with a close and scrutinizing look.

"PI stuff," I answered hastily, fighting the urge to raise a hand to my upper lip. "Every good PI has at least a couple sets."

"A couple? Looks like you have a half dozen."

"Yeah ... well, I'm a damn good PI."

Dylan, I noticed, was looking a little confused, too. Oh God.

"So what brings you here, Dickhead?" There. That should change the subject.

Except it barely got a rise out of him. That snide smile he habitually wore (well, at least in his interactions with me) was gone. And — unless I was badly mistaken — so was a good bit of the confidence he usually carried. "Like I said before, I need your help, Dix."

Dix? He wasn't taking the opportunity to make fun of my name. This had to be serious.

Still, I was suspicious. "*My* help?"

Okay, I've had a couple high profile cases, but my specialty is trailing cheating spouses. In fact, that's how Dickhead and I had met. I'd been trailing him on his ex-wife's dime. Were they back together, and *he* was suspicious of *her* now? No, that hardly seemed likely. She'd taken him to the cleaners. No way were those two living under the same roof again. In fact, Dickhead had been forced back under his mother's roof out of economic necessity, last time I checked. (Did I mention divorce was expensive?) Was he seeing someone else and wondering about her fidelity? Or — oh, wait, hold the phone! — maybe it was his mother! Was the old girl seeing someone? Some old gent who seemed a little too smooth and who needed checking out? (Hey, if you knew *my* mother, you'd know I'm not even kidding.)

Dickhead rasped a hand over his chin. I couldn't help but notice that it was a strong, attractively stubbled chin. (And no, it didn't do anything for me. But just because I despised the man doesn't mean I'm blind. Objectively speaking, he's not a bad looking guy, if you like 'em muscle-bound and lantern-jawed.)

"It's complicated." He cleared his throat and inserted a finger beneath his collar to loosen his already loose tie. Man, he looked uneasy. Stressed. Which made me feel uneasy and stressed ... because it was just *killing* me not to mock him.

"You want me to tail some —"

"No!" The clipped word cut me off, and yet he was still unwilling to elaborate. What was eating at him so?

Dylan cut in, "You're involved with a gang and you —"

"That ain't it either, Foreman."

Dylan and I glanced at each other. Oh, yeah. It was *on*. And it was my turn.

"You lost your badge to a hooker and you need us to track her down!"

Dickhead snorted. "Get real."

I shrugged. Seemed like a pretty real possibility to me.

Dylan's turn: "You … you found out you have an illegitimate son, and you want us to find him!"

Damn, that was a good one.

"Jesus, Foreman."

I was up again. "You … you were looking out the window while recovering from a broken leg. And … and you saw your neighbor across the courtyard acting suspiciously. And now his wife is missing and there's a little dog digging up the flowers and —"

It was Dylan who snorted this time. "That's *Rear Window*, Dix."

Whoops. Hitchcock's best. No wonder it seemed so brilliant.

Dickhead glowered as Dylan and I continued to throw out increasingly ridiculous scenarios at his expense. He clearly wasn't enjoying this as much as we were. In fact, I think it was safe to say he was annoyed. Then again, he wasn't exactly jumping in to enlighten us as to the real reason for his presence, was he now?

And that's when I got it. That's when it really sank in. The guy was *here*, at *my* office. He didn't like me any better than I liked him. This was serious. This was —

"Murder," he said suddenly. "I think someone's been murdered."

I blinked. "You suspect a *murder*?"

His brow furrowed fiercely. "That's what I said, isn't it?"

Testy.

"Why don't you go to the police, then?" Dylan asked, beating me to the punch. "You *are* a cop, after all."

Dickhead cut Dylan a hard look before turning back to me. "It's complicated," he said again. And judging by that look of consternation on his face, I had no doubt of it. "I don't *know* there has been a murder. I only suspect there's been one. I have no proof. No evidence. No motive. And no one willing to come forward."

"Not even you?" I didn't have to work hard to inject the words with incredulity. "You suspect a murder may have taken place, but you're not willing to come forward?"

He glared at me. And if looks could kill ... well, I'd not have made it past the third grade, but that's not important right now.

Then something remarkable happened. The light of battle went out in his eyes as he reined himself in. At that, I felt a frisson of unease crawl up my back like a spider. What the hell was going on here?

"No, not even me, Dix." Dickhead heaved an in-for-a-penny sigh. "It's a club. An exclusive and private club that I belong to. Members are dying."

"How many?" Dylan asked.

"Two in the last month. The M.E. called it natural causes, but it's just ... fishy to me. Feels wrong."

"Did you know the deceased?" I asked.

"Not well. Only by first name and ... well, not well. But they seemed healthy enough. Not at all sickly."

"Old?"

"Yeah, *old*. About your age, Dix."

Mentally, I punched his shoulder. Hard. Oh, and physically, I did the same. Dickhead had been expecting it. Hadn't even flinched in that *totally worth it* kind of way.

"The point is," he continued, "in both cases, each of these folks was at the club one night, dead the next day. No sign of foul play. But I don't like it."

"Yeah, but without any proof —" Dylan started to say.

"But you feel it in your gut," I interrupted.

It was with serious eyes that Detective Head considered me now. "You know it, Dix. In my gut. I know you do."

He was right. I'd had my share of those niggles and nudges of intuition, and I wasn't foolish enough to imagine I was the only one. Hell, cops were famous for it. Gut instinct, jokes aside.

This was it. This was real. This was a case I'd be taking. And I told Dickhead so.

"You'll need to infiltrate the club," he said.

Here's where I got nervous. "Want to elaborate on what kind of club this is?" I was having visions of needing to wear a neoprene cat suit and leather boots with five-inch heels.

"It's a club. An exclusive ... club."

Somehow, I didn't think I'd be at a quilting bee. "Right. A club. So you said."

Dickhead scrubbed a hand down his face. "It's a cuddle club."

"I'm sorry, you had your hand over your mouth. It's a *what* club?"

"I said cuddle club. It's a cuddle club!"

"Ha!" I snorted. "Good one."

He wasn't laughing.

"I've heard of those," Dylan said.

"Yeah, well, I've heard of the Great Wall of China and that doesn't mean it's real."

Sa-lam!

Oh, wait, did I say *Great Wall of China*? Er, not so much of a slam, then. How did I screw these things up? I should have said *the Tooth Fairy* or *honor among thieves* or *monogamous men,* but no —

I realized then that both men were just looking at me, obviously waiting for me to say something (preferably something comprehensible this time). I looked at Dickhead then turned back to Dylan. "He's not kidding, is he?"

He wasn't.

Oh boy.

I cringed. Man, did I cringe.

The phone rang in the outer office and Dylan excused himself to go answer it.

I asked Dickhead a few more questions: When did they meet next? Where? What did I need to wear to fit in? I almost choked on his answers, but I took the case anyway.

And I named it Death by Cuddle Club.

Chapter 2

OKAY, SO FIRST thing I did when the door closed behind Dickhead was to open my desk drawer and rake all those sets of tweezers into it with one swoop of my shirtsleeve-covered forearm, effectively dusting the desktop at the same time. (Martha Stewart, eat your heart out!) Then I went down to the moving van to retrieve one of the office chairs and brought it back up in the elevator. The moment I rolled it behind the desk, I sat. And I did all this, it seemed, in a daze ... a genuine WTF daze.

I'd just agreed to work for Detective Richard Head. I'd enjoy the pretty penny that he was paying me (and knowing it was coming out of his own personal pocket and not the City's coffers would make it all the prettier). I would enjoy showing off to my nemesis, yet again, my mad PI skills. (Did I mention there is no love lost between Dickhead and me?)

But as I sat there, what really hit me — like a sledge hammer — was this: I was going to infiltrate a cuddle club.

A freakin' cuddle club! Dix Dodd does not do close. Dix Dodd doesn't do warm and cuddly. I had a guy in a pretty tight headlock once, but that's about as close to cuddling as I'm comfortable with.

Yet, seriously, what the hell was Dickhead doing hanging out in such a place? Dude, he would be the dead last person I'd want to cozy up with. Shudder. Mind you, I could be (okay, totally am) letting my animosity toward the individual color my perception.

But really, what was he doing there to begin with? It's not like he's a troll or anything. I mean, I imagine he could get a date, as long as he could keep that living-with-his-mother thing under wraps.

Plus he's a cop. Lots of women find a badge hot.

Also — hello? — he's a cop. He gets to grapple with arrest resistors. Wrestle uncooperative prisoners to the ground. What more could a person ask for in terms of physical contact?

Ah, physical contact ... flashlight bulge between us. Dylan's weight pressing me into the sagging mattress of my mother's pull-out sofa bed ...

"Thinking about the case, Dix?"

Dylan's question jolted me out of my drifting down thoughts, and I looked up to see him standing in the doorway, wearing a knowing smile.

I fought the blush I could feel rising in my neck. "Absolutely." Then I went on to fill him in on what Dickhead had said.

"So, pajamas, huh?" That deadly grin of his started slow and spread sexily. "You gonna get a pair of those footie ones for your debut?"

"Smartass." I peeled my gaze away from his mouth. "I don't think they make them in my size." God, what kind of sick, perverted place was it where the patrons wore pajamas? And hugged?

"I could totally get a pair for you. My Aunt Gert makes them."

I lifted an eyebrow. "She makes adult-sized footie pajamas?"

"Yep. Actually, she makes all kinds of pajamas, but I think the footies would be especially fitting." He struggled to keep a straight face. "You know — made out of fleece, little trap door behind you. Soft, cozy ... cuddly."

I couldn't help it — I shuddered at the image.

Dylan dissolved into laughter. And by laughter, I mean he chortled so hard he snorted. Unfortunately, he was too close to the coffee machine for me to throw anything at him.

So I smiled right back. "Actually, Dylan, they sound great. Pick up a pair for yourself while you're there."

He blinked. "Wait — what? Me?"

Ha! I guess the image of footie pajamas wasn't quite so funny when he was picturing them on himself. "Yes, you. You're infiltrating the cuddle club with me."

"But ... um ... wouldn't it be better if only one of us is on the inside? You know, so I can work things from another angle?"

"Not a chance."

"What about our other cases?"

"We have no other cases right now. Unless that phone call was a new client?"

He shook his head. "Just a preliminary nibble. She'll call back; she definitely needs our services. But I imagine it'll take her a few weeks to work her resolve up."

I nodded, knowing Dylan was right. He had an unerring sense about these things.

"But she might call back sooner," he said, brightening. "I should probably be here."

I laughed. "Forget it, buster. You're coming with me."

By the way, it wasn't vengeance on him for laughing at my predic-
ament that gave me the notion we were both needed on campus, so to
speak. I'm not that petty. Oh wait, I am. But it wasn't just petty vengeance. Did I mention Dylan is handsome as hell? Sexy as sin? I could
just picture every female in the joint wanting some of that snuggle-up
action. And yes, Dylan had a way with people that I never would — he
can talk to people. Win confidences. Lend a sympathetic ear. And he
did so genuinely.

I looked at my watch — it was later in the day than I'd thought.
Cuddle club went into cuddle-mode at 6 p.m., according to Dickhead.
We'd have to get moving to be ready.

"Cheer up," I told him. "At least this means we can postpone
the unpacking."

And those mini-bottles of wine ...

Dylan and I drove in silence through the streets of Marport City. Though
it had stopped raining an hour ago, the blacktop was shiny under the
glow of the streetlights and the lights that shone from shop windows.
People milled about. A short man, maybe mid-sixties, eyes downcast
and hands shoved into pockets, made his determined, hurried way along
the sidewalk. At the last moment, with no warning, he ducked into a
doorway and disappeared. Meeting his mistress, I figured. My gaze fell
on a well-dressed man — late twenties or early thirties — who also hurried
along, but unlike the other fellow, his eyes darted around — left, right,
behind. I was guessing he didn't want to be seen in this part of town.
Probably had something to do with the straining closed hand inside the
right pocket of his London Fog. Yep, I'd bet a buck he'd scored what he'd
come for — coke, likely — and was anxious to get back across town. Man
needed to find a dealer who delivered if he couldn't be cooler than that.

Yeah, I know people; I trust my instincts. And so, I had to admit,
did Dickhead.

Shortly after Detective Head had left my office, the fax groaned to
life and spewed out papers with the particulars — who, what, when and
where. Wow. I'd kind of expected a home address. You know, someone's
basement rec room or something. But apparently this club was part of a

franchise. Gaetan Land — with ten locations to serve you.

Nine of them in California.

Though why Gaetan Gough chose Marport City to break into the Canadian cuddle market was beyond me. Why hadn't he given Toronto that ... um ... honor? That would seem more logical. But for whatever reason, Gaetan Gough had picked quarters in my little city — specifically, down on 33rd Street, in one of the newer complexes close to Donatta's Karaoke Bar — to set out his sign, promote his cuddles, and sell his wares.

Yes, *wares*. That last part has surprised me, too, but I'd seen it in black and white on the flyer Dickhead had faxed over: "A large assortment of products ..." What the hell could that mean? I guess I'd soon find out.

"So, tell me again about the deceased."

I glanced over at Dylan. He was driving tonight. Which was fair, I suppose, since it *was* his car. Well, strictly speaking, it was his mother's car — a very comfortable SUV; Dylan drove a motor bike. And I was currently without wheels, having returned Mom's BMW to her in Florida recently. Which, needless to say, sucked.

"Oh, so you're talking to me again?" I tried to sound miffed.

He rolled his eyes at my comment.

Dylan had been a little on the quiet side since I'd sprung the news that he'd be joining me on this escapade. It was not the way he'd intended to spend his Saturday night, clearly, because he'd excused himself to make a call, cancelling whatever plans he'd had. I tried not to listen in as he placed the call from the outer office. But even with the heavy antique door shut between us, it was hard not to overhear at least *something*. Especially when you're crouched down on the floor with your ear pressed to the keyhole.

Had he had a date lined up? I mean, a *date* date on this Saturday night? He'd cancelled something with somebody, that's for sure. And as he'd passed on his regrets, he'd said, "Yeah, I know. Work. What can you do? But I'll make it up to you."

Not that I was jealous.

Well, maybe a little.

Dylan turned onto 33rd. We'd be at our destination very shortly.

"Okay, the deceased," I said. "First to croak was Faynelle St. James, 53-year-old single mother of a 20-year old son. She managed the janitorial staff at Marport General Hospital. Cause of death was massive heart attack. No history of heart problems, but then again, heart disease is statistically more likely to go undiagnosed in women. Two days later:

Telly Smith. Keeled over from cardiac arrest. Now this guy did have a bit of a history — he was taking a cholesterol-lowering drug and some other meds to control his blood pressure. He worked for catering services up at the university. Guy reportedly wasn't very active. Couch potato."

"Well, I can see why the M.E. wouldn't be too suspicious, especially with nothing to link the two cases. Which there wouldn't be." Dylan pulled into the parking lot next to the building on 33rd, and sent me a serious look as he killed the engine and pocketed the keys. I waited for it ... "Because no one talks about cuddle club."

It was my turn to roll my eyes.

As we walked into the building, my insides clenched. Seriously. As we moved down the long, low-lit hallway toward Suite 106 where Dickhead had directed us, it was like every fiber of my body was rebelling against this plan. I distracted myself by studying the building. Half the suites we passed were vacant, but quite a few housed fledgling businesses. Probably an incubation center. Businesses starting up, half of them with government grants, then failing, moving out to make room for the next batch of hopeful entrepreneurs.

"Try to loosen up, Dix," Dylan whispered.

"I *am* loose," I grated.

The sign said WELCOME TO GAETAN LAND. Oh God, there were flowers adorning it, teddy bears and fluffy clouds.

Breathe, Dix. Breathe.

Dylan opened the door for us.

It was the music that hit me first. Sleepy and slow, like a lullaby. The walls of the club were a tranquil sky blue, unadorned with pictures but bordered with a strip of fluffy cloud wallpaper running along the top. The center of the room was a sea of soft, plush carpet, and all the furniture — such as it was — lined the walls. Lots of chairs, but not a good, old-fashioned straight-back job among them. No, not chairs, I realized. Plush, comfortable loveseats. Every one of them built — no, *curved* — to hold two. There were even three kicked-out La-Z-Boy recliners around the room, currently occupied by a few old geezer types. The lighting was low. The fish swimming in the tanks in every corner were serene. Everyone looked so peaceful, so relaxed. At ease. Sipping what looked like fruit smoothies from large glasses (complete with the Gaetan Land cloud-strewn logo on the sides) and smiling as they chatted casually. Two women — one older and one younger — were handing out the frothy drinks. They each got a way-too-appreciative hug from everyone as they made the rounds.

Yeah, this just was not right!

"Er, Dix," Dylan whispered. "They're not wearing pajamas."

"I see that, Dylan."

"And we *are*!" he hissed.

"I know." *Damn.* "This is Dickhead's fault. He said people wore their pajamas," I ground out. "I'm going to kill him."

"Did he actually say pajamas?"

"Yes! No. I mean, I think he said leisurewear or something like that. But that's just code for pajamas, right?"

"No. *Lounge*wear might be code for pajamas. *Leisure*wear, however, would be code for a track suit or sweats. Possibly even pajama pants and T-shirt. But not full pajamas."

"Crap."

And then Gaetan spotted us standing in the doorway. (I knew it had to be Gaetan from Dickhead's description: "Look for a sawed off Q-Tip.")

"Ohhhhhhhhhhhhhh!" Gaetan drew the word out like he was having an orgasm. Like it was a ten-syllable word. The short, smiling man was clad from his neck down to his bare feet in blue velour — the same blue as the walls. His blond hair — oh God, *cloud-like* blond hair — was styled in a perfectly round and perfectly tight afro. Perm. It had to be a perm. He clapped his hands together in a steepled, just-so-delighted/I'm-a-seal fashion as he raced toward us.

"Easy, Dix," Dylan said, noticing I'd gone into a hunched, defensive stance as though to repel a tackle. "Loosen up."

What can I say? It's an instinct. Nevertheless, I tried to take his advice and make my muscles relax. But Gaetan was still bearing down on me.

Please don't hug me. Please don't hug me, I mentally pleaded as Gaetan charged. But oh hell, it wasn't working.

"For the love of God," I shrieked, "Don't —"

He hugged me.

"Ohhhhhhhhhhh," he said. (But it was more of an owww this time, and definitely not an orgasm. I think he hit an elbow. Yeah, that's it — his fault.) "We have a tense one here!"

Ya think?

To Gaetan's credit, though, his smile never faltered as he turned to Dylan.

Dylan opened his arms wide, bent down, and hugged the much shorter man. I watched his uncringing eyes as he did so. Oh, man, how could he do that so easily? Gaetan looked practically lost in Dylan's arms. Oh geez, practically vibrating.

Finally they pulled apart. Gaetan held Dylan out at arm's length — his chubby little hands on those rock hard guns. "My, you're a tall one. Strong." He felt Dylan's arm muscles. "Oh, a natural!" He turned to me. "And you're … you're …"

I waited.

"You're welcome here too!"

"Gee, thanks."

"We're new here," Dylan said, as though that weren't perfectly obvious. Hello? We were the only ones wearing pajamas. I groaned inwardly. Again.

"Yes, yes," Gaetan said. "But there's always room for more."

"Nice place you have here," I said. I looked around the room as if I hadn't already cataloged every inch of it, noting all the exits. But this time I was looking at the people, the faces. Who looked too at ease to be sober? Who looked too tense? I waited for that niggle and nudge of my intuition as I scanned the crowd. But then something else caught my professional PI attention as I looked around the room.

It was a blood-curdling shriek.

Chapter 3

"Dix!" That high, female shriek came again. "Omigod, it is you. Dix—"

"Davidson!" I cut Elizabeth Bee off quickly before she could spill my real name.

And being anything but slow, the girl caught on immediately. I mean, she did not miss a beat. Her eyes met mine in a conspiring way as she played with the straw in her glass. "Oh, yes, Dix Davidson. I remember you. But ... I can't believe you're here!" Then her tone turned serious. Cocking her head, she asked, "I mean, really, you? Like ... of all people? I can understand Dylan being here." She flashed him a brilliant smile before dropping it once more for me. "But ... you?"

"You three know each other?" Gaetan said.

"We sure do!" Elizabeth said, ever so sweetly, but what I heard was Ka-ching! Ka-ching! I could see it in her eyes. This was going to cost me. Of course, any interaction with the young Ms. Bee tended to cost someone something.

Okay. Remind me to take Richard Head off my Christmas card list. Well, if I ever do write up such a list, remind me to keep him off it. Permanently. But for crying out loud, why hadn't he warned me this woman was here? He damned well knew Dylan and I had become acquainted with Ms. Bee a few months back, when I'd solved the case of the Flashing Fashion Queen.

Yes, it was the one and only, the inimitable Elizabeth Bee, massage room assistant at the Bombay Spa (at least, last I heard). AKA former girlfriend of at least two unfortunate souls I knew. AKA blond bombshell.

Surely Dickhead would have recognized her. Yes, she had changed her hair color. Her shoulder length blond locks were now shoulder length auburn locks (so technically now she was a red-haired bombshell), and she'd gone from straight to curly. Her nails were a long and lacquered dark red (so I'm guessing she wasn't at the Bombay anymore; that would never fly there). And I could almost swear her breasts weren't nearly so large the last time I'd seen her (swear, as in holy mother of God, those are some fucking big implants!).

But still, Dickhead was a cop! Also, male. Both characteristics that pretty much guaranteed he'd remember a piece of work like Elizabeth.

"So what are you up to these days, Dix Davidson?" Elizabeth inclined her head again. "Last I heard, you two were between projects."

This complicated things.

I'd have to think fast.

But you see, the thing about being undercover is that you have to be careful what you cover yourself with. Pose as a doctor? Someone will surely go into labor. I mean, if there was only one pregnant woman within three square miles, that woman would be standing in front of you at Tim Horton's when her water broke. Claim to be a plumber? As soon as you pull out the fake business card, toilets start backing up. I posed as a vet once. (Oh God, did you know dogs have anal glands? And that they need to be expressed?)

So guess what I came up with?

"We're designers."

Dylan glanced at me, then smiled as that quick brain of his latched onto the idea. "Yeah," he said. "We're just starting out. Clothing designers. Sleepwear, specifically." He flashed one of his gazillion-watt smiles.

And Elizabeth's smile grew even sweeter. This would cost me at least fifty, I was thinking. "So how's business," she asked. "Bet you're designing a lot of flashing fashion these days."

More like seventy-five dollars

"Peachy," I grated. "Business is peachy."

I was starting to think I was in a bad dream — a certain bad dream. That one in high school where you're the only kid who shows up either naked or in your pajamas. Well, at least I wasn't naked. This was the pajama one.

We had stopped by Dylan's Aunt Gert's after all. She'd been thrilled to outfit us in her homemade PJs (all the while informing her favorite nephew that the silk green striped ones he was currently wearing were supposed to be his Christmas gift). Mine were pink fleece. Fleece! Nope, not even hot pink. I looked like a peppermint. A big fuzzy peppermint that had been in someone's pocket about a month too long. (Yes, I know that from experience.)

Everyone else, however, was in exercise wear, from fairly fashionable Yoga outfits to the standard sweats, pilled with little lint balls.

"Did you ... make these?" Gaetan asked, eyeballing our attire.

"Yep," Dylan said. "Grand, huh? Our specialty is —"

"I ... I'm a designer too."

I turned around, looking for the owner of that hesitant voice, and spotted her standing behind a nearby counter.

The young woman was neither attractive nor unattractive. Her smile was pitifully tentative. She was as nondescript an individual as anyone I'd ever met. Shoulder-length sandy brown hair pulled back in an elastic band, light brown eyes, minimal make-up. And even though she'd spoken out, it was as if her whole demeanor now said, *Please don't look at me*.

"What do you design, Miss ...?"

"Babe," she said in response to Dylan's question. "Babe Gough." She glanced at Gaetan. "My brother and I —"

"Babe works the counter here," Gaetan said. "She does odd jobs around the place. Paperwork. Answers phones. That sort of thing. Nothing spectacular, I assure you — ha ha ha!"

Babe looked crestfallen, yet she spoke up again: "That's true. But I do like to imagine up designs, and sometimes I even sew —"

"*Imagine up?* Yeah, that's all you do, isn't it, Babe? You have quite the imagination — delusions of grandeur if you ask me! So, you're a designer now? What was it last week you were going to be? A writer? A poet, wasn't it? No, that was the week before. Last week, I think it was ... oh who can remember?"

She lowered her gaze to her feet.

Immediately, irrevocably, I did not like Gaetan Gough. He was a bully and a jerk, and if I weren't undercover he'd be a bully and a jerk with my foot up his ass.

I glanced around the room casually, interested in how the Gaetan Land crowd would react to Gaetan's boorish behavior. Incredibly, no one seemed to bat an eyelash. Dylan, of course, was glaring daggers at him. But the rest of the crowd was simply talking amongst themselves as they sipped their smoothies, as though Gaetan's treatment of his sister was just that common. As though they were used to it. Or as though they were so enamored of Gaetan, they were prepared to overlook the fact that he was a complete asshole.

"So you two are siblings then?" I asked.

"Yes," Gaetan said. "Babe's my little sister. The baby of the family. And she was just leaving."

And she just left.

Just that quickly, Babe walked into what had to be an inner office and closed the door behind her without so much of an if, and or (my personal favorite) fuck you. Interesting. Disturbing, but interesting.

Ah, but what's the old saying? When one door closes another door opens.

And as it opened, in walked Dickhead.

And omigod, I'd never seen Detective Head looking less like a cop. Gone were the dress pants and sports coat, the boring tie, the obligatory shades. Oh, and the gun. I think it was safe to assume he wasn't packing heat under those black sweatpants. And certainly not under that body-hugging charcoal T-shirt. What he *was* packing under there was a pretty impressive body. Well, if you liked that much brawn.

I can't say it was a total shock. I mean, I had photographed him *in flagrante* with that dispatcher, after all. But damn. Okay, yes, yes, he was my nemesis. Sworn enemy and all that (I had the paperwork somewhere). But — let me say it again — damn. He actually looked pretty good.

Then he completely ruined it.

He smiled around the room, at everyone. Nodding politely, blowing little kisses (oh Gawd, complete with sound effects!). And then — dear God — he *winked*. At *me*, even. Yes, that sealed it: we were that deep under cover.

"Oh," Elizabeth Bee said. I knew it instantly — she had just made the connection between Head and us. "Let me introduce you new folks. I mean ... you don't already know each other, do you?"

Okay, it would cost me a hundred bucks now. Damn, but I admired that girl.

"Don't think we've ever met," Dylan said.

"Um, he doesn't look familiar," I added.

"Oh, I'd have remembered if I'd met this lovely young lady," Richard Head said, extending his hand. "Hi, I'm Richie."

Richie? Pfft!

Unable to do anything else, I took the hand he'd extended.

"Dix Davidson," I said. "And this is Dylan Foreman, my —"

Dickhead raised my hand and kissed the back of it with a flourish. I yanked my hand away and fought not to wipe off the imaginary spittle.

"Oh, that's our Richie!" Gaetan clapped his chubby hands in that steepling way. "Always such a charmer with the ladies. I can tell you two are going to hit it off just *wonderfully*."

Oh crap, there was giggling all around me. Quickly, I shot Dylan a cut-out-the-giggling look.

"Smoothie?"

The voice came from behind me. I turned to see an older woman standing there with a tray of fruity looking beverages.

"Oh you're new here," she said when she saw my face. "I'm Ruth-Ann Dale. And you are ...?"

"Dix," I said. "Dix Davidson. And this is Dylan Foreman."

"Pleased to meet you," Dylan said.

Ruth-Ann smelled of mothballs and deep-fried donuts (which is to say, like everyone's grandmother.) I didn't break my smile *(face beginning to ache)* or break eye contact with her, but I knew Dylan was giving me a glance. I could feel Dickhead's too. And I knew what they were thinking. *The smoothie*. Presuming there really was foul play involved in the cardiac-related deaths, that foul play might have involved administering a noxious substance. And what better way to deliver the poison than in the complimentary smoothie?

"I'll pass," I said. "Don't want the extra calories, you know."

"Nonsense!" That from the younger smoothie-passer working the other side of the room. "That just makes more of you to hug!"

"Isn't that the truth, Starla!" Ruth-Ann called back to her.

"Oh, I've got lots to hug already," I retorted. Stupidly.

"I'll be passing too," Dylan said. He put his arm around me. "I keep telling Dix she's perfect as she is, but I want to support her in her efforts. You know?"

That drew a chorus of *awwws* from around the room, and a "Couldn't you just hug the stuffing out of them both?" threat from Ruth-Ann.

I watched as Dickhead took a smoothie from the older woman. "Gaetan Grape tonight," she said referring to smoothie. "Your favorite, Richie."

"Wonderful!"

"Gaetan grape?" I asked.

"Oh, it's delicious," Ruth-Ann said. "Though I prefer the Gaetangerine Twist, myself."

Oh, God! Gaetan named the drinks after himself.

Of course Dickhead didn't take a sip of the drink. I knew he wouldn't; he was wary of everything now. And if I knew the detective (damn though I hate to give him credit), he'd be sneaking that drink out for analysis.

Balancing the tray in one hand, Ruth-Ann drew Dickhead into a hug with her free arm and gave him a peck on the cheek before she scooted away. Someone else came in the door — regulars judging from the greetings, and Ruth-Ann rushed her smoothies over to them. They too joined in the happy mingle.

There was about thirty ... er ... cuddlers in the group, and they were all milling around now, talking and laughing. Slapping each other on the shoulders. Rubbing each others' backs. Hugging as if ... as if ... as if hugging were normal!

"Now, before we begin," Gaetan said. "Will that be cash or credit card?"

"Credit card." Dylan answered quickly, thank God, before it got awkward. He pulled out his Amex.

"For the both of you?" Gaetan asked.

"Yes, both of us," he announced loudly. "We're a couple."

"A couple of business partners?" This from a young lady Gaetan had introduced as "our Brandy" when he'd made the round. Her two friends, our Eva and our Zoey, looked just as anxious as Brandy did for the answer to that question. God, I think the three were leaning in. Well, at least Zoey and Brandy were. Eva at least had the discretion not to lean forward (which was a good thing; the young lady was so stacked, she might have fallen over.) As if she'd caught my glance (God, I hope she didn't catch my glance), she crossed her arms over her chest.

"A couple as in lovers," Dylan answered.

Brandy looked deflated. Then she looked at her equally deflated friends. Zoey mumbled something about cougars, jerked her head toward me, then the three of them turned away as if they'd suddenly smelled something foul.

Cougar? Me? A cougar in fluffy pink jammies!

Well, bless her little heart!

I shot the quickest glance at Dickhead/Richie. He was clearly blessing Dylan silently for his lovers remark. Now our Richie wouldn't have to feign interest in me.

I turned back to Gaetan, who had shoved Dylan's credit card into his machine.

All our expenses would — eventually — be covered by Dickhead, but

I was glad Dylan had offered to cover our membership on his card, for now. Yeah, my plastic was maxed out again (curse you online shopping), but that's not the point! The point was, I didn't have a card under Dixie Davidson, the moniker I'd chosen so hastily.

Then Gaetan told us the price. And I was even more thrilled that Dylan was putting this on his card, even if temporarily.

Apparently exclusive cuddle clubs were expensive.

Stupidly expensive.

Which was strange, because when I looked around the club, with the exception of the old geezer holding onto Elizabeth's arm as he wobbled out to the center of the room (or cuddle floor, as Gaetan had dubbed it) whom I recognized as Hugh Dramman, and maybe Brandy and her well-groomed friends, few looked like they could really afford to be here. Maybe I was wrong. I mean, I know a developer who walks around in steel-toed gumboots, work pants, and a plaid jacket looking more like a homeless person than a millionaire. But I didn't think I was mistaken about this crowd.

"Holy shit, expensive," I said.

Yes, I really did want to gauge the reactions.

Gaetan looked at me as though I'd just committed a horrible social gaffe. (Go figure.) I was already rubbing this guy the wrong way. What is it about me? Man, if I could package this charm ...

"Can you really put a price on human touch?" Gaetan said. "On physical affection? On the love you'll find — and only find — here at Gaetan Land?" With that, he turned on his heel. Apparently his questions were rhetorical.

"Amen to that, brother! You can't put a dollar sign on the squeezin'."

I glanced at the speaker, a man standing to my left. And oh my fucking God, he was doing this little squeezy thing, with his hands coming up like he was grabbing someone's tush.

"Albert Valentine," he said, as if I'd forgotten his name.

I had. Which was weird for me. But the moment Gaetan had introduced him all that had gone through my head was *Goatman*.

Albert Valentine had to be the butt-ugliest man alive. (And I've seen a lot of butts ... how do you think my credit card bill got so high? But I digress.) He was short in that squat, tank-like way. He was balding, but not in any discernible pattern. The guy was down to one dark eyebrow, all the way across.

I'm not shallow (okay, not *super* shallow). I know you can't judge a book by its cover. But right now Albert Valentine's *cover* was animating a curvy girl, hourglass figure thing with his hands. So, yeah, I'm judging: what a jerk.

"Albert, you're such an asshole," Zoey said.

"Total asshole," Brandy concurred, with vehemence. All three young friends glared hard at him. Harder when he laughed.

This was one strange establishment.

"Okay, people, now that business and introductions are out of the way ..." — (Gaetan let the pause hang; oh, the guy was a showman) — "... it's time for us to make tents!"

I shot a horrified look at his velour-covered crotch.

"Omigod!" someone exclaimed loudly.

Okay, that was me.

Fortunately, it turned out the tent Gaetan was talking about making (threatening to make?) wasn't in his pants after all. As if on cue, Babe emerged from the office again, this time bearing armfuls of royal blue fleece material. Blankets of a sort. But as she got closer, I saw they weren't really fleece so much as fleece-like.

There were three of these large perfect squares, and I watched in a sort of horrified amazement as Babe spread them out on the large *cuddle floor*. Then, head hanging, she made her exit.

"For those of you who are new to the group, these are my patented — yes patented — GAETAN LAND Cuddle-Uppies." Gaetan spoke to the whole group, but his words were presumably for the benefit of Dylan and me. "I made them myself. Cozy, warm, perfect to cuddle up under with others."

Cuddle-Uppies? *Oh oh oh ... be afraid! Be very afraid!*

"For sale?" I asked. Not that I was looking to buy, but I was curious about these enormous blankets with holes in them. Yes, holes in them. Head-sized holes, laid out in a circle.

"Of course they're for sale."

"I'm saving up for one!" Elizabeth Bee proclaimed.

"I'll buy you one, my dear." Hugh patted her hand as she squealed her delight. "As long as you cuddle-up only with me."

"Oh, no one but you, Hugh-Bear. You are just the sweetest!"

"I thought I was the sweetest?" Albert was laughing again — oh joy.

Dickhead was the first to slide under one of the Cuddle-Uppies. (But first he put down his untouched Gaetan Grape smoothie, very carefully, beside a small table. Yes, he'd know which one was his to gather after.) He poked his head up through a hole, smiling widely. Elizabeth Bee and Hugh Drammen cuddled close under a second Cuddle-Uppie. All the blankets filled in. Starla set down her tray of smoothies on one of the many small tables along the edges of the room where others had stashed their glasses and crawled in with Elizabeth and Hugh. Ruth-Ann crawled in with Dickhead.

Dylan of course, easily stepped up to the plate, and slid his handsome frame under the third Cuddle-Uppie that Babe had spread out. Predictably Brandy, Eva and Zoey popped their smiling heads up, and it was obvious by the motion of those ultra-soft looking Cuddle-Uppies that arms were going around each other, and yep, wrapping right around Dylan and the others in that grope ... er, *group*. Very quickly, the empty spaces beneath the blankets filled up. (And I just bet by the look on some of the men's faces, there were a few little tents being made here after all).

Gaetan chose the Cuddle-Uppie that Dylan occupied, and slid in. "Ahhhhhhhhhhh," he said. "This is sweet."

And that left ... me. Alone. Standing like the ugly step-sister in some unfortunate fairy tale.

Well, you know, I always liked that broad.

"Lights low," Gaetan commanded, raising his voice.

Automatically they dimmed to near darkness, a small whirr sounding as they did

Hands, people! I wanted to shout. *I wanna see hands!*

My intuition was vibrating. Every fiber in my body — hell, every fiber in the room! — was telling me to run. Get the hell out of there. *There's the door, sister!* it urged. *Run like the wind!*

I took a calming breath. A couple of them. Deep ones.

Dix Dodd doesn't do cuddly. That had to be what was making those warning bells clang. But for God's sake, how dangerous could it be? Yeah, yeah, Dickhead has his suspicions, (and I reminded myself yet again, I had his check). But more and more, this just struck me as too bizarre.

"Come on in, Dix. The water's warm." Gaetan called. "Dive right in!"

It seemed to me the dive-right-in reference got way more laughs than it deserved, but then again, it might have been metaphor envy. But I was procrastinating. It was now or never.

And since never never paid, I convinced myself that the chill up my spine was aversion, not my intuition. That the crawling of my scalp was my body's way of saying, "Dix Dodd doesn't do close," and not "Danger, danger!" Or maybe that crawling sensation was just because the only

Cuddle-Uppie spot left for me was between Richard Head and — oh fuck! Albert 'Squeezey-Hands' Valentine.

Chapter 4

I HAD TO maneuver around a sea of bodies, but soon enough, I too was poking my head out of one of the holes at the top of a royal blue Cuddle-Uppie. Yes, right between Dickhead ("our Richie" was smiling still) and Albert. Okay, which way did I cringe?

Suck it up, I told myself. You're on an important fact-finding mission.

The creepiest fact-finding mission on the planet, granted, but this was business.

"I'm a salesman," Albert said. He nodded to Dickhead. "Just like Richie here. 'Cept he sells paper products. How boring is that?"

"Yeah. Boring." Dickhead's answer confirmed that he was indeed posing as a salesman.

"And what do you sell, Albert?" I felt obliged to ask.

"Flowers!" He answered triumphantly, as though I should swoon or something.

"Flowers?"

"Pretty flowers for pretty ladies. Do you like flowers, pretty lady?"

Lady? I looked around automatically, then realized he was talking to me. I managed not to roll my eyes. "Do I like flowers? No."

"No? Not even roses?"

"Can't stand 'em."

Albert looked confused. "How could you not like roses?"

"It's the pricks," I supplied. "I just wanna snap them right off. Take a pair of shears to them. Or pliers, and twist and twist and twist."

Albert's eyes grew wider with every little fantasy ... er, I mean detail.

"You know — the thorns," I said, smiling. "I can't stand the thorns."

From the other side of the Cuddle-Uppie, Ruth-Ann struggled to suppress a smile.

Albert turned away. Which required some awkward butt-walking action, seeing as we were all sitting on the carpeted floor, and our heads were so closely trapped by the Cuddle-Uppie.

Jesus, I felt like I was in one of those whack-a-mole games at the amusement park.

On that thought, I almost giggled, picturing a great big giant inflatable hammer coming down to whack us on the head at any moment. Said huge hammer could start with Detective Richard Head on my left.

Boing. Pop. Got him! Then it would move on to Gaetan and his perfectly round afro. I could almost picture the hammer sinking down and bouncing back.

Yes, I could really picture it. And so, despite everything, I got that warm and fuzzy feeling. Caught myself smiling. Okay, maybe even relaxing.

Weird for me, under the circumstances.

I glanced over at Dylan, who was looking over at me.

I knew that smile — the smart-assed ha-ha-you-like-it smile. Or, maybe he was smiling because he was the only guy under blanket number two with Eva, Brandy, Zoey, Starla and a few others female cuddlers. Geez, there was even a geriatric woman in there, and she looked delighted to have Dylan Foreman so caressingly close. Oh, she was laying on the charm, batting her eyelashes faster than I could … well, bat my own eyelashes. (I still suck at metaphors. Also, I suck at batting my eyelashes.)

Elizabeth Bee and her old fart were under the Cuddle-Uppie to my right. And oh, oh, oh, there was something going on under that blanket, if I knew Elizabeth. There was this little flippy ripple to that royal blue cover. Hands were working on something. That could only be —

"You can quit staring, Dix," Elizabeth said. "I'm scratching an itch on my foot."

Yeah, that.

Okay, so there I was, sitting under a Cuddle-Uppie blanket with my head poked through a hole in the top.

It wasn't like we were body to body, bumping parts better left unbumped. We were sitting there under these huge blankets. Just … sitting. A bit knee to knee — but that wouldn't kill me. Elbow here and there (mine were the pointiest). Of course, Dickhead was practically straining at the neck hole, as was I, so we wouldn't touch each other. (God, you'd think we were in grade school and worried about catching cooties.) I started to relax even more. Yeah, I kind of did.

"It's time, my little buttercups," Gaetan cooed to the crowd of us.

"Time to cuddle. Snuggle in close, now."

"I have cooties! I have cooties!"

"Oh that's funny, Dix!" Elizabeth Bee laughed. "Cooties. You're such a hoot!"

Everyone giggled. (Well, almost everyone. Eva was scratching her head, as if the cooties were catching.)

What would it take to scare these people away? If the threat of cooties wouldn't do it, what would? I really didn't want to play the diarrhea card. Oh boy.

Well, kind of oh boy.

In truth the panic wasn't nearly as bad as I'd thought it would be as people started wrapping up closer.

Still, I watched before I advanced to go.

Dylan was practically folded up in that custom cuddle blanket as the women gathered around him closer.

"Ladies," Dylan said. "Make room for Mabel."

White-haired, eyelash batting (damn show off) Mabel couldn't have been more thrilled as she scooted closer and then cuddled into Dylan. Okay, maybe "latched onto" is the phrase I'm looking for. She sighed contentedly.

"Cuddle, Hugh?" Elizabeth cooed.

"Love to, dearest." Yeah, that blanket was moving suspiciously again. And I was pretty sure it wasn't an itch that Elizabeth Bee was, er, scratching this time.

Gaetan's clap-clap-clapping was muffled under that blanket. (Oh God, I hope he was clapping his hands!) "Come on, cuddlers!" he said, his words clearly directed at me. "Don't be shy. Cuddle right up!"

Dickhead was still smiling as he looked at me. Well, sort of. It may have strained toward a cringing grimace. And was that a sheen of sweat upon his brow?

Do we really have to do this? That was what he was thinking. I could read his very thoughts. (Of course, it helped that he muttered those exact same words as he thought them).

Albert, on the other hand, wasn't minding. And if he'd been miffed by my rose/prick/happy snip-snip remark, that was in the past. As he butt walked in a little closer (honestly it was a rolly thing), the Cuddle-Uppie folded in. Suddenly, arms were around me. Dickhead's. Albert's.

(And yeah, those arms were still attached to the bodies!)

Albert said, "Oh, you're so ..."

What? Sweet? Luscious?

"My God, you're all — jabby. I mean ... ouch!"

I laughed as if it were funny.

"No, seriously. Loosen up, will you?"

"I *am* loose."

"There's not a soft spot on you," Albert complained.

"Wait — are you calling me a hard belly?"

He snorted a laugh. "God, no. Lots of padding there." And he wasn't meaning the pink peppermint jammies.

Undercover (literally!) or not, the guy had just snapped my last nerve, "I'd be watching my prick if I were you, flower man."

That shut him up. It also caused him to loosen his grip on me. Which only served to make me more aware of Dickhead's arms around me. Gah! Well, that, and the fact that he gave me a jab to the ribs, presumably to remind me we were undercover here. (Ha! *Undercover.* That never gets old.)

"This is how we do it, Dix. That's your name, right?"

"Yes, Dickh —"

"*Richie*," he hastened to say. "But that's okay. Sometimes the older ladies do have a hard time remembering all the names. It's just that — *oomph.*"

Ah, once again, a strategically placed elbow does the trick.

"Lay down, cuddlers!" Gaetan sang out. *Clap, clap, clap.*

Lay down? Was he freakin' kidding me?

It took some maneuvering. Twisting, and an awkward bit of rolling. The process was made even more awkward by the way Albert Valentine went down, like an old tom cat flopping himself down on a rug, dragging me down faster than I'd planned.

"Hey, watch it, Valentine," I hissed, giving him a jab. "We're kind of attached here."

He made a grunting noise. I wanted to give him something to grunt about, but restrained myself. It wouldn't pay to get myself kicked out of cuddle club before the investigation even got started.

So we twisted and scooted some more until we'd arranged ourselves into a sort-of prone position with our heads poking out of the Cuddle-Uppies. Beside each other, around each other. Tucked and tethered and leaning in. And yeah, I was lying down with Dickhead's arms around me and my arms around Albert Valentine. And the only consolation was neither man seemed to be enjoying this any more than I was.

But that was the thing ... I kind of, a little bit, was.

Oh God, I should be freaking, straining away from the contact. But somehow, I wasn't. Maybe it was the coziness of the cuddle, the warmth of it (and it was warm in there, believe me).

Nah. I rejected that thought. It had to be the paycheck waiting for me at the end of this. That was the warmest incentive of all.

Suddenly, the office door flew open and light spilled into the dimly lit room.

"Babe, what are you doing?" Gaetan snapped.

"I'm going to join in."

"Oh, wonderful," Ruth-Ann called. "We can make room in here."

Gaetan didn't seem to concur that that was such a wonderful idea. "Not tonight. We've already started. And the rules of cuddle club are simple. Golden. Once the cuddle is cast, no one else can come in."

Once the cuddle is cast?

Oh brother!

No, make that nasty S.O.B. of a brother.

"But ... but I had to lower the lights, start the music ... turn on the fans! You said —"

"No, Babe. Get back to the office." Gaetan was adamant. Babe turned and left.

Richard Head changed his position. Adjusted himself so that a certain part (guess which one) wasn't so close to me. Oh, but Albert Valentine didn't move a muscle. He lay there stiff as a board. (Okay, I do have a few stock metaphors in the drawer.)

"Sorry for the rude interruption, cuddlers," Gaetan said. "Now, where was I? Oh, yes, for those of you who are new ..."

Again, it was just Dylan and me. Was he trying to make us not stand out? My God, we were the only ones who showed up in our pajamas!

"Is everyone settled into their cuddle spots? Everyone cozy?"

There were a few male groans mixed in with an, "Oh, yeah." More than a few female giggles from the general direction of Dylan's Cuddle-Uppie.

"Good," Gaetan said. "Now, sometimes we have a little sing-along."

"Awesome!" Dylan said.

"Oh, do you sing, Dylan?" Mabel asked.

"I do," he told the older lady. "Frank Sinatra, eat your heart out!"

"Oh, I can't wait to hear you."

I tensed. Well, tensed even more. (Something might actually have cracked inside). Dylan Foreman cannot sing. No, I mean, he is the worst vocalist on the planet. All those really bad *American Idol* auditions? Dylan makes every last sorry one of those contestants look good. Except Dylan didn't know it. Hadn't a clue.

Elizabeth Bee — who'd heard him before — spoke up. "Gaetan, maybe we can do something else tonight. Tell jokes or ghost stories ... anything!"

"Nonsense! You have a very nice voice, Elizabeth. Now's not the time to be shy," Gaetan said.

There were snickers all around. Shy was the last thing Elizabeth was, a fact that clearly was not lost on her fellow cuddlers. But I wasn't snickering. As I lay there between tweedle dee and tweedle's ... dick, I had to figure out a way to stop this fiasco before it began. Before it hurt my ears. I was too far from the fire extinguisher. Couldn't reach my cell to call in a bomb threat. There had to be something I could do. Something that wouldn't blow our cover. Something that made perfect sense! Something that would stop this sing-along before it started.

All of a sudden, I knew I didn't have to make something up.

"Omigod! The guy beside me ..."

"Dammit, Dixieland!" Dickhead grumbled, letting his cover slip a little in his exasperation. "What is it? What am I doing wrong now?"

"Not you! It's Goatma — I mean, Albert. The guy on the *other* side of me ... he's dead!"

Yeah. That worked.

Everyone forgot about the sing-along.

Chapter 5

Yeah, DEATH IS always messy, especially when I'm smack-dab in the middle of it. Or in this case, smack dab beside it.

After the "Ha-ha, very funny", "He's just sleeping," and "Oh, that's just our Albert," were done, people actually started looking over. Questioning. Pulling their heads out of their holes (the Cuddle-Uppie holes), getting their socks back on in some cases, and scrambling to their feet.

As Albert lay there unmoving, panic started to set in among the cuddlers.

Eva gasped and started chewing her hair to an omigod omigod omigod beat.

In no time flat, Brandy had her arms around Eva, soothing her.

Zoey, hand over her mouth, started backing away from the scene.

Babe, who'd emerged at the commotion, started gathering the abandoned blankets and ran back to the office with them as if keeping things tidy was important at a time like this! (Yep, panic sure did strange things to people sometimes.)

And Gaetan? Well, he started accusing me.

"What happened?" he yelled.

"How should I know?"

"What did you do?"

"Nothing!" I protested. "I mean, I hardly said a word to him. Well, just that business about twisting off pricks and —"

"Oh, God, no!" someone muttered. (Someone of the male persuasion — maybe they knew me from Florida.)

"On roses," I clarified. "We were talking about the prickly thorns on rose stems."

Judging by some of the expressions around me, not everyone was convinced. Well, that was their problem. I was in no way responsible for

Goatman's death. But as usual, I was in the thick of things.

Or rather, I would be in the thick of things if the crowd hadn't started thinning so rapidly. People were leaving. Grabbing coats, sliding on shoes and hustling out the door. What the hell? Okay, I know we don't talk about cuddle club, but really, people!

At least Detective Head was here to take charge. Off duty, or not, undercover or out from under the covers, he was still law enforcement. Any minute now, he was going to step up to the plate.

Or not.

Ruth-Ann (who, it turns out, was once an RN/PhD ethicist with the faculty of nursing at Marport University) was checking Albert Valentine for vitals.

"Nothing," she announced, her voice clipped. "No pulse, no respiration."

Then she leaned over Albert and started administering CPR.

I glanced up to see a knot of people rushing the door, jamming it in their haste to get away. The bulge of bodies in the door frame would have been amusing if the circumstances weren't so dire. I was surprised to see Elizabeth Bee quickening her pace to get to the door. I really didn't think she'd give a rat's ass about being seen at the cuddle club. But then I realized what her hurry was. Hugh Drammen was standing precariously close to Eva and Brandy near the door. Well, precariously close for Elizabeth's liking, I imagined.

Then, with a move that would have fit perfectly into any old Marx Brothers' comedy, the log jam broke and everyone fell out through the door frame at once. Righting themselves, they darted off for the exits.

A movement from Ruth-Ann drew my eyes back to the resuscitation attempt. I watched her tilt Albert's head back, lift his chin, seal his nose and deliver a couple of breaths. It was eerie watching Albert's chest rise and fall. Then she went back to the chest compressions. There was a rhythm to it, I saw. Thirty compressions, two breaths, back to compressions again. After a few cycles of this, she paused and checked again for breathing.

Dylan, who'd stepped back momentarily to call 9-1-1, came to stand at my side, cell phone still pressed to his ear. "Ambulance is on the way," he announced. Then he knelt to address Ruth. "I've got dispatch on the line, Ruth. If I take over CPR, can you give them a status report?"

"That's the best offer I've had all day." Ruth blew a strand of hair out of her face, sat back on her heels and took the phone Dylan proffered. I listened to her calmly describe Albert's status and the rescue efforts she'd been employing, but my eyes were on Dylan. *Huh.* I didn't even know he knew CPR. Though I shouldn't have been surprised. He'd taken over where Ruth-Ann had left off, and as I watched, it seemed to me his compressions were more aggressive, deeper than the older woman's. Then again, he was younger, bigger and stronger. And he hadn't been doing it for five minutes. Poor Ruth-Ann looked done in.

Those of us remaining (the very few of us) looked on, knowing the efforts were to no avail. I could tell by the grim look on all their faces.

Especially Albert's.

Come on, EMTs.

As I watched Dylan pause and deliver a couple of breaths, it occurred to me that the cops would be arriving soon, too. Maybe they'd even be first on the scene ahead of the ambulance. The thought had me looking for Dickhead. I didn't have to look far. He'd moved right up beside me. In fact, he took my elbow and drew me back.

"The smoothie — it's gone," he murmured in my ear.

"What?"

His grip tightened on my elbow. "Could you keep it down?"

"Fine," I hissed. "What happened to the evidence?"

"Babe must have dumped it out when she was doing her manic Merry Maids routine."

I groaned. I could hear it now. The churning sound of the dishwasher blended in with the sound of the agitating washer from the other room.

"Shit. Nothing to analyze."

"Not exactly. Unless Albert perks up a whole helluva lot, the medical examiner will have the contents of his stomach to work with," Dickhead pointed out.

"Yeah, but they won't necessarily know if it got into his stomach *here*."

"I know." He sighed, looking over at Albert.

I followed his gaze. Dylan was still doing CPR. Ruth-Ann still held the phone. Head's next words ripped my attention back to him.

"Okay, Dixiecakes, I'm outta here."

"What?" This time I managed to keep my voice down. "Are you kidding me? You're *leaving*? Seriously?"

"I wasn't joking," he said, looking flushed and uncomfortable. "No one talks about cuddle club."

Oh for pity's sake! How stupidly far would they carry this cloak ... or rather Cuddle-Uppie ... of secrecy? Okay, sure, I could picture the reaction from Dickhead's fellow cops if they found him here. He'd be drummed out of the blue brotherhood. But I really thought professionalism would override that macho crap. For God's sake, he'd dragged me into this with his suspicions, and he was bailing on me *now*, when there was a body?

"C'mon, Dix, you can handle this."

"Well, duh. Of course I can handle it, but —"

My words trailed off as I realized I was talking to myself. Dickhead was already blasting toward the exit. He paused in the doorway and shot me a meaningful look, as if to say, "You're on this, Dix Dodd."

Fine. I was on it. I gave him an enthusiastic thumbs up. Well, okay, strictly speaking, it was the middle finger I gave him, but it *was* enthusiastic.

Dickhead's eyes narrowed, but he held my gaze a moment longer, his message clear: he found Albert Valentine's sudden demise as suspicious as I did.

Damn it!

As soon as Dickhead disappeared, the first faint sound of a siren reached my ears. Also, the sounds of Gaetan moaning and wringing his hands. Maybe he'd only just started up with this whining, or maybe I'd just managed to ignore it until now.

"Oh, God!" He threw his chubby little hands in the air in a why-me kind of way.

"I ... I can't believe it," a quavering female voice said.

I turned to see Babe standing close to the body, practically leaning over Dylan and Ruth-Ann. After her frantic, compulsive tidying (frankly, I'd seen more bizarre and irrational responses in this kind of situation), she'd re-emerged from the back room, presumably ready now to confront what had happened. Except as soon as she got a look at Albert, she started to cry.

"Our poor Albert!" she sniffed.

Ruth-Ann, on her feet now, put her free arm around the woeful Babe, as she held Dylan's cell phone to her ear. Both of them watched Dylan's grimly determined efforts.

"Oh, God," Gaetan said again. He'd been leaning against the counter for support, but now he slid down to sit on the floor.

This was my chance. I walked over to Gaetan, slowly, wobbly like I was as upset as the other ladies, and slid down beside him. I slid a little too quickly and landed with an involuntary, *"Umph!"* A fleece-covered butt sliding across worn carpet is one thing; a fleece-covered butt sliding down a polished wood counter was quite another.

Gaetan turned his head and gave me a distracted look, then went back to staring intently at Albert Valentine, as if willing him to draw a breath.

That wasn't happening.

"Poor fellow," I said. The sweet, sympathetic approach — that would work best here, I reckoned. "Oh, poor, dear ... our Albert. He seemed fine one minute, and the next —"

"I hope this doesn't hurt business. Oh, God, a *death*. On the premises! That's just ... so unfair!"

Yeah, Gaetan Gough was all heart. The little prick.

Hold your temper, Dix, counseled that little voice in my head. *Just for once in your life, keep your mouth shut.*

Then a bigger voice in my head slapped the little voice down.

"I'm guessing Albert's death is more of an inconvenience to Albert than it is to you."

Gaetan blinked, as though only now really becoming aware of my presence. "Of course. Poor Albert." He shook his head sorrowfully. "Yes, yes, poor fellow. Very unfortunate."

As fake sincerity went, it wasn't bad. I'd caught Gaetan off guard momentarily, but he was clearly back on his game.

The door opened, and two hulking ambulance attendants strode in with a gurney, led by one of the cuddlers, a middle-aged lady whose name I didn't remember. Well, at least one of the club members had conscience enough to hang around to greet the ambulance crew and direct them to the scene. Bringing up the rear were two police officers who'd also responded to the call.

Dylan and Ruth-Ann gave way to the EMTs. Ruth-Ann hung up with the 9-1-1 operator and handed Dylan his phone back. The older woman looked exhausted, but she still had enough energy left to comfort Babe, who was still sniffling. Ruth-Ann wrapped her arms around Babe in a very *there there* way, pulling her gently backward to give the emergency responders room to work.

Once Albert had been bundled onto a gurney between chest

compressions, the paramedics slapped leads from a portable external defibrillator onto his extremely hairy bare chest and zapped him, to no effect, or at least none that I could see. One of the paramedics — the older of the two — rose and asked what had happened. Ruth-Ann handed Babe off to Dylan (a process that resembled peeling off a limpet) and stepped forward to answer the paramedic's questions. Once he realized she was a clinician, the two of them lapsed into medicalese. After a second jolt from the defibrillator failed to alleviate the grim expression on the EMTs' faces, they piled the defibrillator onto the gurney and evacuated without further delay.

The police had questions, too. Mostly for Gaetan.

Yes, Albert had seemed fine when he'd walked in. No, he'd shown no signs of distress. Never had he complained of chest pains or anything like that! Cuddle club? Well, yes, there'd been a few others here, but they'd all been so upset about poor Albert ...

"It was his heart." That pronouncement came from Ruth-Ann, who was standing there with her arms wrapped around herself. The paramedics had gleaned all they could from her and were whisking Albert out the door.

"Are you familiar with his medical history, ma'am?" the female officer asked. She was definitely the senior of the two on this call. I recognized her, actually. Officer L. Pivans — Leola to her friends (of which I wasn't). And though Dickhead still shouldn't have rabbited, I was blaming him less and less for doing so. Pivans would have ridden him hard, and not in the good way.

"Not really," Ruth-Ann said dryly, "but I know sudden cardiac arrest when I see it."

"Did you know him outside of this ... um ... club?" Pivans asked.

"Only casually. The last time I saw him outside of this room was on campus last month. One of my former colleagues was retiring, and they had a big do for him at the Stark Center."

"Ah, Albert did the flowers," I guessed.

"Flowers?" Ruth-Ann looked at me like she wanted to ask if I was on crack. "Hardly. He was tending bar."

I blinked. "But I thought he was a flower salesman?"

She shook her head. "No, he was definitely a bartender."

Ah, of course. It looked like Dickhead wasn't the only one lying about who he was at cuddle club.

"Albert was always so friendly here," Ruth-Ann said. "Such a gentle soul."

Gaetan snorted behind me, in that you've-got-to-be-kidding way. When all eyes turned toward him, he schooled his expression into sympathetic lines again. "Yes, that was Albert. Gentle."

Constable Pivans cleared her throat. "So, did he have any heart issues that you're aware of?"

Ruth-Ann, who'd been giving Gaetan a frosty look, turned back to Pivans. "Nothing specific, though I think he was under some stress. That's why he was coming to cuddle club — to help him combat stress."

Gaetan made a choking noise this time, but turned it into a cough. Interesting.

"Also, he was very short," Ruth-Ann added, then turned an icy glare on Gaetan. "It's been observed that short men are statistically more likely to develop heart disease."

Gaetan's face flushed, and he drew himself up as tall as he could make himself without actually going on tiptoe.

Suddenly, I felt Constable Pivans's eyes on me. I looked up to see that she'd been studying me while I'd been absorbed studying the interplay between Ruth-Ann and Gaetan. Whoops.

"This has just been so upsetting!" I turned to Dylan, clutching at his arm. "We'd better go."

"Of course." Dylan peeled a puffy-eyed Babe away from his chest, revealing big dark splotches on his pajama top. He handed a tear-soaked and snotty Babe gently off to Pivans's alarmed partner.

While the young male cop sputtered and stuttered, Pivans turned to me. "I'll walk you out."

"Oh, that's not necessary. You're far too busy —"

"Oh, I insist. And you alone, Ms. Do —"

"Davidson!" I shouted.

Pivans blinked, then nodded imperceptibly.

Dammit. Now she knew for certain that I was undercover.

Dylan cast me a questioning look, and I shot back an *it's-okay-I-can-handle-this* look.

He inclined his head slightly. "I'll get our coats and meet you out there."

I headed outside with Pivans.

"How do you know Albert Valentine?" she asked.

"Well, Leola ... may I call you, Leola?" I asked with a smile.

"No."

Fair enough. "I met him here at the club."

"Nice guy?" she asked.

"I suppose. Liked flowers."

"Known him long?" She looked at me sidelong. "I mean, you seemed kind of upset just now."

"I'm sensitive," I said.

She laughed with real amusement. I guess my reputation really did precede me.

Pivans asked me a few more questions. *What did I know of Gaetan Gough? How many people had been there earlier? Where did I learn of this club?*

Fair questions. Easy enough to answer or evade. But then she asked me one more question.

"Who hired you to stake out the cuddle club, Dix Dodd?"

My heart gave a little jolt, which I'm sure was just what Constable Pivans was trying to accomplish. "That's confidential information."

Pivans smiled, then turned and walked back into the building.

Dammit. She'd be on this now like white on rice. (Yeah, I stole that metaphor too).

Chapter 6

THE NEXT MORNING was Saturday. I tried to sleep in, but my brain wouldn't quit worrying about Constable Pivans.

I mean, I appreciated that she hadn't blown my cover last night at the club. But I didn't appreciate that she knew there was a cover to be blown.

And yeah, she totally knew something was up. And this young cop had a rep. She was ambitious, tough, and smart. Which kinda sounded like my own bio, actually. No wonder I liked her.

Sort of.

What were the chances she'd leave this alone? Not good. And why hadn't she blown my cover? I wasn't naïve enough to believe it was altruism. On the other hand, she wouldn't be the first cop to give me enough rope to solve a case for them. (Or to hang myself, as the case may be.)

But if I told Dickhead about my conversation with Pivans, he'd hire someone else. That thought bothered me, and not just because of the potential for losing a paycheck. The mystery had hooked me, and I was dog-determined to solve it. There was something going on here, something serious. I felt it in my bones. Something was not right with these people, and I don't just mean in the they-like-to-cuddle way. I didn't for a minute believe Albert's death was from natural causes.

Dammit! If only Dickhead had gotten that smoothie out the door. Of course, he'd have had to come clean about his cuddle club affiliation if he had. He'd have had to open a file, turn the smoothie over to evidence for forensic analysis. It even occurred to me to wonder if it hadn't been Dickhead himself who'd tossed the smoothie out, not Babe. But no, I didn't really believe that. If there'd been evidence on the line, I was pretty sure he'd have manned up, much as I hated to admit it. But since the evidence had been flushed into the city's sewer system, he probably didn't see the point of humiliating himself.

Toss. Turn. Toss. Turn. And then the doorbell rang.

I knew exactly who it was. Like I said, it was Saturday.

Rochelle Banks was my best friend. We'd met years ago, when I was working at Jones and Associates and her little sister needed some help. Little sister got said help in that we got asshole boyfriend out of the picture, and Rochelle and I had been fast friends ever since.

It was nothing for her to pick up tickets for a Stones concert, announce that we were going, and there'd be a road trip in the making. It wasn't unheard of for her to call me in the middle of the night to tell me the woes of her latest lost love (okay, well, maybe not woes so much as snorts of laughter — neither of us were the woes type). And it was absolutely not out of the ordinary for her to show up on my doorstep early on Saturday mornings bearing fresh-brewed coffee, bagels, and news. As personal secretary to one of Marport City's most prestigious and highest-ranking judges, it was usually pretty damn good news. Not good as in joyous. More like good as in juicy. Nothing that was privileged or protected, mind you. Nothing about cases. She was strictly professional about the judge's business. No, this was more water cooler stuff. Court house gossip. And it usually encompassed the cops, from the chief of police to the lowliest constable, as well as lawyers, lesser judges and politicians. She got the dirt before the rest of us knew it was … well, dirty.

This bleary-eyed morning, as I opened the door to her 8 a.m. cheer, Rochelle was balancing a box in her arms in addition to the customary tray of extra-large coffees and the paper bag that I knew contained perfectly-toasted cinnamon-raisin bagels slathered in cream cheese.

"What's in the box?"

"Don't know. It's from your mother. I stopped to chat up the concierge and he sent it up with me. Said he'd missed you with it last night."

The *concierge* was a retired commissionaire by the name of Chester whom the building management paid to keep a presence in the lobby. This was what I'd inherited when I'd bought out mom's condo.

"Yeah, I was a little late getting in." I took the box from Rochelle and motioned her inside. Closing the door behind her, I looked at the package. Yep, that was my mother's handwriting, and that was her address in Florida. I noticed it was marked *Fragile. Handle with Care.*

"Shake it," Rochelle urged. "It rattles."

I obliged and felt the loosely packed contents rattle around a bit.

"So it does."

"What do you bet it's homemade cookies. Mothers are like that."

I sighed. "What do you bet it's not?"

"Oh, maybe it's whoopee pies!"

"This is my mother we're talking about, Rochelle. I think that precludes whoopee pies. Besides, whoopee pies don't rattle."

Moving aside the pile of yet-to-be-put-away (okay, this'll-never-get-put-away) laundry, we settled in on my living room sofa. Rochelle pulled the coffee table closer to unload the Saturday morning breakfast.

I reached for my coffee and sat back.

Rochelle gestured to the box which I'd deposited on the coffee table. "You're not going to open it?" She turned incredulous eyes on me. "Aren't you even a little bit curious?"

Curious wasn't the word. "Fine. I'll open it." I took a sip of life-giving Colombian, then put my cup back down to pick up the box. I opened it slowly, pulled back the tissues and ...

"Oh my sweet baby Jesus!"

"Whoopee pies?" Rochelle moved in close beside me to peer into the box.

Not exactly. But I'm sure my mother had given some kind of cheer when she and her geriatric friends cut out these babies.

Incredibly, they *were* cookies. Frosted pink, sprinkled with sprinkles, and shaped like dicks. Yes, that's right — penis-shaped cookies. And not a droopy one in the bunch. When I'd phoned Mother earlier in the week, she'd said she was having friends over and there had been some mention of cooking. I should have known. Except she could have meant she and her cronies were mixing up cocktails. Or baking those special brownies.

"Ah, breakfast is served," Rochelle grabbed a cookie and took an ... um ... strategic bite out of it. "Your mom's cool, Dix."

"That's one word for her," I muttered.

I took another sip of hot coffee, grabbed a still-warm bagel and started to pick out the raisins so I could eat them first. I know, just one of my endearing habits.

"So," Rochelle said. "Tell me about cuddle club. How's it hanging at Gaetan Land?" (Of course Rochelle punctuated that with another well-placed bite, grinning as she did.)

Yeah, I'd told her how I'd be spending my Friday night, and was dying to tell her more. And also dying to hear what my best friend knew about the same.

Twenty minutes later, Rochelle had the nutshell version of what had happened: the silk jammies, the fuzzy pink jammies, the happy clientele, Elizabeth Bee, Dylan-hugging Mabel, and the rest, the strange proprietor and his kid sister. Making tents. And Dylan telling the group gathered there (so easily, so easily) that we were lovers. And of course I told her about the demise of Albert Valentine.

She opened her purse, pulled out her iPhone. "Let's check the online obits."

"Excellent."

Less than a minute later, she handed over the phone. "This him?"

I nodded. "Yeah."

That was definitely the guy I'd met last night, but in healthier times. Younger times. He was smiling in this picture. I scanned the write-up. He was leaving behind five adoring kids, all grown, married and living in various parts of the country. A wife, Cathy Valentine. (Not a beloved wife ... interesting). Albert was 60, had worked forty years for Marport City Auto Sales before retiring to tend bar part time. Donations? Yep — to heart and stroke research.

Man, that made three heart-related demises in one month for Gaetan Land. And as much as I was tempted to make a wise crack about knowing all that huggy-cuddly stuff was bad for a person, this was serious.

"So ...?"

I looked at Rochelle. "So what?"

"So tell me about the club."

"Hello? Just did."

"Yeah, but tell me about the men. Were there any good looking ones there? Besides Dylan I mean." She bit the end off of a cookie, and grinned at me. "And Detective Richard Head, of course."

I snorted. "Obviously you shouldn't talk with your mouth full of penis cookies. I could have sworn you said something about head."

Rochelle laughed, covering her mouth to avoid spraying me with cookie crumbs. "Oh, come on," she said when she'd swallowed, "you know he's not bad looking. Kinda hot, actually."

"He's a pig," I said. "And to be clear, I'm not talking about his chosen occupation."

Rochelle knew all about my history with Dickhead, which began so auspiciously by me documenting his adultery, so she ceded the point with a, "True," before taking another bite of her cookie.

Bagel raisins consumed, I was carefully pulling the sprinkles off a cookie of my own. Okay, penis-shaped cookies were one thing. Penis-shaped cookies with sprinkles that looked for all the world like a cartoonish portrayal of stubbly pink hairs, was another thing altogether. Hey, even I have boundaries.

I shrugged. "Yeah, there were a couple of guys who weren't bad looking, I guess."

"Single?"

"Possibly. But then, given how many people there were lying about themselves, who knows?"

"Did they have woodies?"

I slanted her a look. "Woodies?"

"You know, were they —"

"I know what a woody is, Rochelle. I just can't believe you asked that."

She looked up, startled. "For real?"

I grinned. "As if! Just messing with you." I sat forward on the sofa, and put the cookie back in the box. Sprinkles or no sprinkles, I just couldn't bite the end off.

God, there must be three dozen of them. Was Mother trying to send me a message? And if so, what was it? Not enough dicks in my life? I'd give Rochelle the lot of them to take home.

"So, these woodies?" she prompted.

"There were a few, I imagine. Of course, I suspected a double meaning when Gaetan clapped his hands and said, *Let's make tents!* Those cuddly blankets have a dual purpose, I'm thinking."

"And when everyone scrambled out from under them …?"

I shuddered. "Okay, I was trying to block that from my mind, thank you very much. But yeah, some evidence of arousal, even considering the circumstances."

"What about you?" Rochelle asked.

I snorted. "Did I have a woody, you mean? Was I wanking under the cuddly?"

"Wanking?" Rochelle snickered. "I guess we're watching British porn again, are we?"

"Blimey! Why would you say that?"

I sat back, suppressing my own grin as I waited for Rochelle to stop laughing.

Minutes later, wiping away tears of mirth, Rochelle asked, "So … what about Dylan?"

I lifted an eyebrow. "What about him."

She rolled her eyes. "You know what I mean. What was it like having him declare his passion for you in front of so many people?"

"Rochelle, get a grip. We were undercover. He hardly *declared* anything. It was all a ruse. All a … fantasy. Let's pretend. All in the line of duty."

"You think that's all there is to it?" Rochelle's voice had changed, the teasing note replaced with a more serious one. "Dix, I know you have the hots for the guy. Hell, so does any woman who's stood close enough to look into those peepers. But he looks at you differently, not at all the way he looks at the rest of us."

That shut me up. That made me smile.

I know, I know, I'm hard-as-nails Dix Dodd (got the T-shirt to prove it). Rochelle knew that Dylan and I had fooled around some in the past. But the emotion of it? I'd hidden that from her. Hell, I'd been hiding that from myself. There was something about the guy. Not just the looks, the brains, the promise in those jeans. It was —

My cell phone rang, and I jumped.

Rochelle had that smart-assed smile on her face as I reached down into the sofa cushions under me to retrieve the ringing cell. Two tossed cushions and a pair of socks (okay, not a matched pair; one white and one black) later, I found the phone and looked at the call display.

Interesting.

I snapped the phone open. "Hello?"

"Dix?" came the female voice on the line.

"Yeah, it's me. Who's this?"

I knew who it was, but I've found that if I pretend I don't have call display, people are more inclined to call me again. Strange, I know. But those people who are reluctant to call, but want so badly to call, will sometimes dial my number, wait until I answer, then hang up before saying a word. Works to my advantage sometimes.

"It's Babe Gough."

"Oh, Babe!" I said, acting both surprised and pleased to hear her voice. "Are you okay? I mean … after last night with Albert Valentine and all …"

"Yeah … that was very sad. I'm fine, Dix. Really. But … I'm calling you for another reason."

There was anxiousness in her voice.

I listened. And listened. Nodding occasionally (which, yes, I realized she couldn't see). Rochelle's eyes never left me. And by the time I closed the cell phone with a click, she was more than curious. Even more so as I punched in Dylan's number.

"'Lo," he answered.

That single syllable, uttered in that sleepy, husky voice, sent a thrill arcing through me. God, that was crazy! Maybe I should start setting my alarm earlier, find reasons to call him so I could hear that sleep-roughened voice. Of course, there were better ways to accomplish that. Ways that would also let me see those warm brown eyes, feel the rasp of his beard-roughened face against my tightening —

"Dix?"

I cleared my throat to make sure my words didn't emerge on a croak. "Saddle up, Mr. Foreman."

"Er, Dix, have you been watching cowboy porn again?"

Dammit! Why do I leave my things lying around?

"No! I mean, get dressed! Get ready; we're starting the day early."

"What's up?" By the shift in his voice, I could tell he was already crawling out from between the sheets. No background noises, no mumbles, no toilet flushing down the hall . . . yes, he was alone.

"We just got an invite. Babe Gough. Big brother's out of town for the morning. She wants us to come over and talk clothing design."

"And while we're talking shop, we'll have a chance to look around, ask her questions without big brother watching?"

"Exactly."

He'd be at my place in twenty, he said, and hung up.

"Want me to leave out the cookies?" Rochelle asked as I closed the phone.

"Bitch." I smiled. "And I mean that in the good way."

"As if there was any other way?"

Chapter 7

DYLAN CALLED ME on his cell when he arrived, and I ran down and met him in the street. I climbed into the passenger seat, turning to deposit the box of cookies on the floor behind the driver's seat before buckling myself in.

"What's that?" he asked.

"Cookies." Yep, the cookies. Rochelle hadn't taken them with her when she'd left. She'd been in too much of a hurry herself. I figured penis-shaped or not, they were still cookies, and they might come in handy if we needed to pull a stakeout.

Dylan nodded as though it made perfect sense. Which I'm sure it did; I'd glimpsed a six-pack of bottled water back there which he probably carried for the same reason. You'd be surprised how palatable tepid water from a plastic bottle tasted when you were parched.

I glanced at Dylan. He was looking particularly handsome (I'm talking fresh-out-of-the-shower handsome). And his attractiveness increased exponentially when he handed me a Starbucks skinny latte. True, I'd polished off the extra-large eye-opener Rochelle had brought me, but I was definitely due for my second caffeine infusion of the day. It was almost nine, after all.

We had time to spare before our meeting with Babe Gough, so he suggested we swing by Aunt Gert's place on our way to 33rd Street. That was fine by me. I liked the old girl.

Gert was Dylan's aunt on his father's side. She'd been widowed young and left with two small boys, he told me. That had knocked her right on her butt. But like any good women, Gert had dusted herself off and risen to the challenge before her. Her parents had wanted her to move back home, volunteering to take care of everything, but that wasn't what she'd wanted for herself and her boys.

Apparently everyone told her that she was crazy to do it, but Gert had used all the insurance money — every last dime of it — to open a little café in Marport City's new industrial park (the first one out there). And when the boom hit, she'd made a pretty penny on the lunch crowds in the newly popular park. Gert had supported her family — and put both her sons through university — with her little enterprise. Two years ago, she'd sold the business to her boys, who'd equipped themselves to build on her legacy.

Dylan had just finished relating that last bit as we turned into the narrow drive of Aunt Gert's house.

"And now that she's retired," Dylan concluded, "she spends her days sewing. She always loved to sew. Always had to. But now she doesn't just do it out of necessity. She creates."

"Good for her," I said, meaning it. "I mean, going into business for herself when no one believed in her and disproving the naysayers? Gotta admire that."

Dylan's lips quirked.

"What?" I asked.

"Sounds a little like you."

Which meant what? That he admired me? Kind of a staid, boring, platonic word …

He reached over and took my hand, stroking his thumb over the back of it. Every single cell in my body, from the top of my head to the tips of my toes, came to attention from that simple stroke. I dropped my eyelids to shutter my reaction. A useless tactic, I quickly realized. There was just no ignoring the instant, palpable current that flowed between us.

"Dix, we never really talked about what happened in Florida."

I resisted the urge to lick my suddenly dry lips. "You mean the crossword competitions? I still say penis fits a five-letter word for cockpit dweller. I mean if the pilot is a guy …"

His lips curved in a smile, but his eyes remained serious. "You can't avoid it forever, Dix. You can't avoid me forever."

He hadn't meant the crossword competitions. I knew it. And he knew I knew it.

"You can't deny it, Dix. There's always been something between us. Right from day one."

I wasn't going to deny it. And I pressed every smart-mouth comment back in my throat till it felt like they'd choke me. It was complicated. So very complicated. I was twelve years his senior. I was his boss. I was loving how this was feeling, yet so scared to let anyone get close.

I hated the lump I felt in my throat, and yet, I did push past it. "Dylan, I —"

The door to the small house flew open. "Yoohoo! Come on in, you two!" Gert yelled. She stood there with her measuring tape around her neck, her sewing apron on. She wore her reader glasses down on her nose, as if she'd been hard at work. Then, as though we could possibly miss her standing there, she waved vigorously, her arm moving in a wide windmilling arc.

Saved by the yell.

"Guess we'd better get going," I said, and jumped out of the car.

Dylan's sigh was audible.

An hour later, the new silk pajamas (yes, thank God, no more fleece for me!) were in the back seat of the car. I was still shaking my head. Let's just say Aunt Gert's designs were getting a little more ... uh ... creative. But our cover was that we were designers. And what better place to hawk one's sleepwear than a cuddle club? We had to keep it up! At the last club meeting — oh I'd heard the whispers — other cuddlers were planning on wearing (or was it threatening to wear?) their PJs.

So yes, henceforth, loungewear designer was now officially on that don't-go-there list with veterinarians, doctors, and plumbers.

But in the meantime ...

Dylan grabbed my hand as I reached to open the stairwell door.

I stared down at his big hand which easily swallowed mine. "Dylan, this isn't the time —"

"We're posing as lovers, remember?"

Oh, crap. Of course. Just part of the cover. "I knew that."

Babe met us in the hallway of the complex, right by the stairwell door. "Come in! Come in, quickly!" She appeared really happy to see us, grinning from ear to ear as she motioned us to follow her back in through the club door. The girl certainly wasn't one to dally!

Sunlight filled the cuddle room. The other night it had been overhead lighting on a dimmer switch. The daylight was much nicer. There was the smell of lilac in the air, as if someone had just lit a candle. Soft music played. Not the music we'd heard last night, but something instrumental, soothing, with a sort of Celtic vibe. The place was really calm. Peaceful. And —

Suddenly, loud and jarring, an industrial vacuum cleaner rattled and sucked to life.

I looked at Babe. For some reason, I'd expected her to be doing the vacuuming. All the cleaning, in fact. Maybe because of her cleaning frenzy after cuddle club had de-cuddled the other night. I reminded myself that just because she did the laundry (and yes, I was glad to know the Cuddle-Uppies were laundered between uses) didn't mean she necessarily did all the heavy lifting.

"Eva will be done in the office in a minute," Babe said, raising her voice over the sound of the vacuum.

"Eva? From last night?"

"Yes," Babe said. "Eva Mulligan. She's one of our most regular cuddlers. She and her friends — Zoey Smythe and Brandy Crotty. They hardly ever miss a night."

I did a double take on that last name. "Brandy Crotty, as in the Crottys of Ashford Drive?" We'd met a Brandy the other night, but we hadn't exchanged last names. Possibly because she'd been eyeballing Dylan like he was about to become dinner.

I glanced at Dylan. From the look in his eyes, he recognized the Crotty name too.

Babe shrugged. "Maybe." She snapped her fingers. "Oh, wait, yes! That's where she's from. I recall the address from her application." She peered at me. "Why? Do you know her?"

Of course Babe wouldn't be familiar with that family name — she wasn't from around here. But, boy, did I know the Crotty name! Definitely an old-money family in Marport City. Mainly doctors, with the occasional lawyer or judge thrown in there for variety. Every single one of them was an overachiever.

"So how come Eva is doing the vacuuming?" Dylan asked.

"Working for her membership. She comes in after class almost every day to vacuum through and do a few other little chores, and Gaetan lets her cuddle for free."

"How big of him," I said, not trying to hide the sarcasm. By the looks of pretty, young Eva, I somehow doubted Gaetan's motives for letting her work off her membership dues were pure.

Babe shrugged. Whether she thought I was really complimenting her brother or not, I wasn't sure.

The whirring sound of the vacuum stopped.

Just then Eva backed out of the office, pulling the vacuum behind her.

"Oh!" she said, "I didn't know anyone else was here. Hi, Dylan."

Yes, yes, just ignore me. I'm invisible. Pretend I'm not even here while you make those eyes at Dylan.

"Hi, Eva," Dylan said. "Nice to see you again."

She turned with a shy smile to me. "And Ms. Davidson, hello."

Argh! Okay, so she *did* remember me. And I wasn't invisible ... just old enough to be out of that first name club.

"Let's move this into the office, shall we?" Babe gestured for Dylan and me to precede her.

"See you later, Eva," Dylan said.

"Well, maybe."

I gave a double take on that odd little answer. What? Did she think he was asking her out?

Dylan was half grinning as I sat down beside him, taking the second of two chairs in front of the desk.

"So," Babe said. She was standing behind the huge desk. "What do you think?" She twirled around. A couple of times.

"You dance?" I said. "That's great!"

She looked crestfallen. "No, Dix. My design. I designed this top. Gaetan tells me all the time I have no talent for design. That I should just ... quit while I'm ahead. But, I think it's okay." Babe twirled again. "Soooo ... what do you think?"

What I thought was — *Babe* designed *that*? Now that she was still, the material — a sort of hippie-chic pattern with browns and blues and greens — draped sedately from Babe's slim form. But when she'd whirled, it had done something weird and eye-gripping.

"You made that yourself?" Dylan asked. "That's really ... creative. It's so cool."

"So, you think it's okay?" she asked. "I mean you two are real designers ..."

"Hey, none of that," Dylan said. "When someone spends her days following her own passion, despite what anyone tells her to do ... well, I guess that makes her *real* in my books."

Suddenly that flowing thing Babe had twirled into life didn't look so bad at all.

And clearly, Dylan's compliment made Babe very happy. (I could tell because she spontaneously started spinning again.) She stopped all of a sudden and put both hands on the desk, though whether for balance or emphasis, I wasn't really sure. (I mean the gal had been *really* twirling.) She lowered her voice, "I designed the Cuddle-Uppies, too. No one knows, though."

"What?" I said. That really did surprise me. While I'd been checking out the obits on Rochelle's iPad this morning, I'd done a quick Google search on the Cuddle-Uppies. Clear as anything on the homepage for Gaetan Land was the trademark registered on the product (along with a wide variety of smoothie mixes, hand towels — oh, why, why, why? — and scented body lotion. Totally Gaetan Gough's.

"Gaetan says I'm not supposed to tell anyone — about the Cuddle-Uppies." Babe whispered even lower now, as though she feared the walls had ears. "He says I have no head for business. Well, maybe that's right or maybe it isn't. But I was the one who thought of the Cuddle-Uppies. I make them, too, by hand. Each and every one. Though Gaetan tells people he does it himself, and that he sews in *luvvvve* with every stitch." She held up her hands. "Well, I do the sewing, and I've got the calluses to prove it."

Yeah, I was not liking Gaetan Gough one little bit.

Babe leaned forward. "Can you keep a secret?"

Dylan and I both nodded. "I love secrets," I said. That was so true.

"This whole cuddle club thing — it was my idea. Oh, not the idea of platonic human touch being good for you, of course! That was the researchers. And I know there are informal cuddle clubs all over the world. But the idea of packaging it and commercializing it? That was mine. The soft music, the fresh air pumping in, the atmosphere, oh heck, the whole franchise! I came up with all of it! And yes, the Cuddle-Uppies!"

"And big brother takes all the credit," I didn't even try to keep the bitterness out of my voice. "That's so not fair, Babe."

She nodded. "I know. And now I have these other designs." She waved a hand over her blouse, which was appealing to me more and more all the time. "But Gaetan says they're dumb. And that I'd better just get all notions of being a designer out of my head. I have enough to do here with the bookkeeping, and making the Cuddle-Uppies, and handling his affairs, and —"

"I'll take two," I said.

"I'm sorry, what?"

"Your design," I nodded at her top. "I'll take two of them. I presume you can do custom orders? I'd like one with some lime green tones and another that would go with a sort of hot pink."

She sat down, flustered. "Of course, but —"

"But they're gorgeous. Not for me; I'm not that stylish." Oh shit, dumbest thing ever for a designer to say! "But my mom in Florida would absolutely love to have a couple of these."

Dylan laughed. "Oh, for sure. It'd look great on your mom. And I wouldn't be surprised if the other ladies at the Wildoh want to order one after Kat debuts it." He angled his head. "Actually, so would my aunt Gert. Can you make one for me to give to my aunt?"

"Really?" Babe squeaked.

"Absolutely. Maybe something in gentle greens. She likes green." Dylan turned to me. "What do you think about Mrs. Presley?"

I laughed. "Perfect! Okay, make me a third one, in blues." (I'd have asked her to make it from blue suede, but I was pretty sure she'd have to stick with the same type of fabric and eye-dazzling patterns to achieve the same life-of-its-own effect when the wearer moved.)

Babe looked like she might cry. "You ... you really think I have talent, don't you? I mean, you two are doing it ... living the dream as designers. I can only hope to do that someday."

I wanted to sink into the chair. Lying to find out information was one thing. Lying to find out information and potentially crushing someone in the process (someone you *liked*) was another thing altogether.

We talked design with Babe Gough for the next half hour. (Dylan very skillfully drew her out about her own work, minimizing our contribution to that discussion. The less said, the better, lest we reveal our ignorance of our chosen "profession".) Babe was all smiles — and all hope — as she walked us to the door. Eva was dusting around when we walked back through the office. She barely glanced at either of us. Even Dylan.

"Oh, I think I'd like to place another order," Dylan said.

Babe clapped her hands together. "You want more of my tops?"

"Actually," he said, "I was hoping for one of those Cuddle-Uppies." He gestured to a stack of them piled on the counter, no doubt ready for tonight's cuddle club meeting. "Do you have any extras in stock?"

"I'm afraid not." Babe bit her lip. "I mean, I do have some almost finished, but I haven't sewn in the Gaetan Land logo yet. Gaetan wouldn't approve if I sold one without the logo."

I couldn't imagine why Dylan wanted one of those horrors. Maybe as a joke for a friend. And who was I to stand between a man and his Cuddle-Uppie. "Gaetan isn't here. And we won't tell."

She gnawed her lip some more. "I really couldn't."

I shrugged. "Then give him one of those." I gestured to the plastic-wrapped Cuddle-Uppies on the counter. "I mean, they must be sanitized between uses, right?"

"Of course!" Babe sounded shocked that there might be any question about that.

"That works for me," Dylan said. "Then you can finish one of the other ones and slide it into the lineup."

Babe look undecided. "I don't know —"

"Let me guess," I said. "Gaetan wouldn't like it."

Babe tipped her chin up. "No, he wouldn't. But like you said, he's not here." She plucked a plastic-wrapped blanket from the pile and handed it to Dylan. "And what he doesn't know won't hurt him, right?"

"Right," Dylan said, tucking the blanket under his arm. "Just add that to my bill."

"Oh, no, just take it." Babe said.

"Are you sure?" Dylan asked.

"Absolutely. What are friends for, right?"

Babe's parting comment gnawed at my conscience as we crossed the parking lot. Some friends. The poor woman thought we were actual designers, qualified to opine on her designs. When we reached the car, Dylan opened the door for me. I'm as independent as they come, but hey, I like those gestures. It shows a man is paying attention.

A moment later, Dylan slid behind a wheel, turning to toss the plastic-wrapped Cuddle-Uppie in the back seat. Which reminded me . . .

"Um . . . Dylan, what possessed you that you suddenly had to have one of those abominations?"

"You'll see." He didn't turn to look at me, but as we drove away, I could see his lips were curved in a smile.

Chapter 8

I ALWAYS FELT sorry for women like Babe Gough.
She was so smart, so talented, so being taken advantage of. Unsure of herself, she was just the kind of women that bullies and users (aka, turds) preyed on. The worst part was that her own brother — that over-bearing, obnoxious jerk of an older brother — had no doubt helped make her that way, undermining her confidence at every turn. And going through life being called Babe? Not so great, even if it was just a family pet name. Grrrrrr.

I'd checked out the degrees on the small office wall as Dylan and I had sat there this morning. They were copies, of course, not originals. The originals were no doubt hanging on the walls of the California offices. Gaetan's diploma in massage therapy (and no, not from the reputed Cornick School of Massage in Chicago) hung at perfect eye-level on the wall behind the solid maple desk. Meanwhile, Babe's (or rather, Rhonda Mary Gough's) honors degree in marketing and business from a reputable university was barely level with the low filing cabinet, and half behind it.

"Is she any good at what she does?" I asked Dylan as he drove us back to the office. (I knew there was no point asking him to elaborate on that "You'll see" comment back there.)

"Eva Mulligan? Well, I guess she is … but honestly, Dix, I don't know much about dusting and vacuuming. No more than you do. Well, probably more than you do, but really, not that much."

My glare bore a steaming hole in the side of his head. Well, not literally, but I think he definitely felt the heat of it. "I meant Babe," I grated. "Do you think her designs are any good?"

Dylan shrugged. "Yeah, I think she's pretty good. I mean, I bet your mom will love those tops, and I know Aunt Gert will flip over hers. Mrs. Presley, too, especially if Babe can make her one that complements her blue suede shoes." He shot me a quick, appraising glance. "Can't see you wearing one of them, though."

"Why not?"

He threw me another quick glance, this one of the "what, are-you-crazy?" variety. (And yeah, I get enough of those to distinguish them.)

"Too trendy," he said.

"How can it be too trendy? As far as we know, there's only one of them, and Babe was wearing it."

He rolled his eyes. "Okay, it looks to me like something that could become very trendy, probably sell enough to make somebody rich, then fall off the fashion map faster than last year's American Idol can fade from memory."

"Like bolero jackets, you mean? Or the shrug." I shuddered. "Remember those?"

"Or tie-dye T-shirts."

"Bell-bottoms pants!" I responded.

"Women's jackets with linebacker-worthy shoulder pads!"

Hey, I'd liked those. Best not to mention that, though. What else could I dig up from the tickle trunk of my memory? Oh, got it! He'd never top this: "The skort!" I announced triumphantly.

He lifted an admiring eyebrow. "Not bad. But consider the leisure suit. The blue leisure suit."

Crap. Okay, that was pretty hard to top. Everything else I could think of had come back into fashion again. It looked like I was going to lose this one. Not that I'd admit it if I could help it. The trick was to distract him ...

"So what are you saying, Dylan? I'm not fashionable?"

He chuckled. "Trying to distract me, Dix?"

Yes, dammit. "Answer the question."

"I didn't say unfashionable. I said not trendy. There's a difference."

"Really?" God, Dix. Way to fish.

He sent me an amused glance, then focused on the road again. "Yeah, there's a difference. You don't chase trends. You don't have to. You're classic."

Pleasure hummed through me. Well, until I started unpacking his words. Classic? Didn't that mean old? Like 80s rock anthems or a 1967 Chevy Impala?

As though he could hear the buzz of my thoughts, he laughed. "Quit it, Dix. It was a compliment. A high one."

"Well, good then." My face burned at his perceptiveness, and I was glad for the darkened interior of the car. Time to shift the conversation back to Babe. "She really has talent then, doesn't she?"

"She has a lot of potential."

"Just to be clear, are we talking Babe or Eva?" I asked dryly.

He snorted a laugh. "Definitely talking about Babe. And she has a helluva lot more potential than she'll ever realize if she spends her life stuck under her brother's controlling thumb." Dylan's voice had taken on an edge I heartily approved of. "And you know, I'll bet you and I aren't the only ones to realize that."

I nodded. "Yeah. Bet we're not."

Not surprisingly, Detective Richard Head was at my office door within three minutes of Dylan and my returning from our meeting with Babe Gough.

Perfect timing on his part? Great luck? Obsession with this hot-as-hell private dick? Cop's intuition?

None of the above. My intuition told me he'd been waiting at Perky Joe's — the little coffee and donut shop around the corner from my office — until we rolled in. Well, my intuition and that giant cup of coffee with the Perky Joe's logo on the side that he clutched.

"Would you like a cookie to go with that coffee?" I asked, hopefully. "They have sprinkles." (Yes, these were the ones I'd packed for the road when Dylan had picked me up this morning.)

He declined with a wave. The kind of wave that made me think he hadn't even really heard me. He seemed distracted. Upset, even. Not his usual demeanor.

Head and I hadn't had the chance to talk since the death of Albert Valentine last evening. This conversation should be a doozie (ha, doozie! — those *oozie* words crack me up).

Dylan went around behind the desk to check for messages, and I perched on the desk's edge. Dickhead glanced around. The only seating in the outer office was a worn sofa which was currently occupied by Blow-Up Betty.

Yup, good old Betty. Normally, we kept her stashed in the closet in my inner office, but after a rash of break-ins, we'd plunked her out here, within view of the window. Overt video surveillance was a non-starter in my line of business, what with so many of my clients being so shy.

Camera shy, that is. Yes, we had an alarm system, but alarms went off so often in this part of town, they were practically white noise at this point. So we'd propped Blow-Up Betty on the sofa, and got into the habit of leaving a low light burning and the small TV in the corner on. (We only got one station, but Betty didn't seem to mind.)

"Have a seat." I gestured at the couch. "Betty's not particular."

Dickhead flopped down on the sofa, his weight depressing the worn cushions in such a way that Blow-Up Betty tipped over onto his lap, head first.

"Whoa. I guess she really *isn't* particular."

Cursing, Dickhead shoved the doll back to her own end of the sofa. Which was altogether too mild a response for the man I'd come to know and loathe. I looked at him closer and realized he looked like hell. His eyes had that heavy look, as if he'd not slept much. He definitely needed a shave, and I'm guessing a shower too. Even his necktie — with the crooked knot a good inch below where it should be — betrayed his worse-for-wear state.

He was worried.

"I checked before I came over," he said. "The unofficial-soon-to-be-official word on Albert Valentine — natural causes. Sudden cardiac arrest."

"Did he have a history of heart issues?"

"Some evidence of coronary artery disease according to the coroner, but it turns out that he wasn't exactly big on doctors. If he had any arrhythmia going on, his family doc didn't know about it. Of course, he hadn't seen his own doctor in over 18 months. In fact, Albert's last interaction with a physician was to wrangle a scrip for ED drugs at a walk-in clinic where he presented himself as an orphaned patient."

Huh. Well, there were enough of those around — people whose family doctors had retired or moved or gone on to specialize or died. "So, it's looking pretty open-and-shut?" I asked.

"Unless something shows up on the toxicology report." Dickhead dragged at his already too-loose tie. "What do you make of it, Dix?"

And yeah, I caught it: Dix with no derogatory suffix. Oh man, the guy really was troubled.

I shrugged. "It does happen," I pointed out. "I hear that younger and seemingly fitter people than Albert Valentine have erectile dysfunction. So don't beat yourself up if you —"

"I mean the cardiac arrest!"

"Oh, sorry." (I wasn't.) "Yeah, could be pretty open and shut. I mean, nothing turned up in the tox screens for the other decedents. What are the chances they'll find something in Albert's?"

"I know. But I still don't buy it." He looked at me dead on. "What about you, Dodd? What's that famous intuition of yours telling you?"

"I don't believe it was natural causes either. I think —" Whoa, wait a sec ... had Detective Richard Head, my evil nemesis, just complimented me? I like it! I like it *a lot*! But this was no time to be talking about me. "Hey, could you say that again? The part about my *famous intuition*?"

Dylan coughed to cover a laugh.

Dickhead ignored me. Not even an eye roll. "But if someone is responsible for these deaths," he persisted, "how are they doing it? How are they inducing heart failure in these victims? Who has the means? Holy hell, who has the motive?"

I didn't have the answers, but I knew I would soon enough. Hopefully before there were any more deaths.

"This ... this could ruin me, Dix," Head said.

"The whole going to a cuddle club thing, you mean?" Dylan asked. "Prolly not great for the rep back at the station, I guess."

"Not at all," I agreed, "but I've got a feeling that's the least of Detective Head's worries now. Am I right?"

"I shouldn't have bailed." Dickhead sat forward, leaned his elbows on his knees, and put his head in his hands. "As soon as I was out of there, I knew it. I ... I shouldn't have left the scene. I'm a cop, dammit! And on duty or not, I was on the goddamned scene. If I truly thought a crime had been committed, then what the fuck was I doing hightailing it out of there? If Leola Pivans digs deep enough on this, I'm fucked. That's one bulldog of a young constable."

No wonder the guy looked like shit. He'd been up all night dancing with his devils.

"That's not like me." Dickhead sat up. "You're not exactly a fan of mine, Dodd, but even you know that's not like me at all! What the hell was I doing, leaving like that?"

"I have a better question," I said.

He looked up at me. "What's that?"

"What the hell were you doing there in the first place? I mean, come on, a cuddle club? Where people *cuddle?* Yeah, I know you went there on a lark weeks ago when your cousin was in town. I get it. I'm sure it was hysterical. But, why go back? Again and again? You see what I'm saying? That's the better question."

Dickhead opened his mouth as if to defend himself, then stopped. His jaw hardened. "Look, that's beside the point. The point is, I had to do something about it. I couldn't just leave it lie like that."

He looked up at me, then quickly glanced away.

"What?" I asked. There was something he had to tell me, but clearly didn't want to.

"What did you do, Detective?" Dylan said. Clearly he'd recognized the uneasy look too.

"I *had* to do it," Dickhead said. "There was no choice."

"Had to do what?" Wherever this was going, I was pretty sure I wasn't going to like it.

"I opened a file on Albert Valentine this morning. An official one."

As I asked the question I knew the answer to, I felt my fists clenching. "I see. So how did you explain Dylan and me being there?"

He cleared his throat, he loosened his tie, and then he ducked his head (quite wisely). "I ... uh ... I sort of told them that you'd come to me and asked for my help."

Instant rage. It flooded every cell as his words knifed into my brain.

That worm! He was the one who'd come groveling to me, asking for *my* help. And now he was spinning that all backwards, like *I'd* gone crawling to *him*?

Miraculously, I did not take a swing at him. Well, not with an ax or something. Not even the easy-grip lamp I keep on the side table there by the couch for just such a purpose. Instead, I lunged for him, prepared to tear him a new one with my bare hands.

"Whoa! Wait." Dylan caught me around the waist and hauled me back. "Listen, Dix. It makes sense. Think about it. If we had managed to come out of there with incriminating evidence, what would we have done with it? This isn't a cheating spouse case, Dix. It's potentially a murder case. If the fruits of the investigation are going to hold up in court, it needs to be an official investigation. If there's evidence to be found, it has to be documented, with a clear chain of possession from the time it's seized to the time it's logged into evidence."

Dammit! He was right.

"Exactly!" Dickhead said. "Listen to the kid."

I think I growled, though I'm not sure whether it was at the position Dickhead had put me in or the fact that he'd just referred to Dylan as the kid. Dylan wisely tightened his grip on my arm.

"It's not the opening of the file I object to, you weasel." I felt my fingernails digging into my palms and forced my fists to unclench. "It's the timing. By fleeing the scene last night, you managed to avoid being tarred as a cuddler, and as a convenient bonus, you get to tell your buddies that I came to you for help."

Head blew out an exasperated breath. "Jesus, Dix, chill out. The optics are fine. This will not put you in a bad light with the cops. On the contrary. It looks like a smart move, the only responsible thing to do under the circumstances."

"Under the *circumstances*?" I tugged my arm and Dylan released his grip. I guess he must have judged me cooled down enough not to assault a peace officer. He was right, but just barely. "Which circumstances would those be? Oh, wait, I remember — the *totally bogus* ones which you manipulated to your advantage."

"Okay, okay!" Dickhead dragged a hand through his short hair. "I was a jerk to leave. I've admitted it. But what's done is done. This was the only way to salvage it."

I turned away, closed my eyes and counted to ten. Then I turned back to Dickhead. "Okay, that's how we'll play it. We don't have any choice now. But you owe me, mister. Big time!"

And I would surely collect.

Chapter 9

YES, EVENTUALLY, I calmed down. Possibly because by the time Richard Head left my office, he looked thoroughly dejected. I made certain of it.

Let me back up a bit. Back when he hired me to work this case, Dickhead had explained he'd originally gone to Gaetan Land on a lark when his cousin, a Pinellas County Sheriff's Deputy, had been visiting from Florida. You know how it is: boys have too much to drink, boys do something stupid. Like get a circle of barbed wire tattooed on their biceps. Or worse, a flaming heart with someone's name on it. (Urgh.) Or — I don't know — hit on somebody's mother (God help them, not mine! Katt Dodd would hit back). Or maybe join the dancers on stage at a strip club and get bounced out of there. (Okay, we women have been known to do that, too. And not just me and Mom, right? Right?) And okay, sure, a pair of intoxicated men might even end up at a cuddle club, just for the giggles.

Yeah, I'd bought his story then, and I still believed it. I could totally see that happening on one of those boys-will-be-boys nights. (Have I mentioned that I've met the aforesaid Sheriff's Deputy?) But why had he kept going back?

He'd effectively deflected me the first time I asked the question, but I put it to him again: "You never answered my question, Detective. After your cousin headed back down south, why did you keep going back to the cuddle club?"

He'd still had no answer, other than to growl, "Jesus, Dix, why does anyone do anything?" Honestly, I think it was a mystery to Head himself, one he really didn't want to ponder.

And while I was at it, I also demanded to know why he hadn't forewarned me that I could expect to encounter Elizabeth Bee at cuddle club. His response to that question was perhaps even more disturbing.

He admitted he hadn't made the connection between Elizabeth Bee and the Case of the Flashing Fashion Queen. At least, not until I rattled his cage about it. I could see that fact troubled him as much as it did me. What was it about that place? Somehow, it not only kept him coming back, but it apparently also took the edge off his observational skills.

So, like I said, Dickhead left looking miserable, thanks to me poking him about things he'd rather not have poked, but he did promise he'd see us again at Gaetan Land for the next cuddle.

Dylan and I would be there, that was for damned sure! Was I overly fond of the cuddle club? Nope. Nor was Dylan. But more and more my intuition was tingling itself all the way up my spine, and slapping me upside the head. Something was not right in Gaetan Land.

So, yeah, we were working for the weekend . . . .

We decided there really was not much sense in working at the office when my condo would be so much more comfortable. More room. More coffee. More . . . everything. So we cleared our schedules (which in my case meant postponing my date with a couple of Torchwood reruns), unpacked the whiteboards and dry erase markers which were still packed in their moving boxes, and stowed them in the trunk of Dylan's car for transport. Then we each went our own way for the afternoon, agreeing to meet at my place at 7 p.m.

Yep. A night for hard work. Brainstorming. Nothing more.

Oh boy . . .

More indeed.

Dylan arrived right on time. He had his own key to my condo, of course. It came in handy on those occasions when I was working surveillance and he had to retrieve something from my place (such as clean underwear; ah . . . memories). Tonight, though, he rang the buzzer.

I buzzed him in, and when I heard the elevator across the hall stop on my floor, I opened my door.

He was grinning as he stepped off the elevator. My eyes raked over his body. He held the whiteboard under one arm and something else in his other hand, but that's not what grabbed my attention. His attire did. He wore his usual leather jacket, of course, and those size 13 motorcycle boots, but between the hem of his jacket and the top of his boots, he sported silk pajamas. "Headed for a sleepover, are we?"

His grin widened and he arched a provocative eyebrow.

Oh shit! With the current of sexual tension that had been humming between us, *that's* what I came out with?

Okay, pulling foot out of mouth now.

To make room for something else, possibly?

Dix! I slapped that sly, dirty-minded little voice down and stepped back. "Come on in."

"Thanks." He followed me inside. As soon as I closed the door, he fished something out of the bag he'd been holding in his right hand and passed it to me. "I brought yours too."

Omigosh, it was Aunt Gert's latest creation, a pair of silk pajamas. I'd left them at the office, figuring I'd be in on Sunday before cuddle club to collect them.

"Thanks." *I think.*

Dylan said, "Why don't you change into them while I get the whiteboard set up?"

I did a double take. Maybe this *was* shaping up to be a sleepover.

"Relax," Dylan chided.

"I *am* relaxed," I squeaked.

"Seriously, Dix," he said. "I just figured the more we're in cuddle club mode, the more we'll be in that mindset."

"Oh. Oh, of course."

"Unless maybe you were thinking something else?"

The lazy, teasing note in his voice made my toes curl. Literally.

But what if he was just teasing? He *had* brought the whiteboard, after all. And it did make sense to get into cuddle club mode. Sort of.

Lord, did I *want* him to be just teasing?

I caught myself and laughed. God, the man had barely just got in the door. Even if he was interested in … more, I wasn't *that* desperate. Well, I didn't want to appear that desperate, anyway.

He smiled as though he'd followed my entire mental process and didn't need to ask why I was laughing.

"Pajamas it is, then." I nodded to the living room. "Set us up in there, would you?"

With that, I took the bag with Aunt Gert's PJs into my bedroom, stripped down to my underwear, and tried them on.

The pajamas were royal blue, and if I do say so myself, royal blue looks pretty damned amazing on me. Seriously. I *own* it. The vee neck was low, plunging even. The soft sleeves were flared, and they floated down over my wrists. The pajama bottoms floated down to my toes. (I bent over, pulled them back up and tightened the drawstring. (God, that would have been embarrassing!) Then I turned to look in the mirror.

Okay, yeah, I'm tough-as nails Dix Dodd, PI. But damn, I love the feel of silk against my skin. And I loved the way these PJs looked on me. Well, almost loved the way they looked. I turned around and glanced over my shoulders. Yep, there they were. Those little bulges right below my bra where it dug in.

Argh! I'm not one for fashion, but even I knew this was not especially attractive. I bit my lip as I pondered the options.

"All set out here," Dylan called.

Okay, I'd have to go bra shopping before the next cuddle club meeting, but for now …

I stripped back down to my underwear, took off the same, then pulled the pajamas back on.

Wow. I looked —

"Fantastic," Dylan said as I joined him in the living room.

"I'm sorry, what's that?" I said, cupping my ear.

"I said you look fantastic," he repeated, his mouth curving in that half smile I loved so much. "But you heard me the first time."

I had. I just liked hearing it. Does the guy know me or what?

He'd set everything up. The whiteboard was on its stand and the various color markers awaited. A couple of the yellow notepads I worked with (I'm a doodler) sat on the coffee table in front of the sofa. Then I spied it — the Cuddle-Uppie Dylan had wrangled from Babe earlier in the day was thrown over the sofa. Was that why he'd wanted it? For us to cuddle up under? Then I noted the other details. Soft music played in the background. Two low candles burned on the coffee table, and he'd poured two glasses of red wine.

Dylan caught me looking at the set up and shrugged. "Just trying to recreate the scene."

"But we drink smoothies at cuddle club," I said dryly.

Another lift and fall of those shoulders. "Yeah, but you don't have the equipment to make smoothies, let alone the ingredients. Whereas you *do* have a shitload of wine."

Well, that was true. "And the candlelight?"

He grinned. "No dimmer switch to lower the lighting like they do at cuddle club. I just improvised."

I laughed, but it had a breathless quality even I could hear. "You have an answer for everything tonight, don't you?"

His grin faded and his face turned serious. "If this scares you, if this is too much, just say the word, Dix," he said. "The candles go out and the lights go up. I'll dump the wine."

Okay, decision time. If I gave the word, it would be boss and employee. If I didn't . . .

God, I'd shut the guy down so many times. Shut myself down.

I swallowed. It didn't help much. "Shame to waste good wine."

We settled in on the couch. Oh God, we more than settled in. We got under the Cuddle-Uppie (though we used it more like a blanket, stopping short of poking our heads through those whack-a-mole holes). Of course, I was as tense as a board to start with — that whole closeness thing. Dylan didn't make any sudden moves, but rather just waited for me to relax. (Did I mention he knows me pretty well?) Eventually, with the wine and the warmth and the talk (we really were here to try to solve the case), I actually did relax into him. It felt good. Better than good, but by focusing on the case, we kinda kept it normal. In fact, by the time I crawled out from under the blanket to pour us a second glass of wine, the weirdness of it had completely dissipated.

"So," I said, handing him his refilled glass and crawling back under the blanket, "why does a macho guy like Richard Head keep coming back to cuddle club?" This time, I let my leg relax against his without having to will the muscles to cooperate. Progress. Or maybe it was the wine. "I'm pretty sure it isn't Gaetan's fine company."

"And why do those women keep going back? Seriously, on a Friday night, why would those beautiful girls find themselves at Gaetan Land?"

"You're thinking of Eva again? Or Brandy?" I felt a little twist in my gut as I thought of Brandy. Eva was sweet. Zoey was cute. Brandy was absolutely interested. Even though we'd only had one cuddle, she'd latched onto Dylan every time she got a chance. Flirted with him. Gave me the evil eye and that little smirk I just wanted to slap off her face . . .

He laughed, low in his throat, knowing. "Brandy's a pretty young thing, but she's got nothing on you, Dix, and you know it. Same goes for Elizabeth, Eva, Zoey, or any of the others."

"Thank you," I managed to say, trying so hard to pretend his words just now hadn't affected me. "Okay, back to the case. Maybe . . . maybe there is a genuine appeal to cuddling." I plunged on, determined to steer the conversation back to safer ground. "I've heard of stranger things, I guess."

I could have added I'd *seen* stranger things, but didn't want to bring up my porn collection just then. Though that 70's classic, *Men Who Keep Their Socks On*, came to mind. *Ooh, ribbed ...*

"Yeah, but most of the cuddle clubs I've looked into online are free. Folks just get together at homes or rec centres or church basements or some such place where it's free to assemble. Why are people paying Gaetan Gough such high fees to join his little club?" Dylan asked. "And why are they staying there? I mean, why not take the activity to a home venue once they'd all met? That guy Elizabeth was with — Hugh Drammen — you know he's loaded. Why doesn't he offer up his place for the group to gather, sans payment? Okay, granted, Gaetan's got this really fine blond Richard Simmons thing going on. Some people might find that appealing, I guess. But seriously, except for Drammen — and you know he's probably footing the bill for Elizabeth Bee — who could really afford those rates? Geez, Eva *cleans* the place for the privilege of hanging out there."

Tingle. Tingle. Tingle. Oh how I felt the tingle.

Yep, something was going on in that mind of mine. This didn't sit right. But what was it? What made all those very different people keep coming back? What made Gaetan's club such an addiction?

But then I realized Dylan had stopped talking and was looking at me. Specifically, he was looking at my mouth. Suddenly the tingling feeling wasn't just in my mind. He was going to kiss me. I tipped my head back and, lest he had any doubts that I wanted this, parted my lips. I had the satisfaction of seeing the heat leap in his eyes, then his face blurred as he leaned in to kiss me. I felt a shudder of anticipation rack me as his lips neared ... then stopped.

"Dix?" My name was a warm breath oh-so-close to my lips. "I'm gonna kiss you."

I sucked in air to fill my suddenly oxygen-starved lungs. "I sorta figured."

"I'm gonna do more, too, if you'll let me. Will you let me?"

I shuddered again. Would I let him touch me? Strip me? Make love to me? Sitting here beneath the blanket, breathing him in, my breasts swelling and an ache starting low in my belly ... damn right I would!

"God, yes!"

I slid an arm around his neck and tried to pull him down that last few millimeters so our mouths would meet, but he resisted.

"Dix?"

Dear Lord, did we have to analyze this before it even happened? "Yeah?" I husked.

"You're hurting my neck!"

"Oh, sorry," I loosened my grip.

"If we start making love, you're not going to suddenly have a brain wave, solve the case and bail out on me, are you?"

Okay, so I'd done that to him once. Okay, twice, if we're counting. I suppose I couldn't blame him for asking. But there was no danger of that this time. I hadn't a clue what was going on at that cuddle club. And just now, I didn't much care. "No, I'm definitely not going to do that."

Finally — finally! — he closed that tiny distance and kissed me.

For a moment, that was our only point of contact — our fused mouths, our shared breath. Of course, he tasted of the Starbucks breath mints he always carried and that other taste that was uniquely him. The clean smell of whatever shaving product he used invaded my senses. It was just exactly as I remembered, and yet it felt new and impossibly exciting.

Then he cupped my face in his big hand *(yes!)*, angled my chin and deepened the kiss *(yes, yes, yes!)*. My hands found his chest, sliding over the silk of his pajamas, thrilling at the hard heat of him beneath the blanket and the strong thudding of his heart.

Then his hand dropped lower. I moaned my approval against his mouth as his thumb stroked my throat. That was enough for a while (God, the man kissed just how I liked!). Then he slid his palm down, splaying his fingers beneath my collarbone. His flesh was so hot against mine, I wouldn't have been surprised to see a brand materialize on my skin. Of course, the moment he did that, I needed more contact. I leaned into him, pressing my breasts to his chest. This time it was Dylan's turn to groan. As I hoped, that big, talented hand slid down further still, to cup my breast through the thin silk of my pajamas. *Yes, yes, yes, yes, yes!*

My hand flexed of its own accord and I dragged my fingernails lightly down his side, drawing a shudder from him, then another as I slid my hand under his pajama top to smooth over the bare skin of his abdomen. Flat, hard, warm, smooth. I soaked up the tactile sensations. Soon I would have to shuck off the cozy blanket so I could see the glorious landscape I was touching, but for now, it was kinda hot — by which I mean *hawt* — being under the Cuddle-Uppie with Dylan. Probably because it reminded me of fooling around under the blanket on that too-short flight back from Florida.

"God, Dix, you feel good." His hand was sure and urgent as he palmed the smallish mound, but his voice was gratifyingly hoarse.

"Oh, I feel good all right," I said shakily. "But not as good as I'm going to feel very shortly." And that was God's honest truth. I was so aroused, it was going to take embarrassingly little effort on his part. But afterward ... after he'd ... um, bounced back, so to speak, I intended to put the man through his paces. The thought sent my excitement soaring even higher.

His laugh fanned my throat now and I arched my neck, the better for him to nuzzle and nibble it. He obliged, his mouth trailing tingles of electricity wherever it touched. When his mouth went to my ear, it felt as though he'd struck a nerve that went straight to my ... um, happy place.

"God, Dylan, I want you so much!" Suddenly restless, I shifted to straddle his lap, facing him, and the blanket fell away.

"Nice move." His hands shifted to my hips, pressing me down so I could feel his hard-on through the thin layers of silk between us. It was all I could do not to totally *grind* on him, but the way I was feeling, I was afraid the festivities would be over before they got started. No way was I settling for a dry hump. I was getting laid.

"I want to see you." I started fumbling with the buttons of his pajamas, but Aunt Gert had made them too well. The buttons were snug in their buttonholes, requiring considerable patience to unbutton. More patience than I had at that moment. I grabbed two fistfuls of pajama top hem and yanked up and out. Some of the buttons popped through the buttonholes, but at least one went flying.

"Dix!" Dylan sounded slightly shocked.

"What? The buttonholes were too small." I grabbed my own top by the hem and Dylan braced as though he thought he was going to lose an eye to flying buttons. But of course, I just whipped the garment over my head and tossed it aside.

The shock in his eyes turned to something else as he stared at my breasts.

Have I mentioned that I'm forty? Yeah. And so are my breasts — both of 'em (especially the one on the left, but that's another story). They aren't perfect and gravity-defyingly perky. Nor are they plastic. But they're mine, and I'm kind of okay with them. No, I'm *better* than okay with them. I refuse to hate my own body, no matter what the media tells me. But seeing the frank appreciation on Dylan's face, the way his eyes darkened with need — damn, that was hot!

He reached up to cup my breasts and I couldn't help it — I ground down on him, just once, then forced my hips to still. *Better things, Dix. Better things.* "God, this is so good!"

"Mmmm." Dylan's voice was muffled against my breast. He'd taken my left nipple into his mouth and was suckling it.

I sank my fingers into his hair, holding him there. "Oh, man, I think we should take that blanket to work. When we're not busy, we could cuddle under it on that couch in my office."

Dylan mouth stopped moving, and I felt a new tension in him.

Noooo! I flexed my fingers against his scalp. "What's wrong?"

His hands were at my waist now, biting in as he lifted me off him and deposited me on the couch. "The Cuddle-Uppie," he hoarsed.

"What about it?"

"That's got to be it. That's why people keep going back to cuddle club. Pheromones, Dix. Or a drug of some kind. They must be spiking the Cuddle-Uppies."

His words sank in, the logic of them inescapable. This particular Cuddle-Uppie had been primed and ready for tomorrow night's cuddle session, sealed in that plastic bag.

My eyes met Dylan's and I knew that I wasn't getting laid tonight. Not when there was a possibility our passion owned something to a chemical stimulant.

Damn you, Gaetan Gough! Damn you straight to hell.

Chapter 10

A s I LAY there in bed, I thought about Mother's cookies. If they weren't sitting in the back of Dylan's car right now, I'd be eating them, sprinkles or no. I'd be taking my frustration out on the penis-shaped sweets with every single dick-snapping bite.

I'm too old to be heartbroken. Too tough to be hurt. Too amazing to be smacking my head in that "doh" kind of way. (And now my hand hurt.)

Pheromones in the Cuddle-Uppies! Why hadn't I seen that right away? Why hadn't I seen it at all?

Don't get me wrong. I'm not that competitive. I'm glad Dylan thought of it. But why'd he have to think about it at that particular moment?

"'Cuz when it comes to getting laid, Dix Dodd, you suck!" I muttered, feeling sorry for myself.

It seemed so obvious now. Of course that's what kept people coming back to the cuddle club. Synthetic hormones. It made perfect sense. I'd heard rumors over the years about such things being pumped into the air in nightclubs and casinos. Had Gaetan moved this questionable technology into his cuddle club franchise? It was a glaringly obvious question. One that should have occurred to me, in fact, the very first night. It explained why I'd kinda sorta almost felt a little twinge of something not entirely repulsive when Dickhead had put his arm around me beneath the Cuddle-Uppie that night. A memory I'd pretty much succeeded in suppressing. (Especially since he'd informed the police force that I'd called him in on this investigation — grrr.)

But damn the bad luck that it had occurred to Dylan when it did. If he could have staved off that epiphany for another five minutes, we'd have shared a yee-ha moment instead of an ah-ha moment. (Yeah, five minutes; I'd been that ready.)

Argh! I'm cursed.

Always so close but no ... cigar. (God, for once a suitable metaphor comes to mind, and it's just that damn phallic!)

I respected Dylan's decision to call a halt. Really, I did. My logical self was right there with him. My physical self, on the other hand ... well, it was sort of a talk-to-the hand thing happening there. (Er, did I mention Dylan and I left our business ... um ... unfinished?).

Dylan had left, and taken the Cuddle-Uppie with him. In the morning, he would deliver it to Dickhead. As evidence, it wouldn't stand up in court, but if the forensic lab found something on this one, it would be easy enough for Dickhead to seize another wrapped and sealed one. One that wouldn't make its way into evidence via my couch.

I cringed beneath the covers. I probably should be taking it to Dickhead myself, but I just wasn't up to explaining how we'd come to suspect the Cuddle-Uppie was doped."Well, you see, Dylan and I were making out under it and I got scarily aggressive and tore his buttons off and was about to rock his world (possibly traumatizing him) when he twigged to it." Frankly, I didn't know how Dylan planned to explain it, but I knew he'd be a gentleman about it. I would come off looking better than I deserved.

Oh, God.

I pulled the covers up over my head.

On Sunday morning, I was awake (in the shower, even) well before the alarm went off. Even before Rochelle called to tell me she'd reconnected last night with a guy (okay, not just some guy, but a rising political star) whose sister could hook us up with U2 tickets. Was I in?

Oh, I was *so* in.

But after that, I spent a slow Sunday. Slow and anxious.

I did laundry, vacuumed, dusted in the not-so-hard-to-reach places, and did a few other chores around my condo. I did go over to the office for a bit and sorted through some more boxes, checked the few voice mail messages and gathered up the couple bills that had been shoved under the door. I even hit the mall. Yeah, me in a mall. I'd remembered I needed a new bra if I was going to wear those silk PJs in public. Recalling the panty line thing, I even bought a pair of thong panties. Around noon, I picked up a pizza so I could have it cold for supper. (See? Domestic as hell). Finally, I dressed for the evening, if putting on pajamas can be called *dressing*, and started counting the minutes until cuddle club.

Maybe a little too longingly. That bugged me. Really bugged me. I mean, I *knew* about the pheromones, after all. Unlike those other people who had no idea why they wanted to go back so badly. Well, they were going to be disappointed; the cuddle would not be cast tonight.

That's right — there would be no cuddling. Dylan and I had talked about it, and our agenda tonight was to thwart any and all snuggling, by whatever means necessary. There had to be a link between the pheromones in the Cuddle-Uppies and the heart attacks, possibly exacerbated by the physical ... um ... stimulation of cuddling. Therefore, until we got the test results back and could move to stop Gaetan, we had to make sure the cuddlers stayed safe.

But how to accomplish said thwarting?

My cell phone rang and my heart leapt. I looked at the caller ID. Dylan. "Hey."

"Hey yourself," Dylan said. "Your ride's here. Or will be by the time you get down to the street."

"Perfect. Thanks. See you in a minute."

I grabbed my jacket and purse, locked up and started down the hall to the elevator. My mind went back to gnawing on the problem at hand. How did we stop them from getting under the Cuddle-Uppies? We had to figure something out, and fast.

"I have a plan," I announced to the empty corridor. "A brilliant, brilliant, plan."

I didn't have a plan, doubly-brilliant or otherwise. But well, hey, I put it out into the universe. And hoped like hell the universe would think of something double quick.

I pushed the call button and stood, waiting for both an answer and the elevator.

Well, at least the elevator came.

Frackin' non-compliant universe.

When the elevator doors closed on me, my thoughts turned to Dylan. I was both anxious and nervous about seeing him after what had happened last night. And what had almost happened. My mind still swam in the warmth of it.

His SUV pulled up just as I exited the building. I climbed into it.

"Hey," he said.

Hadn't we done this on the phone? "Hey," I answered, fastening my seatbelt.

He didn't reach out to touch me or kiss me, and I don't know whether

I was disappointed or relieved. But when I looked at him, it was all there in his eyes. Nothing had changed.

Relief. Yup, that was definitely relief I was feeling.

"How was your Sunday?" he asked. So I told him about Rochelle scoring the U2 tickets and my puttering around. I asked him about his day, and he told me, in the same mundane detail. What we *didn't* talk about was last night.

My cheeks heated (again) at the memory of it, and I was grateful for the darkness in the interior of the SUV. God, I'd gone wild woman on him. The things I would have done to that boy ... Well, okay, not so much the first time, but the second and third time, after we'd taken the edge off. Oh, Christmas! I mean, I'm no prude, but no man had ever driven me crazy like that. And to think the stupid pheromones in the stupid Cuddle-Uppie were responsible. What if Dylan hadn't tumbled to it and called a halt? What if I'd gone on to do those things with him? Where could we have gone from there? I mean, how would you retreat after a night like that?

And now I guessed there were some residual effects from sustained contact with the Cuddle-Uppie, because I was getting aroused all over again just thinking about it. And as we reached our destination and made our way through the building, it was all I could do not to push Dylan into the nearby elevator, hit that stop button and continue where we left off. I had a mental flash of him with his hands on me, all over me. Cupping my butt and pulling me to him. His hand sliding my zipper down, slipping into my panties. Or — oh, God! — sinking to his knees, tugging my jeans down and putting his mouth ...

"Um, Dix?"

Dylan's voice pulled me out of my fantasy. He was some ten paces ahead of me, which confused me until I realized I'd stopped walking.

"Something on your mind?" His voice was silky, knowing, and those lips were curved up ...

"Yeah, I was thinking I might have left my iron plugged in, but I just did the mental replay and nope. I didn't."

He laughed, low in his throat.

As I pulled abreast of him, I punched his shoulder, hard. "Okay, so I don't own an iron. Want to make an issue of it?"

He massaged his shoulder. "No, ma'am."

I tried and failed to suppress a smile. Damn, he made things so easy. Like, I've said before ... the guy's perfect.

He even held the door as we walked into Gaetan Land.

"Hi, Dylan!" It was Zoey cheering and Brandy waving as we entered Gaetan Land. Babe materialized to take our jackets. Even the shy and quiet Eva gave a warm smile.

"Oh, I love your PJs. Did you design them?" Brandy asked. "Can you make me a pair to match?"

"We did," Dylan lied eloquently. "They're from our fall collection." He waved a hand to indicate both of us. I obliged with a little pirouette.

"And hi to you too, Debbie!" That from the smart-assed Elizabeth Bee.

"It's Dix," I ground out.

"Oopsie. My bad." With a giggle, Elizabeth took hold of Hugh Drammen's arm.

"Did you say you're with your dad?" I shot back. "That's sweet, Elizabeth."

Her eyes filled instantly with (fake) tears. Oh, the girl was good! A (totally false) tremble suddenly afflicted her pouty red lips. "Oh, didn't you know? I … I thought everyone did. My daddy died tragically in a fire when I was just a baby. He died saving me. And … and I was raised by my dear old grandmother. My mother was never around. She never had time for me, only for the long line of boyfriends she had after Daddy was gone. But Nanny loved me. We were poor, but we had love. Lots of love. But now … I hardly get to see her at all. Mama's with her new boy toy somewhere, and I'm all alone in the world now. All … alone."

Oh that was just complete BS!

But as Elizabeth blinked back the tears, Drammen's protective arm curved around her. "You're not alone, sweet angel. You have me."

Sweet angel? Elizabeth Bee?

Damn, she was *really* good.

Everyone else was shooting her looks of genuine sympathy. Compassion. The looks they were shooting me, however, were not so affectionate.

And those looks didn't get any friendlier when I turned to the crowd and said, "Let's do something different tonight!" I clapped my hands, Gaetan style, for emphasis.

Everyone looked at me as if I'd grown a third head. (Yeah, third. I was well beyond second-head looks.)

Gaetan was there, looking commanding in his finest blue velour. Babe was there too, looking … well, Babe-like. Which is to say, timid as hell in the presence of her asshole big brother. Hugh, Elizabeth, Amy,

Eva, Brandy, Mabel (so happy to see Dylan), the ever-smiling Ruth-Ann, and the rest of the regulars. Dickhead was there too. He had been working the room, but now had moved himself front and center. In fact, if I had done my calculations right (and didn't I always?), everyone who'd been there the night Dylan and I had signed up was there.

Dickhead and Dylan knew the plan. Knew we were going to — no matter the cost — stop the cuddling for the night.

"*What?* Have you lost your mind?" This from Gaetan Gough, and judging by his tone, I'm quite sure that last question was a rhetorical one. "We don't just suddenly do things differently. Get a grip!"

Dylan tensed behind me at Gaetan's berating tone. Man, he was in full fake boyfriend mode. Or was that (gulp) boyfriend mode?

Babe, who was standing demurely behind the counter, put it a little more tactfully than her brother had: "Dix, this is a cuddle club. We, you know, cuddle here. I mean, we have the Cuddle-Uppies and all —"

It was Dickhead who came to the rescue on this exchange. "I think Debbie —"

"It's *Dix*," I said.

"Oh, sorry. I think Dixie has a point here. Something different might be fun to try. What did you have in mind?"

Dixie. Grrr. He knew I'd have to let that go under the circumstances. I swallowed my aggravation and smiled. "Maybe we could get to know each other a little better if —"

"Oh, we can do that under the Cuddle-Uppies!" Brandy said, eying Dylan.

"Exactly!" Gaetan clapped.

"But it's so warm in here," Dylan offered up. "Why don't we forego the blankets and —"

"Well, maybe these will cool us down." It was smiling Starla, just then walking into the room with a tray full of smoothies. Pink and frosty and yummy looking. "Gaetan's Own, Snuggle-me-Strawberry!" she announced. "I just mixed up a batch."

In a flash, Dickhead, Dylan and I exchanged a meaningful glance. Oh crap! We couldn't let those drinks be consumed. They could contain more of the cuddle-inducing pheromones, which might or might not be responsible for killing three people. Or worse, someone could be putting something even more dangerous in the drinks, something designed to deliberately kill specific people. Either way, we couldn't let the cuddlers drink the stuff.

There wasn't time to rock-paper-scissors this.

I flew into action. Literally.

"Oh, me first! Me first!" I said, in my best impression of a fourth grader, as I raced toward Starla, just as Zoey and Eva were reaching for their own smoothie concoction. Oh crap! I put on a burst of speed and basically dove at Starla before any drinks could be handed off.

"What are you doing?" she shrilled. "I thought you were watching your ... wait!"

And then there was the crash. Zoey stepped back, pulling Eva with her, but Starla and I both landed with a thump on the floor. The tray of drinks flew up. And inevitably — dammit! - came crashing down, splattering all over us.

Yeah, those smoothies had been that cold. I could tell by the drip of the thick frosty liquid as it dripped down the front of my silk PJ top, and the back of my neck.

"Good thing we didn't bring out the date squares we brought, my dear," Hugh stage whispered to Elizabeth.

"Oh, wow, guess you're off the diet." Starla managed to laugh, despite being as drenched as I was with cold smoothie.

Gaetan, however, was not smiling.

"What the hell, woman!" he thundered at me.

His eyes were furious and his chubby hands fisted at his sides. His face turned beet red as he glared at me, and I could not help it — I giggled — at how that red round face looked beneath that blond head of hair.

"Easy, Gaetan," Dylan said, and there was no mistaking the warning in his tone. "Accidents happen."

"Accidents? *Accidents*?" The little poop sputtered. "If your clumsy cow of a girlfriend hadn't — "

Dylan was on him.

Jesus H. Christ. Dylan had moved so fast, I'd barely had time to process it, but there he was, his hands tight on Gaetan's shoulders. He was much larger than Gaetan, had a least a good eight inches on him. I knew Dylan, knew he wouldn't swing, but there was no mistaking the threat he was laying on Gaetan, no matter that it was delivered as tightly edged advice: "I suggest you don't ever talk to the lady like that again."

All eyes were on Dylan. Especially mine. There was no mistaking the fire in his eyes, and he'd reacted way too quickly, too spontaneously, for it to have been mere role playing. His reaction had been instinctual. Visceral.

"Boys! Boys! No need for this! It's a cuddle club! Let's not ruin the atmosphere!" That from Ruth-Ann. Geez, I liked that lady. With one hand on Gaetan's shoulder and one on Dylan's she easily coaxed them apart. Expertly.

Dylan let go of Gaetan, but didn't unlock his stare until Gaetan said, "Well ... I guess accidents do happen."

As if that was her cue, Babe (with Eva's unsolicited assistance) started cleaning the mess up.

And speaking of messes ... I scooted to the bathroom to remove the frosty from all over me. Especially where it pooled in my cleavage. Yeah, how charming was that? The frosty (did I mention freezing cold?) pink smoothie had pooled in my bra-enhanced cleavage. You know, in that area where you carry your cell phone, car keys, those little dogs that Paris Hilton is always carrying around in her purse. (Normal, right? *Right?*) Lots of women keep things in their bras. Peaches Marie is really into crystals and stones. She wouldn't be caught dead at a yoga class without a small piece of amazonite stuffed in her sports bra. My mom's friend, Mona, tucks a lucky dollar in there before every bingo game (and she's oh so lucky at bingo.)

But not me. Apparently, I collected smoothies.

I headed to the slightly bigger family washroom just past the men's and women's rooms. There was one toilet, one sink, and one door, so I would be assured my privacy as I cleaned up. But as I walked down the hallway, I heard the soft sound of footsteps following.

And in a bolt of intuition, I knew who it was, and why he was following me.

The smoothie. It was evidence. And it had to be collected.

I stepped inside the bathroom, holding the door open for Dickhead, who ducked in behind me. I let the door fall shut and sighed. "Just do what you've got to do!"

He looked sick. Apologetic. Oh, fuck, he looked like a man condemned.

"I don't like this any better than you do, Dodd." Dickhead locked the door behind us. He took a few steps toward me, reached into the pocket of his black sweat pants, and pulled out a sealed specimen jar and a pair of latex gloves.

Yeah, he'd come prepared.

"What are the chances of you letting me do this myself?" I asked as he donned the gloves.

"Can't do it," he said. "You're not a cop." One gloved hand went into his other pocket and produced something else. He tore the wrapper off it and I realized it was probably a sterile tongue depressor. No doubt he planned to use it like a spatula to scrape up the smoothie.

Great. Just freakin' great. I started to unbutton my silk top. Slowly. Oh so slowly. And no, I wasn't trying to be seductive, but curse Aunt Gert and her attention to detail! Just like at the condo the other night, the buttons were too snug in the holes. After about twenty seconds of that, I cursed and whipped the damned thing over my head.

Dickhead swallowed audibly.

Oh God, let's keep this professional.

Have I mentioned that Detective Richard Head is my arch rival? My sworn enemy? (And hey, I'm not kidding about the paperwork on that.) Have I mentioned too that I busted his cheating ass years ago? Oh, and have I mentioned he really isn't that bad looking? And so here I was with my top on the floor, and —

There was a knock at the door. "Um, Debbie … I mean, Dix … are you going to be a while?"

Damn it! Starla! She'd have to clean up too. I motioned for Dickhead's silence.

"Um, I'll be a bit, Starla. You might want to use the other bathroom."

"Oh," she said. As patient as she had been when I'd spilled the drinks, it seemed I was wearing that patience thin now.

After a minute, I turned back to Dickhead — he was staring at me.

"This is going to hurt me a lot more than it's going to hurt you," he said. And I mentally, silently, thanked him for that. But I'm no fool, despite the sworn-enemy status, Dickhead was … not unimpressed by what he saw.

"Let's just get it over with!" I said.

I stood perfectly still, closed my eyes even (some would call it a cringe) as he moved in with the jar.

There was a pause. A long, long —

"What are you waiting for?" I asked,

"Could you … assist?"

I looked down at my breasts.

Great, just great. (Yeah, they were pretty great, especially in the new bra I'd just bought, but that's beside the point.) The problem was obvious. While I'm not exceptionally large-chested, neither am I flat-chested, and I've been carrying a little extra padding these past few years. Basically, the upshot was that there was no way Dickhead was reaching in for his smoothie sample without another pair of hands to assist.

"Okay, fine." No way was I slinging my bra off too. But, hey, I am woman ... I knew the mechanics of the situation at ... er ... hand.

Curse you tight and ample cleavage!

I grabbed my boobs from beneath, lifted and separated. "Make it quick."

"Don't worry about that, Dix."

Dix.

Yeah, again without the derogatory suffix to my name. What the hell was wrong with this guy? Dix? Just Dix? I could have slapped him (and he was so close I wouldn't have needed a hand; a sharp turn to the left would have poked him in the eye.)

True to his word, Richard Head did make it quick. And he was careful not to touch me with anything but the tongue depressor as he scooped the pooled smoothie from between my breasts. I held my breath the whole while (no exhales happening here). He gathered the evidence, sealed the jar, then grabbed for the door. He couldn't get out of there fast enough.

Neither could I. While I had every confidence they wouldn't have cast the cuddle yet (and how could they without Our Ritchie?), I did need to hurry this clean up. I slipped out of my bra, and rinsed it and the silk top out in the sink. Oh boy, I did not relish putting either of those items back on. But I sure as hell wouldn't be bouncing around braless. I hung the new bra strategically under the hot-air hand dryer, and that problem was solved within minutes. But the pajama top was another matter. I still couldn't go out —

Another knock at the door.

"Starla, I'm sorry, but I'm still not done."

"It's me, Dix, Babe. Open the door. Quickly, before Gaetan sees I'm gone."

I hurriedly put my bra back on and opened the door a crack. (Nope, not one for parading around in my underwear, even if the audience was just Babe.)

"Here, take this." Babe handed me a shirt through the two-inch crack of open door. I recognized it even as I reached for it. One of her own creations — the very one she'd twirled around in yesterday, if I wasn't mistaken.

As soon as my hand closed on the garment, she was off like a shot.

Even before I could thank her.

It didn't exactly match. I didn't exactly care. I put it on, finished wringing out the PJ top the best I could, then headed back down to Gaetan Land.

Light spilled through the beveled glass in the door. Good, the lights had not yet been dimmed, and yes, when I opened the door no soft music played. Folks were just milling about, minus the usual smoothies, and they were looking a little grumpy and impatient.

Just the way I liked them!

Gaetan made a point of turning his back to the door — thus on me — as soon as I walked into the room.

Dylan smiled as soon as his gaze fell on me. Which was a little unnerving. What was he smiling at? The change of clothing? The way I'd stopped the smoothie consumption? Or — oh, God! — he had to have realized why Dickhead had disappeared down the hall after me. Or was he just smiling at me?

Dickhead stood in the corner. As soon as my eyes met his, he looked the other way.

"Well," Gaetan huffed, still avoiding all eye contact with me. "We'll have to forego the drinks tonight — but no refunds of course. Ha ha ha ... Not kidding." *Clap, clap, clap.*

Well, I was about to become even more unpopular with Gaetan. (Seriously, if that little dude had a shit-list, I was number one on it. But like they say, in for a penny, in for a pound. Or was that a pounding?)

"Sorry about that, guys," I called. "I guess I got a little overexcited about the smoothies."

General mutter and grumbling ensued.

"But since we're off track anyway, maybe we should do something different tonight. You know, rather than casting a cuddle."

"No way!"

I turned — we all turned — to look where that shout had come from. Babe's face reddened as she looked back at each of us, her gaze stopping on me. "I ... I mean, it's part of the ... club. It's ..."

"It's not up for debate!" With that, Gaetan walked to the counter, taking Cuddle-Uppies one by one from Babe as she unwrapped and handed them over.

Dammit.

I was afraid of this. I was afraid I'd have to resort to desperate tactics. Dire tactics. Oh God, *painful* ones. Oh shit, I wanted to puke. But a girl could only wash up so many times ...

"Dylan," I choked out. "How about you lead us in a sing along? A ... tribute to Albert before we ... Cuddle-Uppie."

"Jesus, Dix!" Elizabeth Bee shrilled, clearly panicked. (Oh, so *now* she remembered my name!) She'd been out with Dylan and me and some others over at Donatta's Karaoke Bar one night a few months back. She knew how horribly Dylan sang. His singing should be outlawed (actually, I think they were drawing up by-laws in some small Ontario towns). And the kicker — Dylan had absolutely no clue that his singing voice was bad, let alone paint-peelingly bad.

"I ... I mean, is that really necessary?" Elizabeth continued.

"Well, it's not against the rules," Babe said quietly. "We usually get under the Cuddle-Uppies to sing, but —"

Gaetan whirled on her. "Are you still here?"

She wasn't for long. Head down, shoulders drooping, Babe retreated to the back room.

"I think a memorial hymn would be great," Dickhead said. I don't think he'd had the privilege of hearing Dylan singing, but he knew I had something up my sleeve.

Ruth-Ann shrugged. "Why not? And ... and I ... I think our dear Albert would have liked that. And Faynelle and ... our Telly too. We've lost so many dear friends lately. Maybe we could sing a hymn or two in their memory." She had tears in her eyes. She really must have thought a lot of the gang. Or at least one or two of them.

"Let's all join hands," Dylan said, as if the debate were over. He positioned himself in the center of the cuddle floor. Gaetan's head looked about to explode

I took Dylan's hand.

Brandy was on his other side within seconds. "Come on, girls." She smiled sweetly at her friends. Eva and Zoey latched on too. Soon everyone was filling in on the hand-holding moment.

Gaetan sighed. "Well, if it will shut this one up —" He jerked a hand toward me.

Dylan tensed beside me, and I felt his grip tighten. "Hey," he said, his eyes darkening as they bore into Gaetan Gough. "I told you to watch how you talk to my lady."

I'm no shrinking violet. (Hey, I eat shrinking violets for breakfast. Okay, not literally. Well, unless you count that one time at band camp. And strictly speaking, violets *are* edible ...) Anyway, what I'm trying to say is I'm perfectly capable of sticking up for myself. But you know, the fact that Dylan was sticking up for me right now to this little turd of a man made me feel … great. Also, terrified.

Gaetan looked away from Dylan's hard stare.

"Now!" I whispered to Dylan. "Amazing Grace. Start with that song."

"Got it," he whispered back. "I'll have them in tears in no time."

"I have absolutely no doubt."

My knees were weak. My stomach was turning to lead. My ears were cringing in anticipation.

Dylan cleared his throat, and began, "Amazing grace, how sweeeeet the sound that saved a wretch like me-eee ieee …"

My eyes were watering. Ruth-Ann, who was standing between two older men, leaned on both of them for support. She looked at me, horrified, and I'm quite sure mouthed the words, "Don't have children." This from a bio-ethicist! Eva and Brandy stared at Dylan unblinking, their jaws hanging slack. I was quite sure they weren't that pale when we got here. Zoey wasn't doing much better. Elizabeth was cursing me under her breath. Oh, how I deserved that! Starla threw her hands up in the air, grabbed her coat and headed for the door. Oh, the look she shot me. Mabel from the other side of the hand-holding circle, reached up, turned something in her ear (I'm guessing a hearing aid) then smiled sweetly at Dylan. Gaetan Gough leaned against the counter, or rather over it. Like he needed help standing up.

But the main thing as Dylan finished — no one had tucked under the Cuddle-Uppies.

"Look at them," he whispered to me. "They're speechless. Oh, man, they're *motionless*."

Indeed they were.

Gaetan was the first to recover. "I think … I think we all need to —"

"Quick, Dylan, sing How Great Thou Art! Nice and loud!" I turned to the terrified crowd. "Just wait till he hits the high notes."

"Elizabeth and I were just leaving!" Drammen said, speaking for both of them, but Elizabeth didn't seem to mind. I'd never seen an old guy move as fast as he did then. Never! And Ruth-Ann elbowed past him on her way out the door. So did the guys who'd been at her side.

"Oh look at the time," Brandy said. "I'll be late for … family dinner."

"Take me with you!" Zoey pleaded.

"Wait for me! I'm coming too." Eva was right behind them.

The room cleared out in less than two minutes. The only ones who remained were me, Dylan, Richard Head, Gaetan, and Babe, who just then walked out of the office.

"Gaetan," she said. "Do you still want the lights and air turned — oh!" she looked around at the near empty room. "What happened?"

Gaetan glared at me. "She happened."

Guilty as charged. There was no love lost between Gaetan Gough and me, and I was quite fine with that. More than fine with that ... it tickled me right to death.

"What the hell are you up to?" he demanded.

"Don't you mean, what am I *on to*?"

I was almost ready to finger the guy for murder.

Gaetan turned on his heel and stormed off.

Chapter 11

DYLAN WAS STILL talking about his adventures in hymn-singing the next afternoon at the office. We were both sitting on the floor in the outer office, our lidded coffees beside us, as we unpacked yet a couple more boxes (thankfully the last of them). And yeah, we were waiting for that phone to ring. In fact, the first thing I had done when we got into the office this fine Monday morning was to check the voice mails. Dickhead had said he'd gotten the okay to expedite the analysis on the Cuddle-Uppie and the smoothie sample, and it would have been delivered to the forensic lab by 9 o'clock this morning.

No voice mails.

Okay, maybe five hours was pushing it, even for an expedited order. This wasn't CSI Marport City.

"You shouldn't have picked Amazing Grace, Dix," Dylan said, sighing. With a box cutter, he sliced through the heavy packing tape. When he looked up his eyes were glassy, the smile serene.

Dumbly, I nodded. "Yeah, that song gets 'em every time."

"Especially the way I sing it. It's just too intense, I guess. People just can't handle it. I can't tell you the people who've begged me to never sing that song again. I mean, did you see Ruth-Ann? She couldn't get out of there fast enough. And she wasn't the only one who had to bolt. Starla. Hugh and Elizabeth. They all did. Even Mabel seemed to get caught up in my singing."

Actually I think she got caught in the stampede.

I wanted to cry now myself just thinking about it.

"Where do you want these?" Dylan held up the six-pack of yellow pads.

"In my office. Right-hand desk drawer is fine."

"Done." Dylan stood, and walked into my office. I watched him go. Yes, he looked as good in those jeans going as he did coming. And no, we had not gotten it on last night after cuddle club. Not that we both didn't want to.

I'd told him about Dickhead's um, sample gathering. And I had watched Dylan's reaction carefully. His face was neutral as I explained it all. Yep, detail after detail. Yet his expression remained guarded. What was he thinking? Was he jealous? Angry?

He'd burst out laughing. I mean uncontrolled, snorting laughter. The prick.

Okay, it was kind of funny. He'd had to pull off onto the shoulder of the road to collect himself, so as not to risk an accident. It had taken minutes for the snorts and peals of laughter to die down.

And in those moments — believe it or not — the world felt right. As we laughed at my shirt-tossing misfortune, recalled the smoothie dripping down my cleavage, and even the look on Gaetan's face, it felt perfectly right. Easy. Dylan was a trusted coworker. My dear friend. Someone I really wanted to be with, if I only dared ...

When he'd driven me back home, we'd fooled around in the SUV outside my condo building. I've never been much of a fan of petting in a car, but can I just say, that was so freakin' hot! Of course, I'd never done it before with a guy who was quite so good at it. I'd been about to drag ... er ... I mean, invite him up when his cell phone had rung.

My happy buzz of remembered sexual arousal evaporated a bit as I thought about that phone call. He'd listened a lot, kept his answers mainly to yes and no, with a few whens and wheres thrown in there. Then he'd clicked the phone off, sighed, and said he had to go.

"Er, Dix, did you say right-hand drawer?"

"Yeah, why?"

Silence. Sucking silence.

Oh shit! The right-hand drawer! I'd put my personal stash in there! I leapt to my feet.

"I'm just having trouble getting the drawer open. It seems to be stuck," Dylan called out. He was sitting in my chair, and gave the drawer one more good yank. "Ah, there, I got it — Jesus, Dix!"

His alarm was precipitated by me diving/sliding across the desk. I slammed that drawer shut before he saw my ... um ... special reading material (dog-eared as it was). Except I didn't just slide across the desk. I slid right off it and landed right on top of Dylan.

The chair toppled over, depositing Dylan flat on his back on the carpet, and I landed on top of him. The oomph we both let out at the end of our graceless descent only added to the impact of that body-to-body press.

Quickly, (well, after a minute or two), I started to lift myself off him, mumbling apologies as I did.

"Hold it, Dix." His voice was a little breathy, probably because I'd knocked the wind out of him. "Don't move."

By this time, I was lying half on, half off him, and froze. "Why? Oh God! Are you hurt?"

"Not quite."

He lifted his hands to my head, buried both hands in my hair, drew my face down and kissed me. And oh, Lord, I could get used to this! I skimmed my hands up his sides, delighting in the lean solidity of him. He groaned and tugged me fully on top of him. I could feel his arousal stirring, and it sent my libido shooting through the roof.

"Straddle me," he commanded.

Happy to comply, I drew my legs up on either side of him and sat up, splaying my hands on his chest. Bearing my own weight like this I had much better control. Which I immediately exercised by wriggling against his hardness. He turned the tables on me by palming my breasts, stroking and squeezing. I quickly forgot everything but the feel of his hands on me. After a few moments of that, though, I was going crazy. I dragged my hair to one side, then bent and kissed him. He seemed to approve. But then he groaned and rolled me off him.

Well, someone had to answer the phone.

You know, I was really starting to fucking hate phones.

The phone had gotten swept off the desk along with everything else, but had landed a little more gracefully than Dylan and I. Miraculously, the receiver was still in the cradle.

I picked it up on the third ring. The call display told me it wasn't Dickhead with news from the forensic lab, but it was someone else I was just as anxious to hear from. With a push of the button, that party was on speaker phone.

"Hey, Foxx," I said.

Dylan gave an approving nod. Yeah, we'd both been waiting for this call.

Ryan Foxx was a former co-worker of mine at Jones and Associates.

While I'd left the old firm because that glass ceiling came just up to my skirt, Foxx had left for quite a different reason. He'd left for the love of a woman. And in this case, a woman who loved him back. Specifically, Montana Hall. Montana had been a client of the firm's, looking for the son she'd been forced to give up twenty years before when she'd been in Canada. She'd been a runaway, given the authorities a false name, left the baby at the hospital and never looked back. For two decades, that is. Foxx had helped her find said son (the reunion had even been a happy one). But during the course of the investigation, Foxx and Montana had fallen in love. He'd moved to California, where the two ran a foster home for teens who'd been abused (there was a reason Montana had run away in the first place). That was a full-time proposition, to be sure, but it wasn't unheard of for Foxx to do some freelance work on the side.

I'd emailed him the very day we'd taken the case of Death by Cuddle Club and asked him to snoop around and see what he could find out about Gaetan Land in California.

"Hey, Dixie," he said. "How's it hanging?"

"Well, Foxx, if it were hanging any better I'd have to fold it."

Dylan gave me a curious look on that. Private joke. I waved him off.

"Good to hear from you," Foxx said.

"Yeah, you too. How's it going with Montana and the kids?"

He filled me in. Life was good. Busy, but good. Foxx sounded content. No, more than content. He sounded happy.

"Love will do that to you, Dix," he said, startling me.

But even as Ryan Foxx elaborated about his life with Montana, there'd been that little edge in his voice. That little nudge-nudge that let me know he was more than anxious to spill the beans about what he'd discovered about California's Gaetan Land.

"So what's the suspicious death count in Gaetan Land?" I asked, ready for the juicy details.

"Zero."

Huh? "Come again."

"Like I said, zero. I checked Dix. Dug deep. In the last year, there've been three deaths among the membership of all the Gaetan Lands here in California. Two were the result of accidents — one boating, one vehicular. The other was from complications from pneumonia. Nothing suspicious around any of them."

Dylan looked at me, obviously just as surprised.

"No heart attacks? No sudden cardiac arrests?" I said, just to confirm.

"You're sure?"

"None fatal. In fact, it seems the cuddling might have a positive effect on the heart. But that's not so surprising. Human touch and all ..."

I laughed out loud, until I realized he was serious.

"Most of the club members are thirty-somethings," Foxx said. "That probably accounts for the low rate of heart episodes, too."

"Are there no older members?" I asked.

"Oh, there are some in that over-forty bracket —" (I cursed the fucking speaker phone.) " — but not many. So the clientele isn't exactly in the prime group for heart attacks. And really, don't you find that strange, Dix? That so many younger folks would be attracted to Gaetan Land?"

Of course I did. At that age, I was out clubbing. You know, hitting the bars. Dancing till the wee hours of the morning. Times hadn't changed that much.

"One more thing," Foxx said.

"What's that?"

"I also checked on those Cuddle-Uppies they have for sale down here. Yeah, pricey as hell. But Gaetan's making another small fortune in sales of those ugly things alone."

I thanked Foxx. Told him to say hi to Montana for me, and hung up the phone.

"It's a Canadian thing, eh?" Dylan shook his head. "The suspicious cuddle club deaths are only at this one club in Ontario?"

"Yeah, Canadian. Like beaver tails and hockey." I said.

"Maybe that does have something to do with it."

"Beaver tails and hockey?"

"Er, no Dix. The Canadian thing. Maybe some of us northern folk just can't hack the closeness. Face it, we have the reputation of being a bit on the reserved side. Maybe even a little stand-offish."

"You mean prickly?"

"Hey, I wasn't talking about you."

Well, he was. We both snorted a laugh because we knew it.

"Maybe Gaetan Gough just doesn't like Canadians. What's that all *aboot*, eh?"

"My money's still riding on the Cuddle-Uppies," I said. "Pheromones that somehow trigger a fatal arrhythmia in some people. Like an allergy of some kind. And there had to be pheromones in that Cuddle-Uppie the way I ..."

"What?"

"The way I was acting ... you know ... the other night."

No sooner were the words out than my mind shot back to Saturday night. I think I got a little glassy-eyed just thinking about it, because when I looked up, Dylan was wearing a knowing smile. But all he said was, "We'll know soon enough, I guess."

Actually we'd know sooner than that. Because the phone was ringing again, and it was Dickhead.

"Excellent," I said, smiling widely. This case was about to crack wide open. I picked up the receiver. "What's the news?"

My smile soon faded away.

Crap! Crap! Crappppp!

The Cuddle-Uppies were clean.

Chapter 12

I HAD BEEN wrong. Super wrong.

And I really, really hate that!

The only thing the lab found in measurable quantities in that Cuddle-Uppie blanket (besides the head holes, of course) were traces of detergent and fabric softener.

I just did not get it! I was so sure that Gaetan Land had to be using synthetic pheromones in those cuddle blankets to get the clients aroused, coming back, and absolutely addicted to his clubs. And that that hormone was somehow linked to the deaths.

Damn.

I was so sure I'd be waltzing into that cuddle club and having one of my theme-song-humming, Gotcha! moments where I get to point the finger at the guilty party, after which everyone oohs and aahs about Dix Dodd, best PI ever. Hands high-fiving all around. Confetti flying. Wine pouring. There might even be a small parade . . .

"Damn."

Was I ready to abandon the notion that anything was amiss at the cuddle club? Did I believe that all was right in the Land of Gaetan?

Not a chance.

Even if logic was kicking my butt, telling me to turn the other cheek, so to speak, my intuition was telling me otherwise. Niggle, niggle, nudge, nudge — still. Even if I wasn't on Dickhead's dime anymore. Oh, and by the way, I wasn't.

It had been nice while it lasted, but being the softie that I am, the rest of my time would be on the house. But he still had to pick up expenses.

And then there was the favor factor. He'd owe me one. Big time, especially considering he told the force I'd called him in. (Hey, I'm soft, not stupid. Being owed a favor by one of Marport City's boys in blue had to come in handy someday.) Then there was the whole he-saw-me-topless thing ...

And how was Detective Richard Head feeling about all this?

More pissed off by the minute. The question of why he kept going back after that lark of a night with his cousin from Florida was one he wasn't about to let go of. It was so out of character for him. And it was driving him nuts.

How did I know? Well, my shitload of intuition helped. But too, he told Dylan and me over coffee at Perky Joe's as the three of us sipped our mean coffee, bit into day-old donuts, and plotted what we would do next.

But before the dead bodies started stacking up, one thing we all three agreed on — we needed some face time with the recently bereaved. I was all ready to divvy the work up among the three of us when Dickhead reminded me this was a police investigation now. He would talk to the families of the late Faynelle St. James, Telly Smith and Albert Valentine and I was to keep my nose out of it. I nodded agreeably and suggested he start with the first one to have kicked it, Faynelle St. James, so their memories didn't get even more stale and unreliable.

Predictably, he scowled and told me he knew how to do police work, thank you; he didn't need my advice.

As we watched him stalk out of the coffee shop, Dylan said, "I take it you're going to take them in reverse order?"

I smiled. He knew me so well.

"Would you care for more tea?" Cathy Valentine asked me. The petite, attractive woman was already lifting the delicate pot, ready to pour another small cup of the blend. She was, I'd judge, about mid-fifties.

I put up my hand, staving off that second pouring. "Thanks, but no, Mrs. Valentine."

She looked at me reproachfully.

"Sorry," I said. "Cathy."

Mrs. Cathy Valentine had told me to call her by her first name within the first moments we'd met on her doorstep. That was about half an hour ago when I'd come knocking on her door. We were now sitting in her small, well-kept sun room at the back of the house. Which was fine by me on this bright fall day. One of the consequences of my PI work: I just do not get enough sun.

"Now, tell me again how I can help you," Cathy said, with an easy smile. We'd spent the last half hour talking about the renovations she was having done on the rest of the house (the contractors were just setting up as I'd walked in through the foyer), the trip she planned to Dallas to visit her younger brother and his new wife right after the funeral, and her upcoming vacation to New York City to take in a few Broadway shows. (She kept humming *Mama Mia!* — yes, she was a theater buff.) Was that a new sapphire ring on her finger?

It most definitely was.

Had the Valentine's been well off? Was that how the widow was affording all this? Nope. But there apparently had been a couple very hefty insurance policies on Albert's life and Cathy had every intention of enjoying the same.

"So you said you were from the university?" Cathy said, prompting me out of my daze. (Must have been the sun.)

"Um, yeah." I sat up in the chair, and adjusted my skirt over my knees. I'd gone home to change from my grubbies and into something more appropriate. "I was hoping I could ask you a few questions for my thesis research."

"Master's or doctoral?"

"Master's. In sociology," I supplied before she could ask my discipline.

She still didn't look completely convinced, but she said, "I see. And what are you researching, exactly?"

Of course, I could tell her I was researching the phenomenon of cuddle clubs, but if she didn't know about her husband's activities with Gaetan Land, how awkward would that be?

No, better to steer toward safer ground. People were always more willing to talk about their favorite topic — themselves. "I'm doing my thesis on the bereavement process in recently widowed women. How they cope."

Cathy's eyebrows arched delicately. Yep, interest was piqued. "So you scour the papers, looking through the obits to find people to interview? Looking for grieving widows."

Geez, she made it sound so bad. "Yes."

"Well, good for you, Dix," she declared. "No sense waiting for life to come to you. I did that for too long. Way too long. But let me tell you … if you're looking for a grieving widow, you've come to the wrong house."

I saw the tightening in her face; detected that clench of anger in her jaw before she could hide it behind that tea cup.

"Yes," Cathy continued, after she'd sipped her tea and composed herself. "I spent a good many years waiting for life to give back to me."

"But no more?" I asked.

"No more, indeed."

I said nothing. Just waited, sitting forward now in my chair to encourage the widow to go on. I didn't have to wait long.

"Albert and I were married for nearly thirty years. I had my first child within a year of our marriage and had retired to being a housewife as soon as I found out that I was expecting. Terrible idea. That's fine for some women — don't get me wrong. Especially from my generation. I know some really happy and contented women who did just that. But really, it wasn't for me. And I had three babies within four and a half years. Can you imagine!"

I could only shake my head. Yikes. My own mother was a happy-as-a-clam stay-at-home mom, but that was just with Peaches and me, and we were more manageably spaced. Also, she and Dad had adored each other. I didn't get the feeling it was quite that cozy and adoring in Casa Valentine.

"Albert didn't want me working outside the house, even as the kids grew older. In fact, he didn't want me doing much of anything outside the house. But damned if he'd ever take me anywhere. I'm embarrassed to say that I put up with that treatment for a good many years. But Albert had a temper. And … I learned not to ask." She looked up and caught the expression on my face. "Why did I marry him? That's what you're wondering, isn't it?"

"I wasn't going to ask that." And you know, I really wasn't. The man a woman marries isn't always the man she ends up with. I knew enough about spousal abuse to know it very often came out after the marriage, during or after the pregnancy and when a woman felt the most trapped. It's not always pretty in my line of work.

"Well," she sighed. "The one thing I did insist upon, since Albert wanted me home rather than working out, was that he have enough life insurance so that if anything ever happened to him, I'd be all right. Plus, I'd put away a fair amount of cookie-jar money over the years," she said with pride.

"That's excellent," I commended. "Bloody excellent."

She looked at me strangely. "Do you watch British —"

"No," I said quickly. "Nothing British at all."

She smiled. "Well, Dix, I may not be what you're looking for in research, I'm thinking. If you're looking for the candle-in-the-window grieving widow, you won't find her here. You'll find a bitter one."

"Cathy," I said. "That's not what I'm looking for at all. I'm looking for honesty." And yes, I was looking for information too. But I also wanted to hear what she had to say.

"Bet you're wondering why I didn't leave him?"

Part of me was, but part of me knew — *knew* — it wasn't that simple. It's never that cut and dried. Kids to raise. No job. Changes in the workforce. "I bet you would have eventually, but ... I know it's not that easy."

"You're kind," she said.

"Cathy, it sounds like you've got a right to be bitter. Your husband was controlling. He had a temper. But it also sounds like you made the best of the situation that you could."

"And I didn't even mention the affair."

"You were having an affair? Good for you!" Oh yikes. It was all I could do not to leap up to high five her.

"No, Albert was."

What ... wait ... *Albert* was having an affair? A chill rippled over me. Where there was an affair, there was often trouble. Jealousy. Heartache. And sometimes, murder.

"Did you know who Albert was seeing?"

"Not exactly. I didn't have the name. Nor did I really ever see her. But Albert was careless. Oh, more than careless — he didn't care at all. He practically flaunted the fact that he was sleeping with someone. I knew. I damn well knew. Honestly, I didn't give a rat's ass that he was cheating on me, but it did anger me that he flaunted it." There was no mistaking the wrath in her voice. The snap of it. Her eyes narrowed. The tea cup shook in her hands. "But I do know one thing, Dix. Albert met her at the cuddle club."

Chapter 13

I WAS, FOR a change, alone at the office after my visit with Cathy Valentine. I'd stayed longer than I'd intended, listening to the merry widow. I liked her. Genuinely liked her. There was absolutely no pretense with Cathy, no hiding. And in my line of work, that's incredibly refreshing.

And I liked her all the more for the information she'd provided me.

But I might have stayed just a tad too long. As Cathy was walking me to the door, the doorbell had rung. Muttering something about this being her day for unexpected visitors, she opened the door. And there on the threshold stood Dickhead.

"Good morning, Mrs. Valentine, I'm Detective Head from the Marport City PD. I wonder if I could I have a word with —" His smarmy smile froze and his words died off as he spotted me standing behind Cathy Valentine.

"Certainly," Cathy had replied. "Ms. Davidson was just leaving."

"Yes, Miss Davidson." His voice had taken on a hard edge. "You look familiar . . ."

"Oh, you've probably seen me around. My sociology research puts me in all manner of unusual situations." I smiled brightly. "Now if you'll excuse me, I was just leaving."

He stepped back, but not very far. I had to suck everything in to squeeze by him. Prick. But it wasn't the first time I'd had that macho crap pulled on me and I'd learned a trick or two. I accidentally stepped on his foot on my way past.

He stifled a curse and I turned to see Mrs. Valentine trying to suppress a smile. "Bye, Cathy," I called. "Thanks for the tea."

Dickhead had sent me a venomous look before stepping inside and closing the door. And yeah, I knew I was in for a tongue lashing. Especially when he found out I'd then gone on to visit Faynelle's son and Telly's family. Well, I'd deal.

I went back to puzzling about Albert Valentine's affair. I mean, first off, who'd want to sleep with him? He'd been short and squat in a Danny DeVito kind of way, but minus DeVito's good looks, humor, and charm. Cathy couldn't say who he'd been sleeping with, and didn't appear to really care. But just knowing he'd been involved with someone at Gaetan Land was a giant step forward in the investigation.

And that's exactly what I told Dickhead when he called to rag me out. Of course, I'd gone on the offensive, demanding to know what he'd learned.

What? You found nothing out from Faynelle's grieving son? Only that she was a heavy smoker, and significantly overweight, and under the stress of union/management bickering at her hospital job — prime candidate for a heart attack? Oh, and let's not forget everyone liked her. That's all you got?

Okay, that's all I got, too.

And Telly? All you discovered was that he had slightly high blood pressure (not a shock given his age), that he was pretty fit and lived a quiet life?

And yeah, I didn't mention I hadn't found much more.

I challenged him to impress me. Turns out he'd gotten even less from Cathy Valentine. Of course, he'd blamed it on me. Apparently Mrs. Valentine hadn't exactly warmed up to him after he'd been borderline rude to "that nice master's student".

"Dude," I said, "you're not very good at this, are you?"

Then I proceeded to tell him all that I'd found out: Albert's affair with someone at the club. How unlikeable a person he really was. And how amazingly Cathy Valentine was doing now that Albert was out of the picture.

That took some of the bluster out of him.

"An affair?" he asked. "That can be some volatile shit."

"Hey, you don't have to tell me that. I trail cheaters for a living, remember?"

So lost in thought was he, that didn't even get a rise out of him. The gears must be turning in his detective's brain. Just when I thought we must have lost the connection and was about to hit the switch on the phone and say, "Hello? Hello?", he spoke.

"What do you think, Dix? Did she do it? Is Cathy Valentine in on this somehow?"

I wished that I could give a definitive no. I wished I knew for sure. And where there is adultery, there is usually anger, at the very least, no matter how checked-out of the marriage one may be (or pretend to have been). So I reluctantly told him she shouldn't be ruled out.

"Good work," he said and hung up.

I looked at the receiver in my hand as if it were some kind of foreign object. What the ... was that praise I'd just heard? From Dickhead? My eyes shot wide, and my mouth hung open as I stared over at Blow-Up Betty. (Though her open-mouthed expression wasn't due to surprise, I suspected.)

Okay. It was official now. Strangest case ever.

When next I glanced at my watch, it was a little before three o'clock in the afternoon, as I hung up from my second call of the day with Dickhead. He'd lit a fire under a young techie at the forensic lab who was apparently still green enough to be terrified of growling cops, and the tox report from the smoothies concoction was in. Apparently, the drink contained every perfectly legal herb or food known to man that might boost "vitality", including coriander, ginger root, raw cacao powder, maca powder, raw honey, bee pollen and a bunch of other stuff, but there was no evidence of anything remotely pro-arrhythmic. No cocaine, no monster doses of caffeine. Nada.

I sighed. So the smoothies might, over time, make people feel a little more frisky, but the real, measurable aphrodisiac effect of most those herbs was minimal. They probably owed their efficacy to a placebo effect. Of course, for a placebo to work, the cuddlers would have to have believed they were being given something to boost their libidos. As far as I could tell, they just thought the smoothie was healthful, good for their overall sense of wellbeing.

Frankly, I was more disturbed by what *wasn't* in the smoothie than what was in it. I'd have put money on a pheromone of some kind. Or maybe something inhibition-lowering, like roofies. Old-fashioned rohypnol or maybe the slicker GHB. Man, that would have been a slam dunk for manslaughter. GHB had been known to cause respiratory or cardiac arrest.

Was I disappointed? Absolutely.

I was also hungry and more than a little tired. I weighed which of those needs was the most pressing. I did have a stash of Reese's Peanut Butter Cups in my bottom drawer. The caffeine and sugar boost would have me bouncing off the walls within a half hour. Or ...

I glanced at the folded up cot in the corner of my office. One of the downsides of being a private investigator is that your sleep can really get thrown off. Frequent late night stake-outs will do that to a person. But one of the upsides — at least when you work for yourself like I do — is that when it's quiet, I can kick off my shoes, unfold the cot, and crawl right under those blankets (normal, normal blankets, not tossed over the shoulder coats while I caught fifteen in the car).

Okay, the decision was made. Sleep it was. So I set up the cot, unsnapped my bra, pulled off my pantyhose (I only wear the things when a disguise requires I wear a skirt, like when I'm being Dix Davidson, sociology student), and I was snoozing within minutes.

I love my naps, and I don't care who knows it. There is such a decadent pleasure in those mid-afternoon sleeps. The sound of traffic outside and miscellaneous noises from neighboring tenants didn't exactly make for the quietest environment, but that didn't matter. I'd long ago trained myself to filter the non-threatening stuff into white noise, and yet be alert to the dangers. (Yes, just one more thing my brilliant mind is capable of.)

But my dreams ... well, they're another thing all together. Not so easy to apply those filters. Yes, I do have the normal dreams that everyone has. Naked in the elevator, wading through snowstorms, walking in on Christian Bale just as he's changing into his Batman costume ... Okay, maybe that last one's all mine.

But often, I'll dream of whatever case is foremost in my mind. And well, yeah okay, the case of Death by Cuddle Club was the only one on the books right at the moment. But even if I'd had a dozen cases on the go, my thoughts would still have gravitated to this one. And where my thoughts go, so go my dreams. Sometimes I get clues in that dream state. It's like my subconscious just goes to work on the problem at hand. Sometimes my dreams bring me answers, but sometimes they just bring more questions.

Damn. Why couldn't I have fallen asleep thinking about Christian Bale? I could have been peeling off my Robin costume instead of being stuck with Albert Valentine.

We were alone, just the two of us. I knew I was dreaming, but still I looked down at my attire, hoping like hell I *had* some attire (dreams can be nasty that way). I was relieved to see I was in PJs. And not the silky and stylish ones; but ratty old plaid things. I couldn't help it ... I pulled the waist band back to check. Just as I suspected: granny panties. Bonus.

I love my granny panties too. But I digress ...

Dream Albert looked me up and down. (He was wearing white boxers, by the way, and I did *not* look him up and down).

"Naw," he said when he'd finished the head-to-toe. "You're not my type."

"Pfft. Like that's my loss, you ugly little fu —"

"Nice jammies," he scoffed. "You'll have to wear them to the next cuddle club meeting."

"You're an asshole." Yeah, even in my dreams, I got the 'tude.

He just laughed. "So, you've been talking to my old lady?"

"Your long-suffering wife, you mean? Yeah, I've been talking to her."

"I hope she's doing well?" Suddenly, the Albert of my dreams (gag) was wearing a hat. A fedora, in fact, like one my Dad used to wear. I wanted to smack it off his head when he tipped it my way.

"Maybe you should have been a little more concerned over your wife when you were alive," I snapped, "instead of banging around with ... Ruth-Ann."

I tossed the name out there. Ruth-Ann was the closest to Albert's age, after all.

He snorted. "*Ruth-Ann?* You gotta be kidding me. She's not my type either. Plus she's gotta be at least your age."

I swung one plaid-clad arm his way.

Dream Albert ducked. I'm sure I didn't make a connection as in the fist-to-body variety, but even in my dream, I could feel the shooting of pain in my arm as I did a cartoon-style flop to the ground landing on my butt.

Albert stepped back, laughing.

"Face it, Dix Dodd," he said. "You and your skirt-covered butt are not on top of this one. You're not the man for the job."

"What do you mean by that?" I swung again.

"Oh, wake up, Dix!" he snapped. "Wake the hell up!"

"Oh you fucking —"

He was walking away, but I was feeling the pressure on my shoulders. I swung.

"Wake up! Dix, for God's sake, it's me. Dylan!"

My eyes shot open. "Oh, shit ... again?"

I was on the floor. Dylan was leaning over me, holding me down by the shoulders, but not in an aggressive way. And not in a sexual way, either. More like in a you're-about-to-wreck the place way. And he was trying to prevent my next swing. (From the tension I felt in my body, that would be the swing of my knee, which was placed precariously close to his nuts as he leaned there over me. Damn, the boy was brave.)

Okay, here's the story. I have REM sleep disorder. I tend to act out my dreams, particularly when I'm under stress. Dylan, of course, knows all about this little peculiarity. In fact, he's seen it up close and personal more than a few times. I turned my head to glance at the cot I'd been sleeping on. The mattress and bedding were torn asunder, obviously my doing as I'd struggled to smack Albert Valentine in my dreams.

"Looks like a pretty wild time, Dix. You must have been dreaming of him."

My jaw dropped. "Albert Valentine? How'd you know that?"

He gave me a surprised look. "No, Christian Bale."

Smartass. "Last time I play truth or dare with you," I grumbled.

But I knew what he was doing, adding levity to a potentially embarrassing (for me) situation. God, I ... the guy was amazing.

I could have gotten up right then. Oh maybe I should have, but I made no move to get up as I lay there on the floor, with Dylan over me.

"I dreamed about Albert Valentine," I whispered. "He was laughing at me. Told me that my hot, sexy, skirt-covered butt was not up to the job. That I should get a real man to solve this case."

"That's our Albert. Ever likeable."

For the life of me, I couldn't think of anything to say. Dylan was leaning over me still, though his hands had slid from my shoulders down to my upper arms. I could feel his body heat reaching out to me. His closeness, the smell of his aftershave, his leather jacket, his skin ... it all combined to start up an answering heat in my blood.

And he saw it in my eyes and I saw it in his. *We could do it here.*

Oh, man, it would be that easy, it would be that — oh, wait! Crap. "We can't!" I said. "Dylan, I —"

He surprised me with a nod. "I know just what you're going to say, Dix."

"You ... you do?"

"Not here. Not like this. It's going to be right when it happens for the first time. And this ..." he glanced around the dumpy office, "... is neither the time nor the place."

Dylan rose with a sighing exhalation. He did that little pull to the crotch which, okay, made me want to burst into a chorus of *We Are the Champions.*

"I'll get us some coffee," he said. "Be right back."

The door closed behind him, and I laid my head back down on the floor.

Not the time or place for our first time. That was why he thought I'd begged off, because I wanted it to be special.

Actually, it was because I'd suddenly remembered I was wearing the world's least attractive but possibly most comfortable (used-to-be-white) granny panties, circa 1999. But hey, let's go with *it has to be special.*

Chapter 14

YLAN CAME BACK with Starbucks — a venti skinny latte for me
and a regular high-test black coffee for him. I filled him in on what
I'd learned from my interviews (he snickered when I told him how I'd
rubbed it in to Dickhead about scooping him on Albert's affair). But the
lack of juicy info on either Faynelle or Telly gave me a sinking feeling.
Because that left me with Cathy Valentine. Despite her apparent apathy
about all things Albert, she was the one with the motive right now.

But then again, if Cathy was telling the truth about Albert having
an affair, maybe whomever he'd been cuddling a little too closely with
might have a motive. Could we be dealing with a jealous mistress? Maybe
a mistress spurned? Or how about this — maybe Albert had unleashed
that temper of his on his lover, and maybe she wasn't going to take
it — maybe, unlike Cathy, she didn't have to. Or perhaps he'd drawn the
wrath of someone who stood in some kind of protective role over her?

But if we put aside the idea that something at the cuddle club was
inadvertently causing these deaths in favor of deliberate homicide, how
did Telly Smith figure into all this, if at all? Was it a love triangle we were
dealing with? Passion and jealousy never went out of fashion as great
motives for murder.

Nah, I didn't like that theory. Not that it was that unusual for a love
triangle to leave two of the lovers dead, but usually the last man standing
wasn't a woman. Well, not in an M-F-M triangle.

And what about Faynelle? Did she factor in at all? Somehow I
thought not. First, she'd died of a massive heart attack — an infarction.
Different beast than cardiac arrest. Secondly, from her medical records,
it really did seem likely to have been a natural event. Her own family
described her as a ticking time bomb. It had been clear to everyone that
her high-stress job and sedentary lifestyle were taking a terrible toll on
her health. So much so that her son and daughter-in-law had done a

mini-intervention. In fact, their intervention had led to her joining the cuddle club and making an appointment with a fitness consultant to recommend an exercise regime. Unfortunately, she'd never made it to that consultation.

Which brought me back to Telly. Maybe he'd been just an innocent bystander (bycuddler?). Maybe he'd seen or heard something he shouldn't have. Maybe he didn't even realize that he possessed knowledge someone would kill to suppress ...

Hell, maybe there was no connection at all. Except I didn't believe that, either.

And there was still the question about why people kept coming back to cuddle club. Some of them — like Dickhead — against their better judgment. I'd been so certain it was those damned Cuddle-Uppies and/or the smoothies, but the lab results were definitive. The Cuddle-Uppie was clean (Tide-clean!), and the smoothies were innocent. Well, relatively. They certainly didn't contain anything that was likely to cause sudden cardiac death, let alone create an addiction. Of course, that didn't preclude Gaetan pumping pheromones into the air, like the casinos were reputed to do. And yeah, I know, that's probably an urban legend. It bore looking at, though.

And then there was the possibility — hard as it was to fathom — that people really, really liked to cuddle. Maybe there was some real, physiological cascade of chemicals from all that touchy-feely stuff that created receptors in Cuddlers' brains that cried out to be filled again.

There were too many damned questions. Which left only one thing I knew for certain: we were cuddle club bound again.

And that meant we were in need of more pajamas.

It wasn't like we could just swing past the mega mall and pick up a couple of pairs off the rack. Not when we were posing as designers. Nor could we show up in comfy sweats like everyone else now that we'd established that cover.

Thus we found ourselves again at Aunt Gert's, sitting in her cozy living room in front of a pot of tea and dainty finger food she'd set out for us. Her new business cards sat squarely in the middle of the table, in pride of place. Yep, business cards. Aunt Gert had been so impressed by how very impressed we'd been with her designs that she'd invested a bit of her savings on more materials, better sewing equipment, and glossy business cards.

Well, she did have great designs, even if some of them were a little far out there.

And getting more out there by the minute.

Oh, boy.

"These are for you, Dylan, dear." Aunt Gert presented the one-piece long john delight on a hanger, holding that hanger way up over her head so the attached slippered feet wouldn't drag on the floor. Oh. My. God.

All Dylan would have needed was a stubbly growth of beard, knitted socks, and an ax propped over his shoulder and he'd blend in perfectly as the stereotypical woodsman. The lyrics of Monty Python's *Lumberjack Song* started playing in my head. I couldn't help but snicker into my hand, careful of course not to let Aunt Gert notice. But yet making sure that Dylan did notice.

"This," Aunt Gert said, waving a hand dramatically over the long fire-engine red one-piece, "is from my Canadian Winter collection."

Yep, we were all lumberjacks and fishermen up here in the Great White North.

Aunt Gert must have caught my skeptical look, for she quickly said, "When I go international — and you know I will — I have lots of collections in mind — Toronto Nights, Nova Scotia Blues. Oh yes, I've got big plans for my little business."

Wow. Dylan had said she'd been bored since handing over her small restaurant business to her sons. I guess he was right! I sure hoped she knew what she was doing. I mean, I loved her enthusiasm, but I was hoping she wasn't basing all her business decisions on how much Dylan and I were buying.

Dylan was thinking the same thing. "Well, Aunt Gert, Dix and I really love your designs, but ..."

"Don't worry, sweetie," she said. "I've already opened my online shop."

"You *what*?" Dylan asked.

"I opened an e-store," she replied cheerily. "I got my friend Mary's grandson to build the site, including the merchant piece. He did the SEO optimization, too. And Hal — you know my friend Hal? I hired his granddaughter — she's a professional photographer, you know — to corral some models and take pictures of the wares. It's going very well, I think."

"Yeah, Dylan," I said, giving him a reproaching look. "She knows what she's doing."

Aunt Gert scooted out of the room to retrieve the PJs she'd made for me. She was carrying the garment front and center as she came back into the room. "Here you go, Dix!" Yup that hanger-arm was up high again, another one-piece floating down from it.

I was speechless.

"Part of the Canadian Winter collection again, Aunt Gert?" Dylan asked.

"Yes it is! Do you like it?"

"I sure do!" Dylan was grinning ear to ear as he turned to me. "Don't you, Dix? Dix?"

Oh my fuck! Apparently when Aunt Gert had designed these pajamas, she had the female lumberjack in mind. They were almost identical to Dylan's with the exception of one very fine feature. Where Dylan's had a frontally placed buttons for those jaunts out to the frost-covered outhouse in the middle of the night (or who we kidding, around the corner; he's a man), the pajamas Aunt Gert had made for me had that trap door in the back.

I repeat: Oh my fuck!

"I've blown you away!" she cried. "I can see by the look on your face!"

Oh, she'd done that all right.

Dylan and I couldn't get out of there fast enough. And yeah, we did leave with parcels in hand as we climbed into the SUV.

"Any chance we could solve this case before we don these PJs tonight?" Dylan asked hopefully. I'd told him about my conversations with the decedents' families. And though he didn't really have his money on Cathy Valentine either, he had the same feeling that I did, that this affair Albert had been having was somehow connected to the cuddle club deaths.

I shrugged. "We're close to ... something."

"So who was Albert having the affair with?" Dylan asked.

"My guess is Ruth-Ann. She's about the same age range."

"That isn't always a factor, you know." He gave me a devilish smile. "Age isn't all there is to these things."

Yeah, I got it, he was talking about us.

"True enough," I sank back in the seat. "But you know, Ruth-Ann was on him in no time flat, administering CPR. Yes, I know, she was a nursing instructor, but she seemed so dogged."

"True. And now that you mention it, if she hadn't been totally done in, I get the feeling she wouldn't have yielded to me." He keyed the ignition and the SUV roared to life. "Maybe you're on to something, Dix."

"Hey, don't drive straight back to the office," I said as I buckled my seatbelt. "Let's head over to Gaetan Land. Those shirts we ordered from Babe should be ready by now." (And despite how wonderful it would have looked on my mother, I was keeping for myself the one Babe had slipped to me that smoothie-spilling night. Trendy or not, I looked awesome in it.)"And if Albert was having an affair, I'm betting she'd know about it."

"Babe? You think she'd have the inside scoop."

"I'm counting on it."

I called Babe from my cell en route, telling her to expect us shortly. She sounded upset, but I didn't offer to defer our visit, and she didn't ask me to. And if she had, I was fully prepared to fake some kind of static/cellular interference and hang up.

I was damned curious about why Babe was upset. I suspected her turd of a big brother was behind it. And with any luck, we'd walk in on that family drama. When emotions run high, lips tended to run looser.

"Can you drive a little faster, Dylan?"

He could and he did. We got to the building on 33rd within minutes of my clicking the cell shut. And we heard the crying even as we neared the suite. Hysterical crying. Babe's.

Something smashed against a wall inside, and Dylan stuck his arm in front of me and pushed past. "Hang back, Dix. Let me go first."

I bit down on a growl.

"Relax," he said. "You can quit growling."

Okay, so maybe I didn't bite down on that growl very hard.

"I know you can take care of yourself in any situation, Dix, but the cuddle crowd doesn't. Think about your audience. You can hardly go in there flying your kick-ass colors. Not unless you want to blow our cover." Those dark brown eyes bored into me.

Well, when he put it like that ... "Fine. Go ahead." I shrugged my acceptance. "You be the big, strong boyfriend."

Dylan opened the door to Gaetan Land to the sound of a second object smashing.

A broken vase (one of two matching ones that had adorned the reception desk) was shattered on the floor at Babe's feet.

"I hope you don't expect me to clean that up!" Brandy said from across the room.

Babe glanced our way, and I could clearly read her embarrassment at our witnessing her tantrum. Then she promptly broke into tears. Real ones.

Ah, crap. I so suck at the touchy feely stuff.

Brandy looked at Dylan, the angry, rich bitch tone she'd been using with Babe morphing into sultry vamp. "Hi Dylan," she purred. "I'm filling in for Eva today." She cut a look to me. "Oh, and Daisy, is it? You're still here?"

"Ain't going nowhere," I said.

She chuckled in that *we'll-see-about-that* way.

Okay, I love women. Really. Well, not in the way my sister Peaches-Marie does (which, by the way, is totally fine), but in a chicks-rule, you-go-sister kind of way. Seriously, we women are no less than amazing. But Brandy Crotty was just not that likeable. In fact, I wanted to smack her. But first things first. Business before pleasure. I had to attend to Babe.

"Babe? What's wrong?" I asked.

She snuffled back the tears, noisily, as Dylan and I ushered her into the office.

"What is it, Babe?" Dylan asked, his voice kind as he closed the door behind the three of us. "What's the trouble?"

"Gaetan's going back to California!" she wailed. "That's what the trouble is." With a few more wet snuffles, she plunked down into the chair behind the desk.

"You mean he's closing the cuddle club?" I asked. The notion filled me with a small wave of panic, and let me tell you, I was not at all pleased at the sensation. Dylan and I sat across from the distraught Babe.

"No, not closing it," she said. "He says he'll be back. I'm supposed to take care of things while he's gone. It's just that ... just that ..." She started bawling again. "I have to take care of ... like everything! Starting now!"

Okay, I was getting a little perturbed. Seriously, I mean she was this upset because she had to manage the club for a couple weeks? How hard could it be? Throw a blanket on the floor ... mix up a few smoothies in that ... blending thing. Unless she knew something I didn't yet ... something illegal that she was scared of being caught doing ...

"But you're more than capable of running this place, Babe," Dylan said. "You don't need to be concerned about that."

She waved him off. "Oh, I know. That's not what I'm worried about."

"What *are* you worried about?" Dylan probed gently.

"Well, Gaetan wants me to tell one of the cuddlers they have to go. He says there've been complaints ..."

Ah, yeah. I could see that would suck. No doubt it was that fellow with the hairy ears.

Babe looked at me. "It's you, Dix. Gaetan said you can't come back."

What ... wait ... *me*? I lifted a self-conscious hand to my ear. "Complaints about me?" Um, you see what I mean about tweezers ...

"That's what Gaetan said, but really ... I think it's mostly Brandy Crotty. Though I know Starla Good said something too. And, well, Gaetan himself doesn't much care for you."

Well, that was pretty diplomatically put. Gaetan Gough no less than hated my guts. And he wanted his kid sister to do the dirty work in telling me I couldn't come back. Man, what a total jerk.

"So why's he going to California?" Dylan leaned forward in the chair and handed Babe a tissue.

"He says there's some business he has to attend to back home, but I know for a fact things there are running smoothly. He just ... he just wants to saddle me with all the hard stuff, as always. Doesn't know when he's coming back."

Or if. Dylan caught the questioning look I cast and acknowledged it with a look of his own.

"So he just dumped all this news on you today?" I said.

"Yes." Babe balled up the tissue in her hand. "He came in, signed a few cheques, ordered the tickets, and did some of the maintenance."

"Maintenance?" I asked.

"Yeah, he changed a florescent tube in one of the lights — though come to think of it, I don't think any were burned out, or even flickering — and changed the air filters on the A/C vent. That's why Brandy's bitching," she confided. "When Gaetan changes the air filters, dust and particles from the ceiling tiles and ... all that stuff, falls from them all over the place. Any other time Eva would be doing it, and Eva never complains, but she's sick or something."

"Wow, that's very proactive of Gaetan," Dylan said.

Babe shrugged. "He can be very particular. Well, about *some* things. I mean, he changed those filters when we first moved in, and did it again today. We'll have the cleanest air in Marport City, but with other stuff — the paperwork and paying bills and ordering inventory and stuff — he can't seem to lift a finger. If I didn't stay right on top of those things, this business would fall apart!"

"Air quality is important," I said, shooting Dylan another look.

"I suppose." Babe shrugged. "Anyway, after tonight's cuddle, Gaetan says I am in charge until he gets back." She sighed. "Well, at least there's one good thing."

"Yeah? What's that?"

"Gaetan said that as of tonight, I'm allowed to join in the cuddle too."

Chapter 15

I'VE SAID IT before; I'll say it again (like I need to convince anyone — ha!): Dylan is the shoulder to cry on in our dynamic duo. And Babe practically soaked that shoulder with her tears. Poor kid. Gaetan was such a bully. But you know, I thought I was seeing some encouraging signs.

Rhonda Mary Gough, aka Babe, was getting sick and tired of taking this crap from big brother. Through the sniffles and the hiccups, I could see that something else was budding. Anger. Babe was realizing that she didn't want this life anymore. Even more important, she was realizing that the only person who could change things, ultimately, was Babe. Oh, there was help out there; Dylan assured her of that. But she'd have to take the first step (however big, however small) herself. I knew she would. After all (you know it, sister), that's a woman for you.

So while Dylan consoled Babe, I moved quietly away. With Babe's back to me, her head on Dylan's shoulder, I busied myself around Gaetan Land. That is to say, I snooped through the files marked private in the small filing cabinet. Risky, I know, but Dylan was making it easy for me, keeping Babe focused on him, talking and totally distracted.

Soooooo ... I started with the payment information. How interesting to see that Elizabeth Bee's Gaetan Land membership was indeed being paid for by Hugh Drammen. Albert Valentine's attendance had been frequent right up until his demise. But whoa, hold the phone. There were no recent invoices in his file. The billing had stopped weeks ago. Oh, man, that didn't seem right. If I was any judge of character, it wasn't like money-grubbing Gaetan to let something like that slide. But wait? Wasn't Babe in charge of the billing?

The medical histories were interesting. Holy shit! Drammen was old! Ruth-Ann was diabetic. There were three in the group taking meds for depression (poor Eva one of them; wasn't always easy being a young woman), and one took meds from time to time for erectile dysfunction (I can't believe he put that on there!). Heart problems: Faynelle St. James hadn't listed any, but had admitted in her comments that her weight, lack of fitness, and job stress were motivators to join Gaetan Land. All of those factors made a heart condition seem pretty damned feasible. Telly had disclosed that he had high blood pressure. Interestingly, Albert Valentine seemed to have skipped the section on health information almost completely. He'd ticked yes to a couple of minor things, but failed to tick any nos. Had he been lying by omission?

Frankly, I thought all three probably had heart issues. But did I believe they'd all just spontaneously suffered fatal events? Not a chance. Well, Faynelle maybe.

Alrighty then. Looked like I was back to my theory of pheromones. Pheromones that potentially caused people with heart conditions to keel over dead.

Except we knew that Gaetan wasn't using the Cuddle-Uppies to introduce the pheromones, nor were they being delivered via the smoothies. But that whole changing the air filters thing? I think we had a winner for the mode of delivery.

Presuming my theory was right, the question was, did Gaetan know his secret cuddle addiction-inducing ingredient could cause potentially fatal heart problems?

If so … that was manslaughter, plain and simple. Or reckless endangerment, at the very least.

I was going to so nail Gaetan's ass on this.

There was a loud, shuddering sigh from across the room. One of those I'm-all-cried-out sighs. I slid the filing cabinet door closed (oh so silently), then turned to smile at Babe. Then Dylan.

"Time to go, Dylan, dear?"

"Yes, Dix, darling."

We exited the tiny office.

But our visit wasn't over.

"Hey, Brittney," I called over to Brandy. "You missed a spot!"

I turned to Babe, who'd followed me out of the small office. "She really should clean that, you know."

Babe looked down at the mess, sheepishly.

I meant the pile of glass on the floor where, in her tantrum, Babe had broken the vases. It would take randy-Brandy no more than a few minutes to clean that up with her power to suck. (I mean, she still was holding the vacuum cleaner, after all.) Yes, Babe had made the mess, but in my humble opinion, Babe had better deal with the little brat right now. With Gaetan gone, Brandy'd walk all over Babe if she didn't assert herself.

"Sorry, can't," Brandy said. She'd parked the vacuum and was leaning to look out the window (and give Dylan a nice view of her ass, no doubt). But she didn't look very sorry. "Eva and I are off to have pedicures and manicures." She turned around. "Ta-ta and all that. But I'll see you at cuddle club tonight, won't I, Dylan?"

"Er, yeah," Dylan conceded.

"Babe," I urged her under my breath. "I know she's just filling in for Eva but you really should get her to clean —"

"I'll do it." Dylan crossed the room and grabbed the vacuum from where Brandy had left it. "I don't mind helping out. Especially since Brandy and Eva have appointments at the spa."

What the fuck?

But I really do know better than to ever seriously question whose side Dylan is on. Always mine. "Let me go change the vac bag first, though. Otherwise the glass might shred it and get dust all through the motor. Where do you keep them, Babe?"

Ah. Got it. Smart lad, Dylan.

"Oh, I can do that for you," Brandy gushed.

"No," he said. "I insist. You don't want to be late for your appointment."

"Well, it is at the Bombay Spa . . ." With a superior wave, she floated past Babe and me and out the door.

Babe pointed to an unmarked door that led to the maintenance closet. With vacuum in hand, Dylan went inside. I turned Babe around as he shut the door, drawing her into conversation so she wouldn't think too hard on why Dylan had shut himself inside the small closet.

I knew he'd need time in there. So small talk it was.

"So you went to California U?" I'd seen that on the degree.

Babe seemed to brighten. "Yes," she said. "Oh, that was such a wonderful time! I finished near the top of my class. I wish I'd been able to do more with it."

"Like what?"

She beamed. As if she'd never been asked what she wanted to do with her life, but always wanted to be asked, Babe elaborated. Short version of the long story: she wanted to run her own business, or at least be a partner in some sort of business. And not just the *yes* partner. She was very good at business, and very creative. But the baby of the family had always been seen as the baby of the family. Every one of her siblings and both her parents were against the idea of her striking it out on her own. Education? Fine. Life? Not so much.

Just as Babe was wrapping up, the door opened.

"Richie!" Babe said. She gave Detective Head a curious smile. "What are you doing here?"

He nodded (a tad efficiently) and said, "Dylan needed my help with something."

I pointed the way. Babe looked at me confused as Dickhead shut himself inside the small janitorial closet with Dylan.

"Boys, huh? What are ya gonna do? Can't even ask a woman for directions in changing a vacuum bag."

Seconds later, Dylan and Dickhead came out of the closet. Both nodded to me in a meaningful way. Then Dickhead left holding onto the stuffed-out pocket of his overcoat. He had it — the vacuum cleaner bag. Tagged and sealed no doubt, and soon on the way to the lab for analysis.

Dylan started cleaning.

"I really appreciate this," Babe said, as Dylan picked up the larger pieces of glass and vacuumed the floor.

"Well, we appreciate the beautiful blouses you made. Oh, and Babe, don't tell Gaetan we were in."

"How come?"

Oh, so many reasons!

"Well, if he doesn't know we were here, then he won't give you hell when we show up for cuddle club tonight."

We. Yes, I'd thrown that in on purpose.

"Well," she replied sheepishly, "Gaetan didn't ban Dylan from the club."

Of course he hadn't. He'd have had a small riot on his hands if tall, handsome Dylan were kicked out of cuddle club. Mabel might become deadly.

"I just really want to come back," I said. "Just this one more time."

Babe looked dubious, but with a hesitant nod, agreed.

Dylan and I walked quickly, silently, out to his SUV. Dickhead's unmarked car was long gone from the parking lot, with the evidence.

"The air filters," I said. "That's where those deadly pheromones were coming from."

After a hesitation, Dylan nodded. "Seems like it."

We drove away in silence.

Stupid, stupid silence.

Chapter 16

DYLAN AND I had plans for that evening. Namely: crashing the cuddle club. Again.

Ah, got to love working on an expense account. But oh boy, when Dickhead got the bill for this . . .

Not many things give me that warm and fuzzy feeling, but that did. I sighed.

"You look warm and fuzzy, Dix."

I gave Dylan that cocked eyebrow look. "Huh?"

"I mean, there's a dreamy little smile on your face."

It wasn't just the prospect of lightening Dickhead's wallet that put that smile on my face.

It was the impending aha moment. Yeah, I like those center-of-attention times. Modesty is so overrated. Seriously overrated.

But I knew who wouldn't be shouting my praise to the rooftops alongside me. I knew whose voice wouldn't be ringing out with my own with shouts of "Oh, Dix Dodd, you're the greatest!" That would be Gaetan Gough.

Why?

Because Mr. Heading-to-California wasn't going to be hopping on any planes soon, I highly suspected. I'd told Detective Richard Head to bring his shiny badge along tonight. Unless I was badly mistaken, he'd be coming out of paper salesman persona and going into cop persona to arrest Gaetan Gough himself. (Yeah, Constable Pivans was taking a backseat, and Head was at the, well, head of this operation as far as the police were concerned.)

I couldn't wait for cuddle club to begin. Oh, shit, in fact it was a damn long afternoon. I delivered the blue-patterned Babe blouse to a delighted Mrs. Jane Presley (who then insisted I join her for lunch). When I went home, I played Tetris (new high score!), I changed the desktop background on my laptop three times. Oh, and online, I started my Christmas shopping. (I got myself a Dexter charm bracelet complete with miniature knives, cleavers, syringes, and various other serial killer accoutrements. God, I love that show.)

And then I did one more thing. I made a phone call. It was time to invite someone else to cuddle club this evening. Oh they'd definitely want to be here. And I damn well wanted them there. 'Cuz I was damned sure I'd cracked the case of Death by Cuddle Club.

"I'll be there," came the reply to my invite.

Fine, one more who'd see me in my trap-door pajamas, and Dylan in his lumberjack-style boys-pee-standing-up ones from Aunt Gert's Canadian collection. Ah, but it would be worth it.

Dylan and I wanted to arrive late to cuddle club. On purpose. Well, not late-late, but perfectly-timed late. Yes, we wanted everyone gathered and ready to cuddle before we broke the news that Gaetan Gough, their cuddly guru, was a murderer.

Were we worried about the cuddlers cuddling? About Starla and Ruth-Ann or whoever had the next turn, passing out the smoothies tonight? Nope. Not even a little bit. Gaetan had changed the air filters. He was onto us that we were onto him. I suspected — oh fuck, I *knew* — it was going to be a pheromone-free night.

Didn't I?

Damn, where was that reassuring niggle?

So Dylan drove a little slower along the streets of Marport City to 33rd Street. Then he drove a little faster as I started to sing Monty Python's *The Lumberjack Song*. Repeatedly. (Ahaha! He didn't like the jammies he had to wear any better than I liked the ones I was stuck wearing.) Ah, but then, he joined in on that catchy tune.

"For the love of God, speed up!" I begged.

"Think we're running late, Dix?" he said, pressing his foot to the pedal.

"Yeah … yeah, that's it."

As it turned out, our Gaetan Land arrival was perfectly timed. Or would have been had someone not stolen the show. Instead of pitching tents, they were all gathered around the center of the cuddle floor. Brandy was there, fawning over something. So were Zoey and Eva, though to a lesser extent. Mabel, Starla and Ruth-Ann too were snugged into this huddle. In the background, men were back-slapping each other.

It could only mean one thing.

"Someone's gotten engaged," Dylan observed.

"Yep."

"Squeeeeeeeeeeeee, Dix! Dix! Wait till you see!"

Totally freaking out, bouncing and charging, Elizabeth made a beeline toward me.

The rock on her hand must have been three carats. I'm not an expert on jewelery, but holy fuck! Unless that sucker was one helluva convincing cubic zirconia, it must have set Hugh back somewhere between thirty to fifty grand. My money was on it being real.

"Hugh-Bear and I are engaged!" Elizabeth gushed. She squeeeeed again (argh, right in my ear) as she pulled me into a hug.

Dylan went over to shake Hugh's hand while I extracted myself from Elizabeth's crushing hug. I caught Dickhead's eye, quickly, as Dylan joined the menfolk. Yes, it was just a glance, but I could tell by that glance that paper sales were dropping and Detective Richard Head, cop, was on the premises. The sweats were gone, the obligatory sports jacket and boring tie were in da house.

"Um, congratulations," I said to Elizabeth.

She beamed a smile at me. "You'll have to come to the wedding. All the cuddlers are invited."

"When is it?" (As if I needed to ask.)

"As soon as possible!" she said, sharply. "Maybe even as soon as next weekend at Hugh's place. He has a huge house, a mansion, practically. Well, soon it'll be ours. Imagine, little ol' me, Elizabeth Bee, living with all that splendor! In a mansion of my very own ..."

And yes, there it was, that newly-engaged sparkle in her eyes.

I smiled to myself. Good for her!

"What the hell are you doing here?" Gaetan yelled.

Before I even turned around I knew that was meant for me.

"Babe was supposed to call you!" Gaetan said.

Babe popped her head out the office door, that had for a change, been left open. "I ... I ..." Her face was beet red; clearly the girl was no good at lying.

"I had my phone on vibrate all day. And then forgot where I put it." I said. "Silly me."

"You're not welcome here, Dix," he said.

"What?" I said, pretending shock. And I waited for the gasps from around the room. And waited. Apparently they weren't as shocked as I was.

"Dix and I are paid up for three months," Dylan said.

"You're welcome to stay, Dylan. But that one —" He pointed an accusing finger at me, as if there was a question as to who he meant. "She's a troublemaker."

"And she's all elbows," someone called out. "And they hurt!"

"Plus she uses all those British expressions!"

"It's Coronation Street, people!" I shouted. "Just Coronation Street."

"Can you name one character on that show?" Elizabeth asked, always the smart ass.

Yeah, but I had her this time. "Big Ben!"

Er, wait, that's from the British porn …

The door opened and closed behind us. While this all had been going on, someone else entered the cuddle club. Someone new. "What about me? Am I welcome to stay?"

Gaetan paled. So he recognized Cathy Valentine, wife of the late Albert Valentine.

"Oh … um … Mrs. Valentine," Gaetan said. "I'm surprised to see you here."

She doffed her coat. "My husband seemed to liked it here. Why wouldn't I?"

"Yes, but —" Gaetan looked about ready to faint. A sheen of sweat appeared on his forehead. One velour swipe later and it was gone. But just temporarily. The lady was making him sweat.

Interesting.

He scratched his cloudy-blond head. A small snow of dandruff floated down onto his shoulders. Another sign of nervousness?

"Well," Cathy said. "I called this afternoon and gave all my information to your lovely assistant —"

"Sister," Babe said. "I'm Gaetan's sister."

He glared at her. (Man, I was going to have such fun nailing his ass.) "Enough, Babe!" Gaetan shook his head, templed his fingers at his forehead as if steadying himself, centering himself. "Fine," he said. "Mrs. Valentine, you're welcome to stay."

Gaetan turned to the crowd. He sighed, really sighed. "I … I have something to tell you all." Apparently, kicking me out tonight just wasn't worth the hassle it had been a few minutes ago. "Where … where is everyone?" he asked. "Did somebody leave?"

How closely had he been watching this crowd? Oh, my intuition was just jumping.

Zoey spoke up. "Brandy and Eva had to go to the bathroom. And Ruth-Ann —"

"I'm right here," Ruth-Ann said, raising a hand. She'd sat down into one of those chairs lining the wall. "I ... I just had to sit down for a moment." And she did look pale. Sad, even. Why? The reminder of Albert's death, maybe?

"Well, this can't wait for Brandy and Eva. I have something to tell you all," Gaetan said. "Something important."

"Hummph!" That lovely little exhale was from Elizabeth, again at Hugh's side, who apparently didn't like her spotlight snuffed out so early by Gaetan's spontaneous announcement. (Oh, just wait till I took the floor.)

"I'm ... I find myself having to leave you all, my cuddle cups."

Someone mumbled, and not out of Gaetan's earshot. "The guy can be such a windbag."

I eagerly nodded my agreement. (Or maybe it was just for emphasis, cause, you know, I was the one who mumbled it.)

Yet, this evening no one was rushing to Gaetan's side. No tears were falling. No, "Oh no, please don't leave us!" or ... wow! I looked around the room. Except for the earlier bride-to-be hugs for Elizabeth, this wasn't looking like a particularly cuddly group tonight. No one was hanging off one another. People even looked ... edgy. Young, old, rich, poor, or fresh from the Bombay Spa, no one looked starry-eyed happy to be here. In fact, not even me.

Yeah, I knew I was right.

"I wouldn't be so fast, Cuddle Cup," I said to Gaetan. "I wouldn't be cashing in those Air Miles just yet."

"What are you talking about, Dix?" he growled, not even trying to hide the exasperation.

"Sh-sh-show time!" (No, not a stutter, just well, me drawing even more attention upon myself.) "Let me tell you a tale. Let me tell you all a tale, the tale of Death by Cuddle Club. Dun-dun-dun-dunnnnnnnnnnnn."

Damn. I really loved the drama.

Brandy, back from the bathroom, laughed out loud. "Omigod, she's high!"

"Not even close, Brandy," I said. "Not even close. In fact, I'd reckon to say nobody is high here tonight."

"Er, I had a glass of wine with supper earlier," Ruth-Ann said. "Does that count?"

Eva said, "And I had a shot of tequila on the way over."

Oh boy, with anti-depressants, that couldn't be good.

A very mellow-looking young man said, "I might have accidentally vaped like, half a gram. Anyone bring Doritos?"

"I'm on steroids!" said another.

"I sucked back a Red Bull. Does that count?"

"Do we have to pee in cups now?" steroid man said. "My agent said I shouldn't do that under any circumstance."

I shook my head. "Folks, that's not what I meant." I turned to Gaetan once again, oh so ready to make the accusation. "Let me tell you what Gaetan's been doing here."

Oh geez, he was looking worse by the minute. So that set me grinning, the guy had to know what was coming. "Gaetan Gough, your beloved hand-clapping guru, changed the air filters today."

"That bastard!" Elizabeth shouted. "How dare we have fresh air."

Like I said earlier, smart-assed bitch. I guess she didn't like being moved even further out of the spotlight. I saw it then, out of the corner of my eye as I smiled over at Elizabeth: Richard Head was moving closer to Dylan and me. Yep, now my adrenaline was surging. I was going in for the kill — *and everyone was looking at me!*

"Bastard, indeed," I said. "But why did he change the air filters today? Why did he change them, and book his flight to sunny California? A one-way ticket I might add. Why? *Why?* I'll tell you why? Because he's been drugging you people."

There were gasps all around this time, and not just from me.

"Well, of course he's been hugging us, you daft girl," Mabel said. "It's a cuddle club."

"*Drugging*, Mabel," Ruth-Ann said, loudly. "He's been drugging us."

"Oh. That's not good then." She looked at me again. "Continue, Daft girl."

Ah, there was a vote of confidence. Well, sorta.

"What … what do you mean?" Eva cried. She looked genuinely scared. (Though not as scared as Gaetan, I couldn't help but notice.)

"I mean, he's been releasing pheromones into the air to make you all that much more cuddly," I said. "Through the air system."

"You can't prove a thing!" Gaetan said.

There was a shakiness in his voice — oh that sweet, sweet shakiness — that more than proved it to me that my brilliant intuition had been bang freakin' on. But that might not hold up with the rest of the, er, cuddle cakes.

"Mmmm, kinda *can* prove it." I said.

Well, technically I couldn't. The results weren't back from the police lab yet, but I was just that confident they'd find pheromones. And Gaetan's fear as I smiled only made me feel more confident. I was going for it. I clap, clap, clapped my hands, in a very Gaetan way.

"This morning, Gaetan," I said, "you changed the air filters in the ceiling. Those filters — that's how you were getting the pheromones into the room. Making this one hell of a cuddly environment, huh? Folks would come to cuddle club — on a lark or for whatever reason," — (I shot Dickhead a glance), "and they'd experience an arousal level."

"Ha!" Gaetan scratched his head again. (Oh, yuck, another snowy shoulder shower.) "Prove it! Jump right up there Dix and grab that new filter I put in. Go ahead, make my day. Test it for pheromones or anything else."

I threw my head back as I laughed ('cuz I was going for diabolical). "Oh, but you knew we were on to you. So when you changed the filter today, you put a clean one in there. Then you had the place vacuumed so any fallen particles would be disposed of."

Gaetan had gone from looking pale to sick.

"But that's not all, is it, Gaetan?" I said. "There was a problem with these pheromones, wasn't there? Somehow, it induces major cardiac events in those with heart conditions. Albert Valentine. Telly Smith — they both died after coming to cuddle club and breathing in that shit you put in the air."

"Sounds like manslaughter to me," Dickhead growled. He flashed his badge around the place, and yes, to the genuine surprise of everyone.

"I . . . I have to sit down," Babe said. But she wasn't the only one to slide to the floor on that note.

Big brother Gaetan went down butt first too. And now he really didn't look good. His face looked absolutely pasty, and I could see perspiration beading on his brow. Then Gaetan did something that drew a collective gasp from the cuddle crowd. He reached up and grasped his amazing blond Richard Simmons hair and pulled it off. Yep. It was a wig. Without it, Gaetan's head was as bald and round and white as a cue ball. Ignoring the gasp, Gaetan shook the wig vigorously. I blinked as dandruff drifted down to the floor. Huh? Wigs have dandruff? Now, that's realism.

Gaetan made a stricken noise and dropped the wig.

Dickhead quickly retrieved it with a latex-gloved hand, slipping it into an evidence bag. I'm usually pretty quick on the uptake, but it took a few seconds for it to click into place. Of course! When he'd changed the filters, particles didn't just fall down to the floor; they'd have fallen onto the wig.

Apparently, Gaetan realized this too.

Gaetan clutched his chest, "I ... I swear ... I didn't know ... about the heart attacks. It was supposed to be ... harmless sexually-arousing pheromones! In small doses ... there shouldn't have been any harm. Don't understand ..."

Oh, crap. My suspect was apparently having a heart attack right before my eyes!

Chapter 17

Y OU KNOW, I never did like hospitals. The smell of antiseptic, the too-bright lights (that everyone looks a little bit more sickly under). And that whole squeaky-shoes-on-polished-floor thing gets to you after a while. Brrr, that sound. Makes me cringe every time. And what's up with the chairs in the waiting rooms? There just is no way to slouch properly in those things. Dozing off? Not going to happen. And lumbar support? Forget it.

(Okay, you get it, I'm tired. Hungry. A tad on the grumpy side.)

Dylan and I had driven Babe to the hospital. Ruth-Ann and Dickhead had attended to Gaetan after he'd slumped to the floor clutching his chest (Detective Head was now fully back into cop persona). Head had called the ambulance in a very efficient, police manner. And a shout-out to Marport City EMS, they were there within minutes, and depositing Gaetan in the ER less than ten minutes after that.

I figured poor Babe would be inconsolable. But, well, she was more in control than I thought she'd be. I mean, she seemed almost calm, considering her brother's apparent heart attack. Or maybe she was just trying really, super hard to be more in control ... maybe that's where control really starts?

(Oh, and did I say apparent heart attack. You caught that, right?)

Paging Dr. Crotty. Paging Dr. Lincoln Crotty.

"He's the cardiologist," I said to Babe, who might not have recognized the name of Marport City's most sought-after heart doctor.

"Any relation to Brandy Crotty, from the club?" Babe asked.

"Most likely," Dylan answered. "All the Crottys in Marport City are connected. They have a long history as professionals, mainly in medicine — doctors, medical researchers and the like. Though a few black sheep turned out to be lawyers and politicians."

Babe nodded, obviously only half listening to Dylan. She pulled a tissue from her purse, and again I saw the vial of pheromones. Actually, this was one of two small containers she had grabbed from the locked safe in the office. The other one she'd handed over to the ER nurse upon Gaetan's admittance (though he'd looked at her rather skeptically as he pocketed it, once we explained what it was).

Yes, that's right. He'd given up the pheromones. Once a chest-clutching Gaetan realized that exposure to the pheromone-laced air filter flakes in his wig had likely triggered a heart attack, he'd quickly coughed up the location of remaining vials.

There had been pandemonium back at Gaetan Land after that.

Most everyone had been astonished to learn that Gaetan was filling the air with pheromones to make everyone just that little bit more, er … cuddly. Quite a few were genuinely pissed. (And okay, I have to admit it, Elizabeth Bee looked genuinely worried as she clutched her geriatric fiancé closer.) Ruth-Ann had to sit back down again. Brandy's eyes narrowed in that I'm-going-to-kick-someone's-ass kind of way. Zoey mimicked Brandy's glare perfectly. And poor Eva looked, well, down at the floor.

Babe (I'm quite sure) was the most surprised of all.

Personally, I was enjoying the fact that Gaetan had been felled by his own wig, or rather the pheromone-contaminated debris it had gathered when he'd changed the offending filter.

But a friggin' wig. With my penchant for disguise, I really should have picked up on that.

I turned to Dylan in the seat beside me. "And you thought the pheromone was in the Cuddle-Uppies!"

Being so tall, Dylan was having an even harder time than I was with these crappy waiting room chairs (did I mention they were orange?).

"So did you, Dix," he reminded. "But I guess we can't blame the Cuddle-Uppies for anything, huh?"

Holy crap! He was right. I looked up and caught the melting look in those chocolate brown eyes. Oh, dear God, I'd gone up in flames in his arms that night at my condo, and there was no blaming … anything. It was all us.

He leaned in to whisper, so close I could feel his warm breath on my ear. "The question now is, what are we going to do about it?"

Well, nothing right at the moment — Dr. Lincoln Crotty walked into the waiting room. "Come with me, Ms. Gough." He turned and marched out of the room. Babe followed. Dylan and I looked at each other, scrambled to our feet and followed.

True, we hadn't been invited, but when has a lack of invitation ever stopped me?

Answer: never. (Hell, if I waited for invitations, I'd never get out.)

"Think he's dead?" I mumbled to Dylan as we walked down the hall (squeaky shoes! squeaky shoes!) behind Babe.

"Nope," Dylan answered.

"And how do you know that?"

He angled me a look that plainly said, *Seriously? You really have to ask me that?* "Same way you know, Dix," he said tersely. "Dr. Crotty wasn't all smiles, but neither was he looking like he was about to give the I'm-sorry-we-did-our-best news. He didn't ask which of us was family. And of course there was the eye contact."

"Eye contact?"

"Yeah, those weren't sympathetic eyes, nor were they worried. If anything, I'd say he was pissed about something."

Oh, I was smiling. "Anything else?"

"Yeah. My gut tells me — just as *your* gut tells *you* — that Gaetan Gough is still alive and kicking, or clapping. So can we just drop it now?" Dylan said, effectively cutting off any notion I might have of playing twenty questions.

Okay, Dylan was miffed. He'd get over it.

It wasn't that I was testing him. Okay, maybe I was. Maybe it was just my insecurity showing. But he was my apprentice, for a little while longer, at least. What would I do when he was fully licensed? I couldn't afford to pay him a full salary. Would I be losing Dylan in the next few weeks? Jesus, I didn't want to think about that happening!

Or maybe I was doing what Dix Dodd always does, pushing away someone (not just any someone) who wanted to get close to me. Moments ago, Dylan had been whispering in my ear, now, he grumbled.

Argh! I didn't want to think about that right now. And luckily for me, Gaetan provided a distraction as Babe pushed through the door of his private room.

He looked like shit. Even considering the hospital lighting. The top of his head was so pasty, ghostly-white, he made his light blue velour look blindingly bright. He lay back on the bed as if exhausted, or seriously hung over (been there, done that, have the T-shirt). His eyes were half-closed slits. Yes, he really did look terrible. But he didn't look like a person having a heart attack. Another big clue — he wasn't tethered to any sophisticated equipment that beeped or blipped or flashed.

Oh, and too, Dr. Lincoln Crotty said: "He didn't have a heart attack."

"Thank God!" Babe was at her brother's bedside in a minute. Sitting on the edge of the bed, holding one of his hands.

Good idea, I thought. I really didn't want him to start clapping. That was seriously getting on my nerves.

And where was I during this?

Ducked behind six foot four Dylan, who'd cleverly placed himself out of Gaetan's direct line of vision. Despite their earlier bucking contests (such as they were), Gaetan liked Dylan. (Okay, everyone liked Dylan.) So I hid back here. Seeing but unseen. (Oh yes, stealth super-hero mode. Like Spider-Man, Captain America. Colonel Crossing Guard ... Okay, that last one is a Canadian superhero I'm working on in my spare time.)

Dylan angled his head and murmured so low that only I could hear it: "Stop humming your theme song, Dix."

Damn, I do that a lot.

"So what was it then, Doctor, if not a heart attack?" Still holding Gaetan's hand, Babe regarded Dr. Crotty with confusion. "I mean, I saw my brother fall. I saw the pain he was in. I —"

"Panic attack. Nothing more."

"What?" Babe's confused look intensified. "What's that?"

Dr. Crotty rolled his eyes, as if she were an irritant. Dude had no bedside manner whatsoever. Or maybe he had a load of it, but the whole load sucked.

"Panic attack! Stress-induced. Surely, you've heard of the fight-or-flight reaction?" Dr. Crotty asked, adding a condescending sigh.

Babe shook her head.

Crotty continued, "Your body goes into overdrive when it perceives a threat. For some people, when their heart goes into this overdrive reaction, it feels like a heart attack." He turned to Gaetan, or rather turned on him, "Was something threatening you, Cuddle Man? Maybe someone cuddling you a little too closely? One of the young girls you seduce into going there? Did someone confront you about the way you fleece lonely people, creepy old men, and sweet girls out of their money?"

What the fuck?

Babe's jaw dropped. I'm guessing that Gaetan's fight-or-flight response was kicking back into overdrive all over again. Then again, Crotty wasn't accusing Gaetan of murder, as I had.

"Doctor," Babe began, "Do you really think this is the time —"

He raised a half apologetic hand. "Sorry. Of course. You're right. Mr. Gough, you'll be fine. Just rest. No stress." His words may have been doctorly, but ...

"You must be Brandy's father!" Dylan said.

Lincoln Crotty whirled toward Dylan, as though becoming aware of him just then. "How do you know my Brandy?" he demanded.

"I know her from Gaetan Land — the cuddle club."

"Do you, now?" Dr. Crotty eyed Dylan with astonishment, looking him up and down. "You don't look like a typical cuddle male. You're not squat and ugly, for one thing. Not even a whiff of dirty old creep about you."

At this point, I stepped out from behind Dylan and into view. I was betting Gaetan wouldn't be too inclined to renew hostilities with me with this angry doctor so not in his corner, and me ready to tell Crotty all of what I knew about the club. I extended my hand, "Dix Davidson," I said, still in PI persona.

He looked at my hand, nodded at my hand, but didn't shake it. "You must be from the Club," he said.

What? I was in that squat and ugly category?

Through gritted teeth, I said, "Friend of the Gough family. I'm just wondering about that vial of substance Babe brought in."

"The pheromones you gave to the nurse," he said. "What about them?"

"Well, are you analyzing them for —"

"For what? The man clearly has nothing wrong with him, physically. Does it surprise me that he fills the air with pheromones to induce a feeling of arousal? Not at all. And unfortunately, he's not the only one to use sensory stimulation to manipulate people. Tales abound concerning casino use of pheromones to get people to gamble more. Not to mention the flashing lights in those places. Churches use high ceilings and acoustics. Christ, we paint the wall of the hospital in calming colors to induce that feeling in patients."

(I wanted to ask him about the uncomfortable orange chairs in the waiting room, but I let it slide ... for now).

The next words, Dr. Lincoln Crotty practically spat at Gaetan and Babe, "Don't get me wrong, I think what you do is despicable. But illegal? If it were up to me, we'd damn well be finding out!"

Well, it kind of was up to me ...

Ten minutes later, Dylan and I were leaving the hospital. We'd offered to drive Babe home, but she insisted on staying at her brother's side. He'd be released in a few hours, they'd cab it home from there. No sooner had we climbed into the SUV than my cell rang.

It was Dickhead.

"What do you bet the tox results are in," Dylan said, when I flashed him my left breast, then the phone display. (Remember what I'd said about women keeping things in their bras? See? There are advantages.)

I nodded and snapped open the phone. "What's the good news," I said, smiling. But that smile slowly faded as I listened to Dickhead's words.

Chapter 18

WE MET UP with Dickhead at Perky Joes. Yeah, I'd cut the cell phone conversation short, before I could give him our end of the news. Better to make this a three-way conversation, face to face.

Yeah, the three of us. Dylan was an integral part of my operation now. Oh God, so far from a mere apprentice ...

"He's not dead," Detective Head said even before we'd sat down with our Perky Joe's java and day-old donuts in hand. It wasn't even close to a question.

"No," Dylan said. "He's not. The Cuddle guru lives."

Dickhead's jaw tightened. "Fucker." Not that he wanted Gaetan Gough dead.

Well, not *dead*-dead.

It didn't take bucket-loads of intuition to read the anger Detective Head was feeling. He was an open book of four-letter words right now, and he was so not ready to wipe the slate clean where Gaetan was concerned. Dickhead did not like being manipulated. Tricked. Fleeced. Drugged.

And I suspected (oh damn, more than suspected) he wasn't the only one of the cuddle cakes to feel that way.

"So was it a heart attack?" Dickhead asked.

"Panic attack," I said. "Stress induced. I'm pretty sure they gave him an Ativan or two, but other than that, they didn't even have him hooked up to a heart monitor when Dylan and I were there."

"Shit!" Head said. "Of course it wasn't a heart attack."

All things considered, it was worthy of a grumble.

As he'd informed me on the phone and I relayed to Dylan, the tox report was back from the lab. That vacuum bag contained lots of things: good old-fashioned dust, a few pet hairs, a couple of dimes, and one gold stud earring. Yes, there were traces of pheromones in there mixed in with the white particles from the air filters and the dropped ceiling tiles, just as we'd suspected. These were the same particles that had snowed down from Gaetan's blond wig and freaked him out. But though the pheromones were strong and powerful, there was nothing — nothing — in them that would induce a heart attack.

"So nothing deadly." I put forth. "Is that what you're telling us, Detective?"

We — all three of us — let that question hang.

Maybe they weren't directly responsible for the deaths. But indirectly?

It started as a chill. A very thorough and very real chill on my shoulders. It crawled along my scalp and it crawled along my spine. It lasted just seconds, but these were the most real seconds for me — this you're-on-to-it nudging sensation.

On that thought, I stood. "Gentlemen, I bid you adieu."

"Where are you going, Dix," Dylan said.

"To see a man about a crime. Wanna come?"

Oh, of course he did.

"You going to see a man about the murders?" inquired Dickhead. "You got an idea, Dodd?"

I answered with a sly smile (and yes, I know it was a sly one, I've been practicing in the mirror). "No, not about the murders. About a different crime, blackmail. And yeah, I got an idea."

"I'm coming along too," Detective Head said. Oh, yeah, he was in total cop mode.

"I'm going undercover," I answered. "And you, officer of the law, just don't —"

"Let me guess, Dix," he interrupted. "And I just don't want to know."

He was right on that.

"Paging Dr. Crotty. Paging Dr. Lincoln Crotty ..."

I glanced at my watch (Actually, it was Dylan's watch; we'd swapped) under the low lighting of the broom closet as the monotone voice sounded through the PA system. It was after midnight and Crotty was still on duty, or at least still hanging around at the hospital. I'd heard he was a workaholic. Maybe it was his weekend covering emergency? Whatever the reason, Lincoln Crotty was still in the building.

Perfect.

My cell phone buzzed. I knew it was Dylan even before I pulled it out of my bra, and glanced at the call display. "Mission accomplished?" I inquired.

"Yeah hi, Sis, I'm having coffee with a friend. Would you mind letting the cat out?"

"Meow," I well, meowed. "Letting the cat out." I clicked the phone shut.

That was the signal. Dylan was in place. Now, it was go time for me to get in place.

Squeak, squeak — damn these floors!

I edged myself carefully out of the closet, then proceeded down the hospital hall with my head down, as if studying the floor. Blue tile, white tile, blue tile, white tile — I was a quick study.

Visitors were gone, of course, but naturally, there was still staff around.

Though, who would recognize me? I was in amazing PI disguise mode. Yes, yes, I was employing my famous transformative powers. It was past visiting hours, so I couldn't just stroll through as a worried mom, and there was always that risk in feigning sick (Ms. Dodd! It's time for your enema!). And yeah, picture it, me running down that hall with that stupid hospital gown flapping out behind me. Been there! And as I've said, I have this rule against posing as anything that might neces-sitate real medical intervention. That's right, I wouldn't be delivering any babies tonight.

So ... what was my disguise?

"Excuse me, Father, is the cafeteria on this floor?"

"Damned if I know."

The young woman looked at me strangely.

I lowered my voice. "Er, I mean, yes. Yes it is. Go in peace my child."

"Um, okay ..."

That's right, I was disguised as a priest.

As for the obvious gender difference: I had on a killing-me sports bra to flatten my already not-so-ample chest, and a fake mustache that would make even the most well-endowed 70s porn star jealous. My blond locks? Pinned tight and tucked up under a black padre hat I got for twenty bucks on eBay. (Pfft ... and Rochelle thought I'd sober up to regret it.) So yeah, I was well and spectacularly undercover as I made my way to Gaetan Gough's room, and hurrying like a demon to get there.

Gaetan was sitting up in bed, but leaning heavily into a couple of pillows as I walked into the room. Yep, he still looked like crap, but maybe a little less so. He still didn't have his wig back on, and oh, where were the magic markers when you needed them!

It really was strange the transformation that wig had had on the man. Gone was the cloud headed, clapping cuddle fuck from Gaetan Land, and here was ... well, an angry bald guy in a velour jumpsuit.

Gaetan absolutely did not look happy to see me. Padre hat, fake mustache, flattened chest and all, he knew me the moment I walked into the room.

"Dix," he croaked. "I figured when Dylan took Babe out for coffee a few minutes ago, you'd come skulking around. What are you doing here?"

"I'll give you three guesses."

"I only need one. You're not Dix Davidson, you're Dix Dodd — a sleazy, two-bit PI from the wrong side of town."

Offended? Well, I probably should have been, but I was more surprised. "How did you —"

"Let's just say I have my own sources, Dodd. My own suspicions. I've heard about your near-famous intuitive abilities. Well, I have a bit of that myself. I suspected you and Dylan Foreman from the moment you walked into Gaetan Land. He's way too young for you to really be his love interest."

Okay, yeah, now I was offended, and dying to give this sawed-off little fucker a piece of my mind. But first things first: "Just how famous did you hear I —"

"What do you want, Dodd?"

Always a loaded question!

"All right, Cuddle Man," I said. "Here's what I want, exactly what I want — tell me about the blackmail."

He chuckled in a kind of dark, kind of groaning way. "I don't suppose there's any point in my saying '*What blackmail?*'"

Oh shit, I was right! There was this whole happy dance thing going on inside my head now.

"Fuck it," Gaetan said, his voice suddenly decisive. "I want it out in the open now."

"Off your chest?"

"Out of my hair!"

Stifling laugh. Killing me.

"This has gone on long enough," Gaetan continued. "Albert Valentine was blackmailing me."

Yes, dear reader. Just as I'd thought.

"For free cuddle sessions?" I'd seen his lack of payment on the books of course, but couldn't very well admit to going through those ledgers in the cuddle club's office. "Maybe some Cuddle-Uppies for the black market —"

"Don't be an ass, Dodd!" His tone suddenly changed. "Bless me father, for I have sinned."

I blinked. What the hell? Then I realized the door had opened behind me.

"Excuse me," the nurse said in an apologetic voice. "I'll come back later." She let the door fall closed behind her.

I looked at Gaetan. "Why did you do that? Cover my butt?"

"Contrary to what you might think, I'm not a monster. And I sure as hell don't want to be a killer. Yes, I use pheromones and lighting and music and this fucking roly-poly, cuddle-me, non-threatening persona to get members and keep them coming back. But I'm a business man, Dix. A damned good one. If, as you say, people are dropping dead at my club, I want my good name cleared and the problem rectified so I can get back to business as usual. The doctor was kind enough to inform me that there was nothing in the pheromones to cause heart attacks. Nothing. But if something else is causing them — someone else — I need to know what the hell is going on."

Yeah, that Gaetan, he was all heart. "Tell me about the blackmail."

He sighed. "Albert Valentine found out about the pheromones. He said he'd tell the whole club about them if I didn't give him what he wanted. I know a few of them wouldn't have cared, but others ... God, they'd have had a big hairy fit." He raised a self-conscious hand to his head. "As you saw tonight when you so inconveniently spilled it, Dix Dodd. This knowledge could make things in Marport City very difficult for me. Not how I wanted to break into the Canadian market. So I had to buy Albert's silence."

"With what?" I had a pretty good idea, but dammit, I wanted him to say it!

"He cuddled for free. And believe me, that horny little bastard cuddled often."

"And?" No way. No way in hell could that be all there was to it.

Gaetan wiped a hand over his suddenly-sweaty brow. "Pheromones!" he said. "I gave him free pheromones. Vials and vials of the stuff."

I wanted to get up and smack Gaetan Gough right about then. *Hard.*

And more than once. (And, oh, wouldn't that be a sight for a nurse to walk in on — porn-starrish priest smacking around a patient.) "So Albert was using the pheromones to get close to someone that he'd otherwise have no chance of being close to. Is that what you're telling me?" My stomach roiled as I pieced this together further.

"Yes, he was using them to seduce someone. Jesus H. Christ, I think he practically bathed in the stuff! Albert used to brag about it. Laugh about it — how turned on he used to make this certain individual. How he'd gotten away with … so much. And I couldn't do anything to stop him."

"You could have said no."

"And lost the Canadian business? Hardly."

"Who was Albert manipulating?" I asked.

"I don't know."

"Bullshit!"

"No, I really don't know. He wouldn't give me a name. Just the sordid details. But I swear, if I knew, Dix Dodd, I'd tell you in a heartbeat."

I have every confidence he would. Because whoever Albert was manipulating with those chemicals would have enough anger inside to do almost anything. Maybe they'd even be angry enough to kill him.

Oh, I was more than betting on that.

I jumped up. "I have to go."

"Fine by me," Gaetan said. "You really are an asshole, Dix Dodd.".

"And you're a jerk off," I countered.

And with that we were done for the night.

I still didn't know who had done the murder. I still didn't know how. But damn it — I more than had a hunch — I *knew* — why death had come to the cuddle club.

I left the room, pulled out my cell, hit the newest entry in my speed dial.

"Detective Head," came the gruff answer.

"We need a serious toxicology panel on our dearly departed Albert."

"I take it you found something out from Gaetan?"

"Yeah, I found out he's as much of a prick as I thought he was. And Albert Valentine was a dirty, rotten, manipulative, lascivious pig. And someone killed him because of it."

Chapter 19

A s I was heading down the corridor, my cell phone buzzed again. I knew it was Dylan.

"Yeah, Sis, I'm thinking you want to let the cat back in now. It might rain. Might come pouring down all of a sudden, in fact, so get the cat back inside! Now!"

Translation: My cover had been blown. Crap! Perhaps it had been the direction-seeking bystander who'd figured I was out of place and mentioned something to someone. Or maybe it was the nurse who'd poked her head into Gaetan's room. Was it the padre hat? I'm no fashion maven, but don't tell me those things had gone out of style! Or was it Gaetan himself, maybe not so interested in cooperating after all?

So yeah, priest-robes and all I was hightailing it down the hallway back to the maintenance closet. Quick-change artist? You don't know the half of it! I was back in my jeans within seconds. I took a few seconds to struggle out of the too-tight sports bra (God, it qualified as a freakin' torture device), then hauled my shirt on.

As much as I hated to lose a good disguise, I threw the priest attire in the big grey garbage receptacle in the maintenance closet — wide-brimmed hat on top. I doffed the socks and shoved my feet into killer high heels (well, high for me; two-and-a-half whole inches). Ten tissues later, I was hiding my face behind the wad of Kleenex as I boo-hooed/snuffled/honked my way down the hallway. Yep, right past security who really didn't want to start a conversation with such a distraught (and snotty) damsel in distress as myself. Yeah, gross as it sounds, the more loudly one honks into the tissues, the more likely one is to be left alone.

I rock! I just do.

Dylan got back to the car a few minutes after I did.

I saw him, jogging across the moon-lit parking lot to the SUV. Oh, God what a sight. Handsome. As I sat there in the silence of the closed-up SUV, watching this guy crossing the parking lot to come to me, it made my heart do that little fluttery thing.

Yeah, nothing to do with my functional heart murmur.

He opened the door and climbed in. Given his urgency in there when my cover had been blown, I expected him to strap himself into the seat in full let's-get-the-hell-out-of-here mode. Instead, Dylan Foreman, all six-foot-four of him, and twelve years my junior, leaned across the console, hooked a hand behind my head and pulled me close for one hell of a kiss.

"I was so worried about you, Dix," he said when he pulled back. "When I heard that woman talking to security about a creepy preacher up on the third floor, I knew she had to be talking about you." (Oh, if I had a dime for every time I'd heard that!)

His hand tightened on my neck, which he hadn't released. "I know you can take care of yourself in any situation, but impersonating a clergyman to access a patient ... If they'd apprehended you, they might have taken a hard line. God, they might have arrested you."

Well, when he put it like that, I guess it did look pretty ugly. And if security had nabbed me and turned me over to the local PD ... I couldn't quite suppress a shudder at the thought. Can you just imagine Dickhead's reaction? And the press would have had a field day. That would be just weird and kinky-sounding enough to sell newspapers.

I lifted a hand to his chest, partly to soothe him and partly because ... well, I wanted to lay hands on him. "Thank you for the heads up. You saved my butt. Again."

He pulled me close and kissed me again. I let my hands wander.

This time, it was me who broke the kiss. "Why, Mr. Foreman," I said, breathing into his ear in my most seductive, yet teasing voice. "Is that a flashlight in your pocket or are you happy to see me?"

Dylan pulled back. "Dix, that's the hoagie. You told me to get you a big sandwich while I was at the cafeteria, remember? Extra onions and jalapeños, heavy on the mayo."

"Er, yeah, how could I forget?"

I sat back in my seat.

Dylan reached into his pocket, drew out the plastic-wrapped sandwich and tossed it onto the dashboard. *Mmmm, jalapeños ...*

But Mr. Foreman had something else in mind. He pulled me close again and kissed me.

Can I just say this? The man knows how to kiss. His mouth slanted over mine, those full, sensual lips hard and thrillingly possessive. But then he pulled back until his lips barely grazed mine. I moaned a protest, clutching at his shirt, but his fingers tangled into my hair, restraining me.

"Easy, Dix." He angled my face, tormenting me with the warmth of his breath and yeah, the heat of my anticipation. Oh, God, he was *killing* me with those almost kisses, grazing and retreating, nibbling.

When I couldn't stand it anymore, I caught the back of his head with my own hand, pulled him to me and kissed him. Full on. With tongue. That was the end of those butterfly brushes, but I couldn't regret it. Not with him kissing me senseless. Not with his big hand splayed on my chest, hot and exciting, and sliding south (or souther) to — *oh yeah!* — grasp a breast.

I released the handful of hair I'd grabbed and dropped my hand to his chest again. He stopped the kneading-my-breast thing, which drew a moan from me. But then he grasped my hand and placed it somewhere much more interesting.

"This," he said thickly, "is what it feels like when I'm happy to see you."

Oh, God! Now I got the difference.

(Oh, boy, did I ever get the difference!)

"Come home with me, Dix."

"Your place?" I pulled back. I'd never been to his place. "Really?"

"It's five minutes away," he pointed out. "Yours is at least fifteen. Plus we might not be able to find your bed."

"Ha ha," I said, but he had a point. He'd seen my bedroom, of course, when I'd sent him to fetch a change of clothes for me while I was on stakeout. My wardrobe, or most of it, dwelled on my bed. Well, the stuff that wasn't in laundry baskets in my living room.

He trapped my hand against him and squeezed. "Five minutes or fifteen?"

"Your place it is."

Four minutes later (yeah, I didn't spare the horses), we pulled up outside Dylan's place. I didn't require directions, having picked him up a time or two outside this giant Victorian monstrosity, but I'd never been inside.

He took my hand when we got out of the car and led me along a paved walk that carried us around to the back of the house.

"Hope you don't mind steps," he said, gesturing to the metal fire-escape stairs that had clearly been added to the building in its latter days as an apartment house.

"Not at all."

I preceded him up the stairs, which felt a lot sturdier than they'd looked at first glance. At the first landing, he grabbed me and pulled me back against him. "I'm in the attic," he murmured against my ear. "Might be best to pace ourselves."

I couldn't have agreed more as his hands roamed my belly and that big, rangy body curved around my smaller one, enfolding me, surrounding me. Oh God, I couldn't wait to be under him! Or over him, or beside him ...

He released me. "On second thought, the hell with pacing. Come on."

Taking my hand, he drew me up the next two landings to his door. As he drew his key out and worked the lock, I sidled up behind him. I slid my arms around him and splayed my hands over *his* abdomen and chest. To my gratification, his hands fumbled on the lock. At last it gave and he shoved the door open. I followed him through and he slammed the door shut behind us.

"Dylan?"

He had me in his arms by this time. "Yeah?"

"You left the keys in the door."

"Crap." He whipped the door open, yanked his keys out and shut it again. "And I was trying so hard to be smooth there."

I smiled. "Oh, you're plenty smooth, Mr. Foreman." I glanced around, the only light coming from a streetlight outside. "You think maybe we could have some lights so I can get my bearings?"

He reached to the left and hit a switch. Warm yellow from a suspended fixture illuminated the room. Or should that be rooms? Kitchen, dining room and living room seemed to blend into one another. Much as I wanted to get skin-to-skin with him, curiosity about his living space kicked in. The space was tidy and organized, which I suppose such a small space demanded. But even if he'd had ten times the space, I knew he'd still be organized. That was Dylan, through and through.

"Welcome to Casa Foreman."

I scanned the room(s). Where was the bedroom? Or was that sofa a Hida-a-Bed? "Is this ... um ... all of it?"

He laughed. "Not quite. I don't think it'd be legal to rent an apartment without a john."

"Oh, right."

He took my hand again. "C'mon. I'll show you the rest."

As he led me across the room, I absorbed all the detail I could. The floors were wide softwood planking, painted a darkish brown color. The walls were sort of taupe or a sage green — it was hard to tell in this light — and the furniture was nice but mismatched. I spied a leather chair that looked expensive and a couch that looked like a yard sale find. The flat-screen TV was smallish, but the computer station in the corner looked very well equipped with a large-screen Mac. The kitchen I would have to inspect later, because we were entering Dylan's bedroom.

I don't know what I expected, but this wasn't that. The small room was made smaller by the fact that the ceiling on one side sloped sharply until it met the wall a few feet up from the floor, reminding me that I was in an attic. The room was dominated by a queen bed. It had no headboard nor footboard, but rather butted up against the wall with the sloping roof. But what caught my attention was how masculine, yet elegant, the bed was. The duvet bore a pattern of small tan and white checkers. The pillows at the top of the bed were a crisp white, as was the utilitarian looking coverlet or sheet or whatever it was folded at the bottom of the bed. A nightstand stood on the right side of the bed with a reading lamp on it, and a tall, old-fashioned dresser hugged the windowless wall to the left of the bed. The two pieces were mismatched in style, but both were virtually clutter free.

That sealed it — we were never having sex at my place.

I turned to tell him so, only to find him right there, so close I brushed him as I turned. His hands came up to grasp my upper arms and I forgot what I was going to say. In fact, I tried to press closer, dying to feel my breasts crushed against that lean, hard chest, but he held me back.

"You want this, don't you, Dix?"

"God, yes!" I blinked up at him. "Don't you?"

"Oh, hell, yeah," he said, and from the heat in his eyes, I believed him. "I just wanted to give you one last chance. Because once we start, I'm going to do my damnedest to make sure you can think of nothing else but me, the next touch, the next sensation."

My excitement took a leap. *Keep talking like that, Mr. Foreman, and you might not even have to touch me to set off the fireworks.*

"You know," he added, "just in case."

Oh, yeah, bring that up again. I could see he was never going to let me forget that time — okay, those two times — when I'd interrupted ... um ... proceedings after having a big *aha!* realization about the case of the day.

"Hey, last time it was *you* who called the halt," I reminded him.

"True, but I thought there were pheromones involved. Now we know better."

His voice had dropped into that low, gruff, sexy-as-hell register as he delivered that last part, and I knew he was remembering how greedy I'd been for him. I shuddered, remembering too.

"So we do."

He released his grip on my arms and slid those big hands around my back. Which left me free to press myself against him. He groaned and his arms tightened, crushing me as close as I could have wished while his mouth found mine. Just as he'd promised, I didn't have a chance to think of anything but sensation as his hands scorched over my back. When they dropped to my butt and urged my pelvis into closer contact, it set up a delicious tingling.

I realized then that my own hands were doing nothing but clutching his shirt. I skimmed them down his sides to find the hem of his shirt, then slipped them under to glide up his back, feeling the heat and texture of skin and the muscle beneath.

That broke both of us. It was a race then to unbutton and push each other's shirts off. As mine fell at my feet, I took a moment to thank God for having shed that too-small, boob-compressing sports bra with the rest of that ill-fated costume. Dylan seemed content to just look at me for a moment, but I was having none of that. He still wore the black T-shirt he'd had on beneath his shirt. I grabbed a handful and pushed it up his chest. Taking the hint, he yanked it over his head and dropped it on the floor. A part of my brain noted — gratefully — that he could be as messy as me in the heat of passion. But the rest of my brain was still stuck on the picture he'd made doing that peel-off-the-T-shirt thing, the way his muscles bunched, the glimpse of armpit hair when he —

Oh, shit. Hair! On my legs! "Wait! I have to shower."

"No, you don't." He put his hands on either side of my neck and started sliding them south over my collar bone ... "You smell great."

I clapped a hand over one of his to stop him from reaching his destination. "No, I definitely need a shower." Did I have a disposable razor in my purse? Surely I must. I had everything else in there.

"You can shave your legs afterward, Dix."

I closed my eyes, suppressing a groan. I should have known he'd know what the trouble was.

"Seriously. I don't care. And there's not much I can do down there anyway until I've had a shave myself." He waggled his eyebrows. "If you're walking funny tomorrow morning, it won't be because you've got stubble burn on your thighs."

My brain hazed over with lust and my haven't-been-shaved-since-Tuesday legs were forgotten. This time, I didn't resist when he slid his hands down to shape my breasts. Their already hardened nipples budded still tighter.

Then it was fingers undoing belts and sliding zippers, jeans being shoved down, until we were both naked. Part of me wished I could slow things down, take the time to savor the magnificence of his six-foot-four frame, from the top of that glossy brown head to his big, well-shaped feet (sockless, darn it!), and everything in between. But I knew it wasn't going to be like that. He backed me up until the back of my legs hit the bed. I sank down on it then scuttled backwards. He followed me down, his weight pressing me into the duvet-covered mattress. Then his head was at my breast and all I could do was writhe. (Well, once. I saw what he meant about the beard stubble. The growth wasn't long enough to lie down and it rasped my skin.)

I grasped his head with both hands. "Beard."

"Sorry."

I felt the fullness of his erection against my thigh. This wasn't going to take long. "Condom?" I asked.

He rolled away and pulled the drawer of his night table open to retrieve one. For a moment, I pictured the other women — no doubt *younger* women — he'd entertained here. But then he was sheathing himself and I let it go.

It was amazingly easy. I thought it might be awkward because it was Dylan, but it turned out to be easy precisely *because* it was him. We'd already built a foundation of trust between us. On a different level, sure, but it was there. Between that and the fact that I'd been anticipating this for so long, I knew it wouldn't take much.

It didn't.

He moved to lie beside me. I drew him onto me, thrilling to feel his hair-roughened skin on mine. He touched me intimately, and groaned to find me wet and ready. I guided him home, and then he was inside me, stretching me, invading me. Oh, God, his strong arms on either side of my body caging me. That's all I needed to think to put me on the knife's edge. I lifted my hips to meet his every thrust, seeking more of that thrilling friction. My excitement coiled tighter and tighter until orgasm took me. Dylan followed shortly thereafter, his breath harsh in my ear.

Afterward, as he dealt with the condom, I lay there looking at the ceiling. I must have been smiling, because when Dylan came back to bed, he laughed softly.

"Geez, Dix. Usually I have to work a lot harder to put a smile like that on a woman's face."

I jabbed him with my elbow, drawing an *oof* from him.

"You *will* have to work harder next time, Mr. Foreman." I scowled at him. "Much harder. I was just … primed." I could have added that the whole trust thing was a big part of that. Also, that for women of a certain age, it just came easier for us (pun intended), but somehow I didn't feel like reminding him of the age difference.

He grinned wickedly. "I'm looking forward to it."

I let him pull me into his arms. We lay there for a moment, his arm draped loosely over me while my hand rested over his heart. His fingers traced slow circles on my back, soothing now rather than arousing.

"So," he said, "who's going to shave first?"

This time when I jabbed him, it was more of a definite *"Ow!"*

Chapter 20

REALITY CHECK: I was naked under the covers with Dylan Foreman. Omi-freakin'-God! I had to pull those covers back to look at the two of us all over again. Yup, there we were, the two of us, in all our naked glory.

I got laid!

Twice!

The second time wasn't quite as fast as the first, mainly because Dylan kept distracting me by exploring areas that heretofore I would have said were not especially erogenous. His newly shaved face (and luscious, luscious lips) made acquaintance not just with my newly shaved parts, but also with the inside of my wrist, the crook of my elbow, the point of my shoulder. And I'd explored right back.

"Want me to get the flashlight, Dix?" Dylan asked with a chuckle.

Ah, as tempting as that idea was, I declined. And I lowered the covers once more. "I should get going."

"You don't have to go yet." Dylan said it like he meant it.

"Well, okay ... maybe a few minutes longer." It was more symbolic than anything. More, okay, I'm not just doing the screw-your-brains-out-for-a-few-hours-and-running thing. But I wasn't foolish enough — nor was Dylan, I'm sure — to think this wasn't going to complicate things. I snuggled back into his arms again. "We do have lots to do, though."

"I know, but what are we gonna do in the middle of the night? Everyone's sleeping."

(Ohhh, frig! Where I could go with that!)

"By the way, mind if I take my socks off now?" He was already looping the big toe of his right foot into the rim of his left sport sock.

"Of course." I blushed at the reminder that I'd asked him to put the socks on after his shower. Rushing a guy into bed before he could take his socks off was one thing; asking him to put them back on again was quite another. Naturally, he'd razzed me about it, but being Dylan, he took it in stride. More than in stride. He'd turned it to his advantage ...

Okay, Earth to Dix. Come in, Dix Dodd. (Or should that be come again?)

Oh boy. We'd done it.

Everything changes now, I thought, and felt a pang.

All change didn't have to be bad change, though. I angled my head on his chest just enough so I could peer at him through my lashes. He was wide awake, staring at the ceiling. Not in a troubled way, but definitely lost in thought. I lowered my gaze again, tracing a finger through the light patch of hair on his chest.

What had I expected? That he'd be freaking out? Was it better that he wasn't freaking out? Or maybe he was, but was just doing it quietly. Maybe he'd suddenly say something about having to get up early in the morning and would I mind locking the door on the way out?

Oh, God, had I looked up at his handsome face and expected to see —

"Regrets, Dix?"

Did I? A dozen thoughts flitted through my mind, but with the weight of Dylan's eyes on me, I shook my head. "No. No regrets."

He looked at me steadily, those brown eyes unreadable. Damn that pause between his question and my answer. He'd caught it. "What about you?" I asked.

He didn't miss a beat. "Not a one."

And I believed him. So yeah, I had places to go. People that I definitely had to talk to. But, maybe, just maybe, I could spare a few more minutes wrapped up in Dylan's arms. But just a few. This investigation was still under way.

We were getting closer, though. On that thought, my mind started churning again, worrying at the "facts" as we knew them. I know I tensed. I know I tightened and clenched my fists as I began sifting through the details — every single one of them. Mentally, I lined them up. Turned them around. Bumped them up against each other. Then a couple of them bumped back.

Oh, I love when things bump-bump back.

I'd run everything I'd learned tonight by Dylan earlier, of course. Filled him in on the blackmail scenario.

But what was I missing? Who was Albert Valentine having an affair with? How did Telly, and Faynelle for that matter, fit into the whole thing?

Did they, in fact, fit into it?

And when I sighed, Dylan did too. Then we both were sitting up in bed. And then ... I clutched my chest and groaned experimentally.

"Jesus, Dix! What is it? Are you okay?"

"I need to go to the hospital, Dylan. Now!"

"So do you want to run this by me again?" Dylan said. "Just what do you hope to accomplish here?"

No, the guy wasn't slow by any means. And though he wasn't agreeing with me wholeheartedly on this excursion, he wasn't exactly protesting.

I was currently flat on my back on a narrow, not-too-comfy hospital bed in the ER exam room, sprouting wires from beneath my johnny shirt, with one hand on my chest, a grimace on my face.

Dylan poked his head out from behind the sliding beige curtain, then returned his attention to me. "Safe to answer."

I dropped the grimace, then looked at the little johnny shirt the emergency nurse had insisted I put on. My white, white legs (yeah, the ones I'd shaved just hours ago) looked practically scraped under the blinding white lights, all the way down to my grey sport socks.

Wow, that really was sexy. I crossed my legs at the ankles, waggled the upper sock-covered foot in that attractive way.

"Dix ..." Dylan was getting impatient as he waited for my answer.

"I'm having chest pains." I said with a smile.

"No, you're not."

I shrugged. "You know that and I know that. But Dr. Lincoln Crotty doesn't know that. I want to talk to the man."

"He'll know you're faking it."

"Maybe I'm having an anxiety attack too," I said calmly.

"Lincoln Crotty surely is not the only doctor on duty tonight."

"True, but chances are he's the only cardiologist on duty tonight."

"What if his shift's ended?"

Okay, now Dylan was just trying to burst my bubble. "Always have to have a cardiologist covering. I'm betting they do 12-hour stints. We brought Gaetan in about six hours ago, and he was attended by Crotty, so —"

"Would you care to make a wager about that?" A slow grin was starting to spread on Dylan's face, like a pat of butter melting on a griddle. "Want to bet Lincoln Crotty is gone for the day?"

Oh, I knew that smile! That was his competitive grin. He already thought he was the winner.

Yeah, well, I had a grin of my own. "Twenty bucks," I said. "No, fifty!" Didn't want to sound too confident.

Dylan pffted. "Don't be such a wuss, Dix. Money's boring. Make it an interesting bet. Something worth our while."

"Okay, here's an idea," I said. "If you win, and the good doctor has departed, then I clean your apartment. If I win and he's still here, you clean my condo."

Dylan looked at me, slightly horrified. "Are you crazy? That's hardly a fair bet."

"What?"

"Where do I begin? The last time I asked, you were still dusting with your hair dryer."

"Hey on high, that sucker will blow the dust off anything."

Dylan leaned close. "I have a better idea."

"What's that?"

"Oral sex."

I was going to make a comment to the effect that he'd already blown the dust off something else, but I left that alone.

"Dylan, do you really think you should say things like that to a woman who's having a heart attack?" Well, the old ticker must be hammering like that for some reason! I'd just finished making love with Dylan not an hour ago, and yet that stirring in the belly was, well, stirring, again.

What was it with this guy? Oh, yeah. Lean, fit body, great kisser, sure hands and a really big —

"You are most definitely *not* having a heart attack," he said dryly. "But hey, if you're too chicken to make that bet, I totally under —"

"You're on."

His smile was smarmy. Ah, but mine was just a tad smarmier as Dr. Lincoln Crotty walked into the room, and pulled the beige curtain aside.

"You again!"

I feigned surprise to hide my delight (I'd just won a bet with Dylan! For oral sex!). "Why, Doctor Crotty, I'm amazed you're still here! Would you have bet that Dylan?"

Being an obnoxious winner — yet another thing that's underrated.

"What are you doing here, Ms. Dodd?"

Yes, Dodd. I'd had to give my real name when I registered. It's on my OHIP card.

"My chest hurts." Shit! In my bet-winning delight, I'd forgotten the whole grimacing, chest clenching thing. "The pain's right about —"

"Horse shit."

I was pretty sure that wasn't a technical term. Wow, this guy's bedside manner really sucked.

Crotty pulled a rolling stool over beside the bed. (Jesus, I had one of those *slide down* pap smear flashbacks — from the 90s! Yeah, seriously overdue.) I clenched my knees as he sat.

"Why are you really here, Dix Dodd, PI?"

He left the *extraordinaire* part off my moniker, but I let it go — this time.

Then he glanced at Dylan. "And I see you've brought your young *assistant*, Mr. Foreman," he said, his tone completely condescending.

Dylan tensed. "No need to talk over me, Doc. I'm right here. Can handle the really big words myself and everything."

"Oh, really? Well, here are some words for you both: I should have the two of you ejected. Gaetan Gough didn't say so, but I know damned well it was you, Dodd, dressed up like that priest earlier in the evening. I should call —"

"But I'm betting you won't."

His eyebrows soared. "Oh? And what do you want to bet?"

Dylan guffawed.

And at that reminder of the bet I'd just won with Dylan, my heart started tripping faster. I could tell because we could all hear it, thanks to the monitor I was plugged into. I saw Dr. Crotty's attention zoom to it.

"Sure you don't want to check out my heart, Doc?" I asked.

"I guess I'd better," he muttered, clearly not pleased at the prospect but also not wanting to risk the very slight possibility that I might have a real, actual problem.

Dylan turned discreetly as Dr. Crotty opened the hospital gown and applied the business end of his stethoscope to my chest. But already my pulse rate was slowing. I knew it, and so did the tattletale monitor.

"Are you aware you have a heart murmur?" Crotty asked.

Dylan turned then, surprised.

"Yes. But it's nothing. I've had it since I was a teenager. Probably longer." Crotty straightened and I pulled my gown closed. "My doctor says it's functional."

Dr. Crotty slung the stethoscope around his neck again. "And he would know this from imaging your valves?"

"'scuse me?"

"Did he send you for a cardiac ultrasound?"

"No, nothing like that." Why were we talking about my itty-bitty murmur?

"Then how can he know it's functional?"

"I don't know — because I've never been pre-medicated for dental work and haven't dropped dead?"

"That could be proof of nothing more than the fact that you're damned lucky." His brows drew together sternly and he picked up my chart. "I'm going to send you down the hall for cardiac imaging so we can see what those valves are doing."

"Right now?"

"No time like the present. I mean, that's what you came in for, right? Your heart condition?"

"No! I mean, yes. I mean, maybe I could come back?"

"Fine." Crotty scribbled something on my chart. "Central Scheduling will be in touch, and follow up will be through your family physician. Hopefully that'll be the end of it." What he really meant was hopefully he'd never see me again. He tucked the pen back in his pocket. "Well, then, I've checked your heart. OHIP will be happy. Now, how about you tell me what the hell you're really doing here?"

Ah, straight to the point. Maybe I did like his bedside manner after all. "Why do you hate the cuddle club so much?" I asked.

"You're kidding, right?"

I shrugged. "Humor me."

Crotty wasn't hooked up to any monitors, but I could definitely tell his blood pressure was rising. "Where do I begin? They take money from unsuspecting souls, manipulate them, addict them to that damned club. Kids like my Brandy ... sweet, innocent young people get hooked and then —"

He cut his words off before his head exploded. Yep, it was that red. "Brandy spends a lot of money at the club," he continued. "And no, money's not the issue. That daughter of mine is just too damned smart to get mixed up in a foolish thing like that. She's going to follow in the family footsteps and become an MD. Or an MD/PhD researcher, if her mother has her way."

"This must piss you off to no end."

"What pissed me off was that those old men had their hands on my daughter! And her friends."

"Eva and Zoey, right?" I prompted.

"Yes, Eva and Zoey. They practically grew up in our home. Zoey's family lived next door, and Eva's mother worked for us. Brandy is very close to them still, especially Eva. She's such a fragile girl. Brandy has always thought of her as a kid sister. I never did like the idea of them going to that club, but now ..."

"But now that you know that Gaetan Gough has been using hormones to arouse the clientele, you like it even less?"

"I suspected it was something like that all along. Why Brandy didn't see it for herself, I don't know. But now maybe — finally! — I'll be able to talk some sense into her. Now —"

Paging Dr. Crotty. Paging Dr. Lincoln Crotty.

"Sounds like I have an actual patient." He stood and looked down at me. "No more chest pains, I trust?" Without waiting for a reply, he moved toward the door, but turned back to say one more thing. "Get him."

"Pardon me?"

"Get Gaetan Gough. I don't know who hired you to investigate that club. But close Gough down. What's going on at that club is just wrong."

He had no idea.

Dylan waited outside that curtain as I tore out of that oh-so-fashionable (not!) hospital gown and put my clothes back on.

As we left the hospital parking lot, I glimpsed Dr. Crotty's distinctive white vehicle in the physician's parking lot. I bit my lip. Okay, confession time. "Dylan, about our bet ..."

"Yeah, you won, Dix. I know."

"Well, actually, it wasn't a fair bet. I saw the white Lexus with the L CROTTY license plates as we drove in."

"So did I, Dix," Dylan answered. "So did I."

Chapter 21

I WENT HOME after the hospital.

Yes, I did kind of feel bad about faking an illness to the hard-working medical staff. But, you know, I use hospital emergency services ... or any kind of medical services ... so rarely, I figured it all evened out. I'm just not a run-to-the-doctor kind of gal.

Dylan and I parted company outside my condo. No, he didn't walk me to the door. Though there was an awkward pause on his part when I could tell he was wondering if he should. Nope, he didn't lean in to kiss me good night, and I didn't lean in to cop one last feel. (Though we both hesitated as I reached for that hoagie on the dashboard.)

Sleep? Like a rock! A happy, happy rock who'd shaved her legs.

And wow, the dreams I had were peaceful. Rare for me.

The sheets were undisturbed (well, except for where I'd tried to rub that tiny mayo stain out — note to self: stop eating hoagies in bed!). I woke to the ringing telephone. I sat up to answer it and — argh — hand squishing down on a tomato slice. (Okay, it was now a rule to self, not a note.)

It was Dylan on the phone.

"Hey," I said, sinking back into the pillows.

"Hey, yourself."

It was kind of sweet, and just that little bit awkward, then it was all business. Dylan was off to the university to do a little research, a little checking around. Something he half-remembered, or thought he did, and wanted to check up on.

"Feel right?" I asked (oh the double meanings.) "Is your intuition telling you —"

"It totally feels right, Dix."

Yeah, double meaning there too.

After I hung up with Dylan, I called Rochelle and arranged to meet her for lunch. She agreed and a few hours later, we met at a local pub (her choice). We chose to sit in the busier section (my choice). Yeah, I know, I'm not usually such a people person. What the heck had gotten into me?

Oh right, Dylan Foreman.

(Sa-lam!)

"Hi Katie." Rochelle greeted the young waitress (young as in, wow, is she even legal to serve liquor?). The waitress was at our table as soon as we sat, despite the lunch hour rush. Clearly, Rochelle was a good tipper.

"I'll have my usual," Rochelle said.

"Perfect." Katie turned to me. "And for you?"

I wanted to get this out of the way quickly, so I ordered the first thing that came to mind. "Coffee, please. And bangers and mash."

The waitress looked at me strangely. "Er, have you been watching British —"

"No!" I said. "I do not watch British porn!"

"Um, I was going to say British films."

Oh, man. Head desk.

Rochelle and Katie both laughed.

I rose, rubbing the sore spot on my forehead. "Can I get a steak?"

"Certainly, how would you like it?" Katie held her pen poised over her pad.

Through tears of laughter, Rochelle put in, "She likes her steak like she likes her men."

The poor waitress looked all the more confused.

"Rare," I grated.

Smiling, Katie walked toward the bar. Finally I doffed my coat, relaxed back into the seat.

And Rochelle was looking at me in that knowing way that only best friends have.

"Oh my God!" Rochelle squealed. "I can't believe it!"

"What?" I said, innocently.

"You got laid!"

"Geez, it is that obvious?" I didn't even try to fight the grin. "What is it? Do I have that certain glow? Is there a special look in my eyes? Do I exude that contentedness of a woman well-loved?"

"No," she said. "You're finally wearing your 'I got laid!' T-shirt." She reached across and ripped the sales tag off the sleeve. Damn, I'd missed that somehow. "When did you buy that anyway? Three, four years ago? Good God, has it been that long since —"

"That's not the point!"

She was laughing at me all over again. Laughing until the tears were rolling down her cheeks.

"So, I take it you're happy for me?" I finally said.

Katie had brought our iced tea during Rochelle's laughing fit, and Rochelle toasted me. "Delighted. I always knew you and Dylan would become a couple. Eventually. When you stopped fighting it."

That straightened me up. "A couple?"

"Yeah," Rochelle said. "Together, Dix. It scares you."

"Scare me? Pfttt."

Rochelle cocked an eyebrow. "Right."

Busted. Rochelle knew me too well. She understood. I'd been so burned in the past. Myles Gauthier hadn't just broken my heart, he'd *shattered* it. Myles was long gone, but those scars remained. Few things scared me. Close scared me.

"Okay, it scares the hell out of me. But only when I think about it."

"Well, don't think about it today." Rochelle lifted her glass in a toast again, drawing me from my darker contemplations. "Just enjoy the afterglow."

Well, I could drink to that.

"So how's the case going?" Rochelle stirred the ice in her drink with her straw. "Anything new on the Death by Cuddle Club case?"

"Where to begin?" While we waited for our lunch to come, I told her about the pheromones, Gaetan's anxiety attack, the lab results, and about my clever disguises and visits.

"So," she said. "Gaetan may be guilty of doping the club air with pheromones. Albert Valentine was definitely guilty of blackmail."

"And whoever Albert was manipulating with those pheromones, I'm betting, is guilty of murder. Mad as hell — guilty as hell. It just makes sense."

There. Ta-freakin'-da — I'd said it.

But where was the *aha?* Where was the feeling of complete brilliance? (Oh yes, there it was — never far away — but not front and center, like it should be.) Most of all, where was that niggle of intuition that told me I was bang on.

It just wasn't there.

"So did you figure that out while you were rounding second or third base?"

I looked at Rochelle. "What?"

"Oh come on, Dix! You usually get those aha moments while getting it on with Dylan, don't you? Remember the Case of the Flashing Fashion Queen? "

"We were at the Underwood motel —"

"And then again with the Family Jewels —"

"Hey," I said. "What happens in Florida, stays in Florida." My turn to laugh, 'cuz I'd told her all about Florida.

"Forget about Florida. I want to hear what happened with Dylan last night."

Over lunch, I let her wheedle it out of me. Okay, so there was no wheedling involved, and yeah, I spilled the glorious details before the entrée had even arrived. But why wouldn't I? We're best friends. And there is a loyalty between close women friends that is just amazing. I trusted her; she trusted me. I'd do anything for her and — you got it — she'd do anything for me.

But that was women for you. Right?

Yes, it was.

Chapter 22

Y ES, I KNEW I needed a car. Like, one of my own.

And with any luck, I'd find a cheap one soon. But in the meantime, I borrowed Rochelle's Smart Car for a couple of hours. It was lime green, which is so Rochelle. She loves green and she loves that funny little car. And yeah, it suited her right down to the ground. But whenever I borrowed it, it felt like I was scooting around the city in a Granny Smith apple.

(And Rochelle's customized license plate — BITE ME — didn't help.)

But I wanted to go see Mrs. Jane Presley over at the Underwood Motel. I'd not been to see her in a while, and well, with Dylan doing research up at the university and everything else stalled right now, I had some time.

It was a quiet afternoon at the motel. Mrs. P insisted I stay and talk for a bit. I was happy to oblige, but I had to pass on joining her in a piece of cherry cheesecake — I was still stuffed from lunch. She made herself a tea while I grabbed a Diet Coke from the vending machine in the corner of the lobby. Then we sat down in the office just behind the small front desk. From there, she could hear the ding of the bell if anyone came to the front desk. But perhaps more importantly, it gave her a view of the parking lot, and she always kept an eye out for troublemakers coming to her no-tell motel.

But as we sat there, I knew she was watching me.

The lady knows me. She loves to razz me, teases the hell out of me every chance she gets. But well ...

"So," she said. "I see you and Dylan finally got together last night."

Ack! I mean, I had my coat on over that tell-tale T-shirt. Maybe there really was a sparkle in my eyes ...

"You're a little too old for pins that say *I just had sex* aren't you, Dix?"

I removed it sheepishly from the lapel of my coat and shoved it into my pocket.

"But I would have known anyway," Mrs. P said, grinning over the rim of her tea cup.

I chuckled. "Yeah, I suppose after what you've seen here with people leaving the motel and all …"

"This isn't anything like that, and you know it, Dix."

I guess I did, but she told me, just the same. Boy, did she tell me …

"Sweetheart, you have to crawl out from under that pickle of a rock and face the coffee." (Yeah, she's never lost for a metaphor; she just fucks them up.) "Don't get me wrong — there's nothing wrong with a quickie or a little fling. But that's just not what you and Dylan have — and don't try to pretend. Not to me. Not to yourself. And I sure as hell hope you're not stupid enough to pretend to Dylan. You two have been circling around each other for way too long. I was ready to smack you both. And I see the way he looks at you, Dix. No way was that man looking for a fling. And you know what else, Miss Smarty Pants PI, I see the looks you give him when you think I'm not paying attention, or dozing in the back seat of the car."

Ah, the Florida trip again.

I shrugged. Hesitated. Finally, had to acknowledge what she said. "Thanks, Mrs. P. You know, it's not that easy for me."

Her tone did not soften. "I know. I was the one pouring the Baileys for you that night you found out what a scumbag Myles Gauthier really was." Her hand tightened on her china tea cup. "Sometimes I wonder if I did the right thing, calling you."

"I'm glad you did, Mrs. P." Yes, she'd called me. Of course I hadn't wanted to believe her. I absolutely did not want to acknowledge what I couldn't help, but really already knew deep down inside. But finally, I'd driven to the Underwood, and found my then most-serious-ever boyfriend with someone else. I wanted to kick some ass! Starting with mine for trusting him again.

"I'm not trying to bring up bad memories, Dix. But I'm just saying, don't be stupid. Myles is in the past. Let that dog lie there. You've got a chance at something good here with Dylan in the present. Don't be such a chickenshit and let one stupid prick who cheated on you be an excuse to keep running away. You're a woman, Dix. Act like one. Move on with your life."

Yep, I'd been told.

"You're right. Thanks, Mrs. P."

"You're welcome."

The door behind us swung open, and Craig Presley walked in. "Safe to come in, Ma?"

Guess he'd heard part of that earful meant for me.

Mrs. P nodded. "Come right on in, sweet baby."

Sweet baby? I always had to smile when she called one of her twins something like that. They were twenty-eight and roughly Hulk-sized.

"I brought the cheesecake like you wanted," Craig said. "Two pieces."

"Thank you, sweetie," she said as Craig set both pieces down on the table — in front of me. "And did you remember —"

He reached high in the cupboard and retrieved a bottle of Bailey's Irish Cream and two small glasses.

Told you Mrs. P knew me.

"A toast to your new life," she said.

I'd have a drink to that. With the cheesecake I was about to scarf down, it wasn't a concern for driving. Yeah, she knew me — I never pass on cheesecake.

I had just finishing the last decadent bite of piece number one and was wrapping up piece number two (I keep plastic wrap in my purse for just these occasions), when my cell rang.

"Dylan," I mumbled glancing at the call display.

"I knew by the smile."

I snapped open the cell. "Hey," I said.

"Hey yourself."

He'd found something. I could tell instantly by the leashed excitement in his voice.

"Can you meet me, Dix? Right away. I found what I was looking for at the university. You're not going to believe it! I mean, holy shit! I — I know I'm onto something. And if I'm right … no wonder the coroner didn't find anything … Holy shit!"

I was already carefully positioning that extra piece of cheesecake in my purse. "I'm on the way. Where shall we meet? The office? Perky Joe's?"

"Better make it Detective Head's office. I'm calling him next."

I snapped the phone shut and was out the door within moments.

But not without promising Mrs. P I'd take her to bingo one last time before Christmas, and that I'd call as soon as Dylan and I cracked this case, and most especially that I'd remember her words about Dylan.

I'd try … on all accounts.

"Bite me?"

"Well, yeah, screw you!" And here I was starting — just starting, mind you — to think maybe Dickhead wasn't a complete asshole. But that's what he greets me with as I walk through the detectives' bullpen to his desk, where he and Dylan waited for me.

"I was referring to the license plate, Dix," he said, coming away from the window overlooking the parking lot. "I saw you drive in. That's Rochelle Banks' car, isn't it?"

"I borrowed it," I said.

I only briefly wondered how he knew it was Rochelle's car. That little green orb probably was hard to miss parked behind the Justice Building. Marport City wasn't that big. The lawyers, cops, and those inside the system all had to know each other to at least some degree.

Dickhead nodded and his lips sort of twisted.

Oh shit, wait — was that a smile? Yes, by God, it was! It was just a flicker, but definitely some lips-through-cheek action.

Where was the familiar sneer? The mean jabs about my business? The derogatory way he always said my name? I missed it.

Dickhead sat down at the desk where Dylan was poring over piles of papers. Seriously poring over them. The coffee to his left was untouched and no longer steaming. Dylan not pausing to take a drink of his coffee?

"This is it," Dylan said. "I know it."

He was talking to me, but not for a minute did he lift his gaze from the pages before him. I'd seen this intensity in him before when he was onto something — when he was that dead serious about not missing a thing, about getting it right. And I gotta tell you, it was hot, seeing him so focused like that.

"So what's up?" I asked.

"Between my first and second years of law school, I dated a woman who'd just finished her master's in biochemical engineering. Wendy Chance. She's from here, and she'd come back to work on a project for the summer — you know, one of those studentship thingies — before going on to get her PhD."

"Okay?" What made him think of this Wendy woman? Was he making the point that he liked older women? Because her PhD candidate to his first year law ... yeah, she'd likely have had a few years on him.

Or was he saying he liked them smart? I perked up at that thought.

"We only dated about a month," he continued. "Really bright girl, but we didn't have that much in common once we — um — got to know one another."

Once the newness wore off, he meant. Once the novelty was gone, the mystery dispelled, the uncharted territory charted. That did have a way of happening with men.

Actually, it had a way of happening with men and me. That thought did not perk me up.

"Oh, man, been there, done that," Dickhead said in masculine solidarity. "Said no thanks to the T-shirt."

I glared at him. A fact of which he was totally oblivious. Or pretended to be.

"The point is, I remembered her talking about the research project she'd been hired to help out with," Dylan said, finally looking up from the documents before him. He'd stopped flipping through papers and stared at me. "This is it. I know it! This is the drug that killed those people."

"What drug are you talking about?"

"Deleonex."

"Never heard of it."

"And neither has anyone else. Well, no one outside the pharmaceutical or biomedical research community. It was an experimental drug that died at the animal test stage. Apparently, in the initial stages, it showed incredible promise for inhibiting the proliferation of cancer cells. But when they moved to the next stage, they found that it was a powerful pro-arrhythmic."

Pro-arrhythmic? "Translation, please."

"Way too many of the test subjects suffered fatal arrhythmias."

"No shit?" I blinked. "They died of cardiac arrest?"

"No shit," Dylan assured.

"And you knew this all from dating Wendy Whatshername?"

"Unfortunately, no. If I had, I'd like to think I'd have tumbled to it a lot sooner. But I did remember her saying the animal trials went poorly. So I tracked her down, reached her early this morning. She filled me in on the specifics of the failure, i.e., the whole dying of cardiac arrest thing before the drug had a chance to impact the subjects' cancers. She even pointed me to a scientific paper about Deleonex published in more optimistic times," — he gestured to some of the papers on Dickhead's desk — "when they still thought it was going to be the next big cancer breakthrough."

I looked at Dickhead. "Why didn't it show up in the toxicology report?"

"Jesus, Dix, it's not like they push a button and a computer spits out everything that's in the stiff's system. They kinda need to know what they're looking for. And since this drug never made it to human trials, they sure as hell wouldn't be looking for it."

Okay, he had a point. "Makes sense. What about now? What does the forensic lab say now?"

"They're on it," he growled. "I sent them the chemical composition for this kill juice from that paper Dylan mentioned. Sent them the whole paper, in fact. They've pulled Albert's tissue samples, and I've got 'em working on retrieving Telly's and Faynelle's as well. It'll be given the highest priority."

My mind raced, sifting through this new information. An experimental drug that this Wendy person had been working on, right here in Marport City ... Oh shit, of course! The answer lay right before me. Well, now that Dylan had dug it up. "Was this drug being developed by a certain MD/PhD researcher by the name of Crotty, by any chance?"

Dylan grinned. "Janis Tascar-Crotty, to be specific. Brandy Crotty's mother."

Oh, God, it was poetic. Old goat uses pheromones to seduce young woman; young woman realizes what's happened and exacts her own chemical revenge. But there was still the matter of proving it. "Where's this Delayonex now?"

"Deleonex," Dylan corrected.

"That's what I said."

"No, there's a subtle difference. It's *Deleonex* as in Ponce de Leon."

I still couldn't hear the difference. And who was this Ponsay guy? I gave him a blank look.

"You know, Ponce de Leon?" he prompted. "Spanish explorer who searched for the Fountain of Youth?"

I narrowed my eyes. "Are we going to get to 'where is it?' any time soon?"

He shrugged, completely unwithered by my withering squint-eyed look. "My guess is they never destroyed all of the stuff. I'm guessing it's under lock and key at Marport U, which is where Dr. Tascar-Crotty — and Wendy — were working out of. Part of a little bio-med cluster that they were incubating there."

"Then Dr. Tascar-Crotty should be able to tell us exactly where to look, right?" I said, looking at Head. "Just pay her a call."

"That could be a little hard," Dylan said. "Dr. Tascar-Crotty is on a six-month sabbatical, on a bio-prospecting expedition somewhere in the Amazon basin. She's been gone two months now, according to her department head."

Dickhead didn't seem all that dismayed. "Well, it's not like anyone figured Dr. Tascar-Crotty for the murders, is it?" he said. "I think we've all got our money on her daughter Brandy, the pre-med student. She'd know where her mother kept her research. I'd lay my last dime that Brandy Crotty is the one Albert Valentine was using the pheromones to seduce."

"There are others in that age bracket," Dylan pointed out. "Like Starla, Eva, or Zoey."

"Yeah, but only Brandy Crotty has access to this drug."

"That doesn't make her the killer," I said, more to play devil's advocate than because I truly believed she was innocent.

"No," answered Dickhead, "but it does make her the prime suspect. And in my books, that usually turns out to be the guilty party."

Dylan and I shot glances at each other. The drug? It absolutely felt right. The connection to Brandy? Definitely there. But the niggle and nudges? Oh fuck! Just not lining up!

"I'm going to get a warrant to look for this Deleonex stuff," Head continued. "And presuming the lab results come back the way we think they will —" he gestured to Dylan's research on the table, "I'll be bringing our Miss Crotty in for interrogation."

As if waiting for that opening, the door swung inward. It was Constable Leola Pivans. "I don't know what kind of dirt you have on those lab geeks, Detective, but the toxicology report is back already."

"No dirt involved," he said as he reached for the thin folder that Constable Pivans held out to him. "I just gave them motivation. Told them they had a crack at recording a forensic first."

Brilliant move on Head's part, I had to concede, even though it pained me. I could see from the expression on Constable Pivans's face, though, that her appreciation was less tinged with reluctance than I would have thought. Was she coming to admire our Richie?

Dickhead opened the file and scanned it quickly, his eye going to the bottom line.

He looked at Dylan. He looked at me. "Bingo! We have a match."

Chapter 23

"ALL THREE OF them?" I asked.

"Valentine only." Head glanced at Pivans. "Did they say anything about Smith and St. James?"

"Yes, sir. They're going to see what they can do with the other two, but if they don't have sufficient samples to work with, we may need to apply for exhumation orders."

"Excellent work, Pivans."

"Thank you, Detective."

As the two cops left the room, Head mumbled to Pivans, "It's a good thing Dix Dodd called me in on this with her suspicions about the cuddle club."

Yeah, Dylan and I were just that quickly dismissed. We saw ourselves to the door.

I shook my head.

The police station was close enough to the justice building that I didn't mind calling Rochelle and asked if she could pick up her Bite-me-mobile behind the station. When she agreed, I jumped into the SUV with Dylan for the drive back to the office. I glanced at the familiar hand-stitched bag in the backseat. More pajamas — had to be. And when I asked he confirmed he'd hit up Aunt Gert's for a couple more pair, in case there was a next cuddle club meeting.

Well, looked like that wouldn't be necessary.

Case solved.

Wasn't it?

"That was brilliant work, Dylan."

"Thanks." He shot me a quick look before returning his attention to traffic. "We nailed the murder weapon, all right."

In the silence that fell between us, I could almost hear what he *didn't* say: *Why doesn't it feel right?*

When we got back to the office, I checked the few voice mails (nothing pressing) while Dylan made the coffee. He tossed Blow-Up Betty (damn, she's a floppy thing) aside, while I snapped off the old black and white TV. We did all this in silence so deep it was dead. Then we sat, both of us, on the small sofa in that outer office. Sighed and leaned back.

"Everything points to Brandy Crotty," Dylan said, sounding very matter-of-fact. "She had access to the drug. She clearly didn't like Albert Valentine."

"Certainly no love lost there."

"Nope."

"And we know — Gaetan told us — that Albert was having an affair with some young thing."

"Well, she's a young thing."

"Yeah, everything points to her. But ..."

"But she didn't do it."

Dylan looked at me. I stared at him. There was an unopened package of yellow legal pads on the table before us. I ripped the pack open, tossed one to Dylan and grabbed one for myself. Doodle time. Thinking time.

"You do realize all we really have to go on at this point," I said, "is our gut feelings?"

He answered as I'd hope he would, "Good enough for me."

Dickhead called just before four o'clock, again reaching me on the cell phone.

"I tried to call you at the office," he said.

"Not there," I answered. Nope, not giving him any more detail than that. He was dying to ask though. I could tell.

Detective Head filled me in: Brandy had been brought in for questioning mid-afternoon. Questioning had consisted of four senior lawyers from the firm of Whitman and Crotty (yeah, same family, the black sheep who didn't go into medicine) who promptly had Brandy out of the station in about thirty minutes. But Detective Head was all the more certain she was the murderer. She was apparently pretty shaken by everything.

"Her father, the doctor, picked her up at the station. I'm guessing he took her home."

Yeah, well I could pretty much guarantee it from my vantage point.

"I know Brandy Crotty is guilty, Dix. Everything points to her. She didn't cop to anything, but we're building a case and not even her fancy lawyers will be able to stop us."

"Thanks for the call," I said.

"You're welcome." Pause. "Bye, Dix." The phone clicked off.

Bye, Dix?

I cringed as I put my phone away. Detective Head had just said, "Bye," to me. Like ... *me*? Man, this was too close for comfort! Okay, I had to do something to make this right! Get us back to the way it should be.

After a shake of the head, I relayed the conversation (well, except that, "Bye, Dix" bit) to Dylan. Neither of us was surprised that Brandy's stay at the behest of the City was a short-lived one. In fact, we'd been so sure that it would be, we'd abandoned the office after less than an hour of brainstorming to park where we were currently staked out. Ashfield Drive, just down the street from the Crotty house. About twenty minutes ago, I'd watched Lincoln Crotty drive his daughter home, and now ...

"There he goes."

At Dylan's words, we both slumped down in the seat as Lincoln Crotty drove back down Ashfield Drive. Yes, I knew it was him. Who could miss that humungous car and those wager-winning Crotty plates? But of course, now wasn't the time or place to tell Dylan he owed me oral sex.

"Yes, yes, I know," he said, reading the note I'd hastily written. "I still owe you oral sex." With a smile, he tucked it away in the inside pocket of his leather jacket.

I was quite sure the good doctor hadn't seen us, but I sure as hell got a good look at him. The expression on Lincoln Crotty's face was a blend of anger, worry and disbelief. And he drove just a little too fast.

Dylan and I straightened in our seats as he rounded the corner.

"Time to go," I said. My hand was already on the door handle.

"You sure you want to take this one, Dix?" Dylan asked. "You know Brandy's not exactly in your fan club."

"I have no doubt her father has told her who I really am and that I was hired to investigate the cuddle club. If we make the approach now, she'll expect it to come from me, the licensed PI."

"Yeah, you're right." Something in his voice made me look up at him. "She'd be more likely to talk to you than the lowly apprentice."

Oh shit. "I didn't mean it like that."

And I hadn't. It's just that I had the credentials on this one. Crap. Crap. Crap. I didn't want to hurt Dylan's feelings. But for now ... "I have to go."

I started to open the door, and would have jumped out, but Dylan grabbed my hand. I eased the door closed again.

"What?"

"I know you didn't mean it like that."

He reached across the console and pulled me close for a kiss. I was reaching for something else when the back door of the SUV jerked opened. I jumped like a horny teenager caught parking in the graveyard. (Come on, like you haven't parked at a graveyard? I mean, it's a perfectly normal place to make out, right?)

It was Brandy Crotty, and she parked herself in the back seat before slamming the door.

"Oh, Brandy. Fancy meeting you —"

"Cut the crap, Dix Dodd. You two have been watching the house ever since I got back. I know you're a PI — Dad told me. And he told me you were in the hospital snooping around. What the hell's going on?"

She'd been crying, and by the looks of her, ready to start crying again at any moment.

As much as Brandy was trying to play the hard-assed, in-control young woman, right now she looked like a frightened kid. And despite the snide remarks she'd thrown at me, the cutting glares she'd cut across various rooms, I felt sorry for her. I don't have a motherly bone in my body, but I really did feel for young Brandy just then.

"So what do you know?" Dylan turned in the seat to ask her.

"That Albert was murdered. And about the pheromones. The blackmail." She shook her head. "I ... I suspected the pheromones a few weeks ago. I mean, come on! Though, honestly, I didn't think they were affecting me. But Zoey and Eva ... kept wanting to go to cuddle club."

"Why did you go there in the first place?" I asked. (Seriously, I could not wrap my mind around that ... people voluntarily cuddling!)

"Zoey was taking some stupid anthropology class and for extra points she had to visit three different places where people gather and write a report. Eva and I just tagged along. So we went to a karaoke bar, a coffee house and — leave it to Zoey — the cuddle club."

"You went there purely for academic purposes?" Dylan asked.

"Yeah," she said. "Purely academic. Well, at first."

"Then what happened?" I asked.

"Eva happened. Man, she couldn't get enough of that club. She even started working there to pay for it. But, Jesus, it became an obsession with her. Or rather, it was an obsession before —"

Dylan and I exchanged a glance. Of course, Brandy saw that silent communication, which we didn't make any attempt to hide. I sort of expected her to rush in to fill the conversational pause with information, but she didn't. Clearly, she wasn't anxious to spill all.

So I prompted her. "That was before she found out you were having an affair with Albert Valentine."

"What the fuck?" Brandy just about hit the ceiling of the SUV. Literally. "What the *actual* fuck? You think I was screwing around with that hairy toad? Holy crap, Dix Dodd, you're not the quickest dick on the deck, are you?"

I wanted to say something about how quick dicks are overrated unless you have to get up early, but I didn't. Um, that could have been one of those metaphor things again.

Brandy (oh so eloquently) elaborated, "Albert Valentine was the most obnoxious man I've ever met. Pure jerk. Total troll. Piece of crap. If he were the last man on the planet, I'd switch teams."

"We know someone was having an affair with Albert," Dylan said. "If not you, then who?"

She bit her lower lip. Zoey. Or Eva. It had to be one or the other for her to go into protection mode. Brandy turned to gaze out the window into the night. She did not want to betray her friend, and so I wouldn't ask her too.

"It was Eva Mulligan, wasn't it?" I said.

Brandy's silence stretched. A moment too long to go into denial. And it was all that I needed for confirmation. That and the tears in her eyes.

"Eva was as innocent as the day is long. Trusting and sweet," she said softly, yet with an edge of anger. "We've been friends forever. Her mom came to work for us when Eva and I were both just five years old. She couldn't afford a sitter, so we just played together. Right away we were friends. And Eva's needed me. She's fought depression all her life. Been on medication for it for quite a while now. And honestly, it has done her wonders. That is …"

"Until powerful and potent pheromones were added to the mix."

"I won't break her confidences — but let's just say it wasn't a happy home life even after her father left. My parents saw how close we were, and they liked Eva, so they sent Eva to school with me — private school. Even now, they're helping with her tuition." Brandy's eyes filled with more tears now that she could hold back. "Eva's like a sister to me. And

Albert Valentine, that fucking bastard —"

I continued that thought for her. "And Albert Valentine used Gaetan's drugs to seduce Eva."

"Yes!" Brandy said. "Yes, he did."

"Why did you guys keep going back, after Albert took advantage of Eva?" Dylan asked. Then, as though hearing his words and thinking about how they might sound, he threw his hands up defensively. "And no, I'm not blaming the victim."

No, he wasn't. Neither of us were of that mindset, that it was the woman's fault for being there, or just being. And it drove us both nuts when we saw that mentality in the media. Albert was in the wrong, Eva was victimized. But I knew what he meant, how could she face that man again and not spit in his eye? Or better yet, push him down a well.

"I made her go," Brandy said. "You don't know Eva. She had to go back and face him or she'd crawl up in a ball and just … die. I had to push her to be strong. So I did."

"You must have wanted to kill Albert Valentine," I said, keeping my voice as even and cold as I could.

Brandy looked at me straight on. "Want to kill him? You bet. I wanted to kill him slowly and painfully. In my darkest fantasy, there were tweezers involved."

I could have helped her there, but I digress.

"But I'd never kill anyone," she said.

Her words confirmed what I'd felt all along. It was in her eyes and on her face and in her posture and every fiber of her being. She hated Albert Valentine, wanted him dead, but Brandy did not kill him.

"Ask me if I'm sorry he's dead, Dix Dodd," Brandy said.

"I don't have to; I think I know."

"Damn straight."

"The problem is," Dylan shifted in the seat as he slid back into the conversation "you had access to the Deleonex." He held up a hand before Brandy could protest, and profess her innocence again. "I believe you didn't kill Albert. But, Brandy, who else could have gotten to the drug?"

"Eva?" I suggested. "She could potentially have access to that drug. Gotten your mother's office keys. I assume she didn't take them with her on sabbatical." No, I didn't suspect Eva. But I wanted to raise that edge of protective anger in Brandy, so she'd let her guard down.

"That's ridiculous! Eva wouldn't have even known *what* she was looking for! Even if she did, she wouldn't know how to find it. Hell, I'm not even sure where to look! You think there's one big cabinet labeled *Old research stuff*?"

Well, okay, not anymore I didn't.

Brandy groaned her frustration. "Mom worked on Deleonex way back in '05 or '06. I knew about it like I know about all her research — we really are like-minded. But that stuff's been mothballed for years!"

I closed my eyes. Tightly. I swallowed hard.

"Dix?" Dylan said. "You okay."

I was more than okay. I was feeling it. The bang-on beat of it. And it pounded and it pounded — that intuition of mine. I knew. I knew as sure as I knew my own freakin' name, who killed Albert Valentine.

"You've got that look on your face," Dylan said.

I opened my eyes and looked at him. "Bet it matches your own."

"Yeah?"

"Yeah."

"Because we both know who killed Albert Valentine."

"Who?" Brandy asked. "Oh God, you gotta tell me."

"We will," I said. "Tonight. At a special meeting of the cuddle club."

And with that I grabbed my cell phone, and started calling that meeting.

Chapter 24

WE DIDN'T GET to call the cuddlers personally. Not even the most cooperative company would share its membership list with a PI, for obvious protection of privacy reasons. However, Babe agreed — with Gaetan's grudging consent — to make the calls for us. We told her to tell everyone that this wouldn't be your typical cuddle club meeting. (Of course, after the last one where Gaetan had his panic attack and revealed all about the pheromones, how could it be?) We further instructed her to tell them that if they wanted to know who killed our Albert — and possibly others — they should plan to attend to get a briefing from Dix Dodd, PI.

Suffice it to say, no one refused the invitation. Everyone would be showing up at Gaetan Land tonight.

Dickhead, however, was less enthusiastic.

"What the hell are you trying to pull?" he'd roared. "If there's something the police should know about —"

"Just show up," I'd said.

He would.

I was excited. I was so very pumped up. Not to mention thrilled that I didn't have to wear pajamas in public again.

Yeah, that's right. Dylan and I would get to dress normally this time. By which I mean we'd not be wearing those extra PJs that Dylan had picked up from Aunt Gert. Though I'd checked mine out — they were from Gert's Moonlight Nights collection and were made from a beautiful indigo satin. Yes, I was keeping them.

Dylan dropped me off at the condo, with an assurance that he'd pick me up on the way to the cuddle club later. (That settled it. I was getting wheels — pronto! No more borrowing from Rochelle or waiting on Dylan.)

So how to kill the time? What does any normal 40ish woman with time on her hands do?

Yeah, I laid down for a nap.

Well, I *lay* down anyway. And the longer I looked up at the ceiling, the more I knew sleep wasn't coming my way. And the more I knew what I had to do about Dylan.

It didn't take a dream. And it didn't take (just) Mrs. P strong talk. It didn't take just this case of Death by Cuddle Club where the young, handsome and sexy Dylan Foreman had pretended to be my boyfriend. It didn't take just his brilliant work on this case. It was all of those things.

My relationship with Dylan Foreman? It was about to change. It was changing.

I knew what I had to do. But no, that wasn't all. Damn it, I knew what I *wanted* to do.

But what would Dylan think?

"What's in the box?" Dylan asked. We were in the building, and walking down the hallway to Gaetan Land. Dylan was just now noticing the package I'd brought in from the car.

"Oh, just something I thought might come in handy later on."

Dylan was so focused on the scene to come he let it go at that. He glanced at his watch as we arrived at the door to Gaetan Land. "Eight minutes past eight o'clock. We told everyone to be here at eight, so ..."

"So chances are every one's been here for at least fifteen minutes. No one would want to be late tonight. And just think," I said. "We won't even be casting a cuddle."

Dylan and I had planned our arrival for just after eight bells just to make sure everyone that we'd called, had arrived. Also we were late just to make sure the tension and suspicion were running just that little bit higher.

"Ready?" Dylan asked.

"Oh yeah."

Dylan opened the door and we both walked through. I set the box of cookies down on the table by the door and we moved deeper into the room. We were greeted with the familiar low murmur of conversation, but as people realized my presence, one by one, a hush fell over the crowd. Eyes widened. And everyone was looking at me.

Correction. They were looking at *us*. Me and Dylan. I surveyed the room, slowly, thoroughly. Everyone presented and accounted for. "Thank you for coming," I said to the lot. "But then again, I didn't expect that any of you would miss such a jolly good show!"

"Jolly good?" Mabel cocked a hand to her ear. "Did she say jolly good? Why, I haven't heard that expression since I was a little girl back in London!" She looked at me. "Do you watch British TV?"

"No!"

"Oh," she nodded, thoughtfully. "Must be British porn then. I love that stuff too."

Okay, we all did a WTF double take on that (mine was with admiration).

"Can we just get on with this please?" Gaetan was close to shouting now. And not even trying to hide it.

Yes, not surprisingly, the guru of cuddle was out of the hospital. Looking alive, but like crap. He wasn't wearing his blond-cloud wig, nor his blue velour. He was wearing plain old tan dress pants and a very normal-looking Eddy Bauer button up shirt. And those hands were not clap-clap-clapping so much as fisting at his sides.

Babe was right beside him. But she wasn't jumping now as Gaetan spoke. Wasn't fretting. If anything she rolled her eyes at her big brother's outburst, and yeah, I was glad to see it. Maybe she was getting tired of his bullshit. By the looks on the faces of everyone else, they were getting pretty irate with Gaetan themselves. Without pheromones floating around, folks weren't so very enamored with the cuddle man.

Brandy was there on the other side of the cuddle floor, with one arm protectively around Eva. Zoey was close by, as was a hovering (not to mention angry-looking) Dr. Lincoln Crotty. Though Zoey seemed curious (and slightly perturbed) to be there, both Eva and Brandy spared me a hopeful smile. And no, I wasn't surprised that Brandy had filled Eva in on what was going on, given the powerful friendship between them.

Dickhead had an expectant look on his face. The guy knew me. Despite his earlier bluster, he knew I wouldn't have called this meeting unless I was onto something. As if waiting for the moment, Constable Leola Pivans came through the door behind Dylan and me just then, carrying reports. She quickly crossed the room and handed them to her boss.

I waited the nearly full minute it took for him to look the papers over. Then Detective Head nodded at me, with the slightest smile on his face.

No smoothies were being passed out tonight, and both Ruth-Ann and Starla leaned against the front counter as if not knowing what to do with themselves. The rest of the group — and that included a snuggled-up Elizabeth Bee and Hugh Drammen — occupied the various cozy, built-for-two chairs around the room. And sitting quite alone in one of those chairs built for two, was someone else I'd invited this night — Cathy Valentine, Albert's non-grieving widow. She looked like a million bucks in her designer pant suit, with her new jewelery gleaming.

And everyone, without exception, was looking at me. (And I wasn't even wearing my PJs!)

And I was liking this very much. So it started — my theme song playing in my head. (Weirdly, it was taking on a strange Benny Hill beat ...) This was the moment that I lived for. Oh yeah, big time. I was center stage, life of the party, queen of the PIs. Smartest person ever! Albert Finkelstein, eat your heart out! (I know what you're thinking, but no, I don't mean Albert Einstein. Einstein didn't defeat me in that grade-school spelling bee, did he?)

It was my time to shine, baby!

Except it wasn't. Not entirely.

It was Dylan's time to shine too.

"Go for it," I said to him. "You've earned it. We wouldn't be here without your work."

"You're the PI, Dix. This is your show. I'm just —"

"Just the one who cracked this thing wide open."

Dylan smiled at me. Okay, I gotta admit to it, as I stood there on the cuddle floor, his theme song was playing along with mine. Then he clicked off his cell phone and silenced that KOL tune. "Let's do it together," he said.

"Amen to that."

Dylan began. "By now you all know that Gaetan Gough has been using pheromones at this cuddle club of his. Putting the stuff into the air filters so that you'd have a nice pleasant feeling here. A feeling of arousal. Sexual arousal"

"Son, when my lawyers get through with you ..." Hugh Drammen was clearly addressing Gaetan.

"Oh, please, Mr. Drammen." Dr. Crotty's request was pleasantly sinister. "Let my lawyers take the first crack at him."

Both men nodded approvingly. How much those lawyers could actually do was yet to be seen, but I must confess I did enjoy seeing Gaetan squirm. But if Dylan and I had our way, he'd soon be squirming more.

"Well, before the lawyers get involved, I think we can all agree it was a pretty sleazy thing happening here at Gaetan Land," Dylan continued. "Filling the place with chemicals so you'd keep coming back, keep paying those outrageous fees."

"But that wasn't the biggest crime committed on these premises," I interjected. "Not by a long shot."

Dylan turned to Gaetan — or rather turned *on* him. (Okay, since that day Gaetan had insulted me, Dylan has wanted to let loose on the guy. And yeah, that gave me a warm fuzzy — I'll cop to it.) "Murder's the biggest crime committed here. Faynelle, Telly and Albert. Three heart-related deaths in such a short period of time? Dix and I were sure it was the pheromones. And we blamed you, Gaetan, for introducing those pheromones to this environment."

Gaetan looked as if he were about to have a panic attack all over again, or maybe this time he was heading for an actual coronary episode. "I didn't kill anyone!" he protested, looking around for help. His desperate stare shot to Starla, Ruth-Ann, and finally to Babe.

Babe turned her gaze away from big brother.

"No, Gaetan," Dylan said. "You didn't kill anyone. All you're guilty of is being an obnoxious and unscrupulous creep using chemicals to manipulate people without their consent or knowledge."

"Oh, yes! Christ, thank you!" Gaetan said. "Er, wait —"

Ah, there was Dylan's legal training! Hugh Drammen's and Lincoln Crotty's lawyers would have a field day with that admission.

"And then there was Babe," I said, before Gaetan could backpedal or go on the defensive.

"What about me?" Babe cried.

"Yes, the bullied little sister. All that pent up anger, all that frustration! It's not too much of a stretch to imagine you being responsible for the deaths at the cuddle club."

"That's ridiculous! If I were going to kill anyone …"

I finished that sentence before she could: "It would be Gaetan."

"I'd never do it, though." She gave an almost apologetic shrug. "He's my brother. As tyrannical and opportunistic as he can be, I could never kill him."

"Yeah, I know you didn't do it. You're not the killing kind."

"And, in fact," Dylan said. "We were wrong about the pheromones inducing those fatal cardiac events. They were potent — crazy potent — but not especially dangerous and certainly not deadly. Clearly, someone else wanted death to come to the cuddle club."

"But why would they?" Starla asked. There was an ache in her voice. "I mean, Faynelle was a sweetheart. Telly, just a quiet guy. Albert was …" Her words petered out as she glanced at Albert Valentine's widow.

"Albert was an asshole," Cathy Valentine said. "And everyone here knows it."

"Yes," I said. "They do. But none so much as you do, right, Cathy."

She looked at me steadily. Her eyes narrowed. "I believe you are right about that, Dix Dodd."

I'd explained to her on the phone that I wasn't a student, but actually a PI. Cathy Valentine had seemed more amused than annoyed. She still seemed amused, and not too damn concerned that I'd turned the pseudo-accusatory finger her way.

The only thing she was guilty of was relief. (And hey, that's no crime.)

"My husband was a controlling, manipulative, misogynistic bastard," Cathy said. "I know it, you know it —"

"Pfft, we all know it!" Ruth-Ann, interjected. She raised a hand hastily to her mouth as if to cover that ill-spoken thought. "I'm sorry, I don't usually blurt things out like that."

Everyone did look a little surprised by her outburst. Everyone that is, except for Dylan and me.

Dylan said, "Well, Ruth-Ann, Albert Valentine brought out the worst in a few of us. Not just you."

Ruth-Ann sent Dylan a grateful smile. She blinked. Looked at me and looked at all the other cuddlers. Her eyes settled on Eva Mulligan. "He … he really wasn't a very nice man."

"No, he wasn't," I said. "And that's why murder came to the cuddle club."

"What about Telly and Faynelle?" Babe asked. "They were … nice."

"Faynelle St. James's death was by natural causes," Detective Head interjected. He held up the papers Pivans had delivered to him. "Our labs ran tests. Multiple tests. Our Faynelle really did just have a heart attack. But Telly Smith and Albert Valentine … those two men were both murdered."

"How?" Eva asked, anxiously.

"They were given an overdose," Dylan said. "The toxicology tests missed it the first time because it's an experimental drug that never got past trials. Initially, it seemed like it had a lot of promise for impeding the growth of cancers, but all that promise evaporated in the animal trial stage when it was found to be associated with an extremely high rate of sudden cardiac arrest. It was being developed right here at Marport University by Dr. Janis Tascar-Crotty. And someone who had access to that research — to Deleonex — killed Albert and Telly."

Dr. Lincoln Crotty straightened and he absorbed that last part. "What the hell are you doing, Foreman? Are you accusing me of murder? Oh hell, are you accusing *my daughter*?"

"We're not accusing either of you," I said. With a nod I turned to Dylan.

And Dylan turned to Ruth-Ann. "We're accusing you."

The older woman straightened. She stood there silently for several minutes, saying not a word in either defense or denial. And then, finally, she sagged and asked one very simple question. "How did you know?"

I closed my eyes a moment. Straightened my thoughts. Mentally high-fived myself again.

"Why are you clapping, Dix?" Elizabeth asked.

Oops! Sometimes my mental high fives slip into reality. I lowered my hands to my sides.

"Professor Ruth-Ann Dale, you worked at the university," Dylan said. "Your specialty was bio-ethics, was it not? And you served on the Review Ethics Board in your last years there before your retirement, just about the time when Tascar-Crotty sought approvals for the Deleonex trials. From that position on the REB, you had to have known about the trials going south."

"Oh, my, yes," Ruth-Ann said. "The drug had unforeseen, wildly pro-arrhythmic properties that couldn't be mitigated. It was a huge disappointment." She sounded almost conversational. "But help me out here, young man — if nothing showed up in the initial tox panel, what made you pursue it further? What made you dig deeper to discover Deleonex?"

"That's a long story," I said. "Suffice to say our investigation moved in a certain direction which caused Dylan to remember a conversation he'd had with a bio-chem master's student who'd done a summer studentship with Dr. Tascar-Crotty."

"I see." Ruth-Ann's face looked perfectly peaceful as she digested that, except for a small furrow on her forehead. "And why did you connect it to me so quickly?"

"When Brandy told me this afternoon that the drug had been mothballed, I thought of you, Ruth-Ann. It slammed into place."

Ruth-Ann drew herself up. "Was that a comment about my age?"

"Of course it wasn't!"

Of course it was.

Dylan said, "You would have had access to the Deleonex. You would have known where such things were kept on campus, and since you have professor emeritus status and still teach the occasional ethics course, you can pretty much come and go without arousing undue suspicion."

"That's all?" The furrow in Ruth-Ann's brow deepened into an expression of bewilderment. "That's all that led you to me?"

"Not quite all," Dylan said. "There was something else. Something that I really didn't pick up on until later. When our Mabel misheard Dix, and said, *Of course he's been hugging us,* you retorted not with, *She said, he's been drugging us,* but with, *He's been drugging us.* You already knew about the pheromones. And you knew that they couldn't induce a heart attack. When Gaetan had his panic attack, you weren't the first to rush to his side."

"But wait," Starla said. "Ruth-Ann performed CPR on Albert! If she wanted to kill him, why would she try to revive him?"

"Why not?" Dickhead said. "She knew it was likely going to be a lost cause. Or maybe she figured if she did it poorly, it would prevent someone else from moving in and doing it more effectively."

Oh yeah, the guy was getting the picture. He gave an almost indiscernible nod to Pivans, and the young constable moved closer to Ruth-Ann.

"And don't forget access to Albert," I said. "You and Starla were passing out the smoothies on the night that Albert died. You slipped the Deleonex into his drink. And I'm guessing on the night Telly died, you were on smoothie duty then too."

Ruth-Ann closed her eyes. "Yes. I never meant to kill Telly. But somehow ... the drinks got mixed up." She sighed and opened her eyes. "That was very unfortunate. I ... I feel badly about that."

If she was looking for a there-there, she wasn't getting it from this crowd.

Constable Pivens removed her handcuffs and stepped up to Ruth-Ann. "Hands behind your back please, ma'am."

Ruth-Ann complied with Constable Pivans's direction.

Detective Head stepped in. "Ruth-Ann Dale, I'm placing you under arrest for the murders of Albert Valentine and Telly Smith." As the constable secured the bracelets on Ruth-Ann and Detective Head recited her rights, Ruth-Ann finally looked shaken.

"Why?" Eva said, her voice quiet. "Why did you do it? I mean ... you're an *ethicist*!"

Ruth-Ann offered a shaky smile. "He ... he wasn't a nice man. I saw the way he looked at you girls. And I saw ... more."

No more needed to be said.

Chapter 25

As Eva had pointed out, Ruth-Ann Dale was a really bad ethicist. I'm sure somewhere deep down inside her cool, logical brain, she felt completely justified in her actions. She'd rationalized what she'd done, viewed it as perfectly acceptable. Right. Just. Ethical. But really, to cuddle with strangers? That was just wrong, wrong, wrong!

Oh, and that whole murder/vengeance thing wasn't very ethical either.

We'd all been asked to go to the station. Although Ruth-Ann had essentially confessed in front of multiple witnesses, the authorities still wanted statements from all the cuddle club members. For me and Dylan, they were agreeable to our submitting our written reports within the next twenty-four hours. We could have left the station at that point, but we chose to hang around as the crowd slowly dissipated after each took his or her turn with a detective. Most everyone stopped to say something to us as they left, a few with tears in their eyes. Many with a grateful handshake. And Elizabeth Bee with a whispered message to me. ("Dix, I need to talk to you. I'll be in touch.") What was *that* all about?

Gaetan was cursing the day he ever set foot in Marport City, and yeah, I was betting the closed sign on the Gaetan Land door was a permanent thing. And I'm also betting that the cut-the-crap attitude Babe laid on Gaetan when he started in with her, was going to stick. She was already speaking about plans of her own.

Brandy surprised me with a hug on her way out the door. "Thanks so much, Dix."

Her father, Dr. Crotty, was in a corner of the room, talking to Eva. Even from the distance I could tell it was a good conversation. Eva was even smiling as her father figure dished out what had to be fatherly-advice.

When it was obvious that Brandy had something more to say, and that it was of the my-ears-only variety, Dylan excused himself. "I think Mabel needs a little help with her coat," he said. She didn't need it, but she'd revel in the gentlemanly assistance. This older woman was sweet on him too.

Brandy hesitated, chewed her bottom lip a moment, and then said. "Sorry I was such a bitch to you. I mean about your boyfriend and all ..."

There it was on the table. Yes, she let that sentence hang to see if I'd correct her. If I'd deny the relationship with a we-were-just-under-cover explanation.

"Apology accepted," I said. Then I nodded toward Eva. "You have a wonderful friend there, and you've been an amazing friend to her. Take care of each other."

"Thanks, Dix. We will."

While Dylan chatted away with Mabel and helped her into her coat; Lincoln Crotty, Eva, and Zoey said their farewells to me too as they left the station.

"Don't forget to turn up for that cardiac ultrasound," Dr. Crotty said. "Tell your doc to send you my way if there are any issues."

Oh, and then there was Detective Richard Head. I turned around, and there he was.

"Well, I guess we're just about ready to head out," I said to Head. "I'll be in touch about the bi —"

"You're welcome, Dix Dodd." Dickhead's words cut across mine before I could get the word 'bill' out there. "Glad the Marport PD could help you out with the case. Good call, calling me."

I did a double take, then saw that Constable Pivans was standing in Dickhead's wake. Again.

"Yes, it was a very good thing you called the detective in on this," Pivans said. The glance she sent Dickhead was clearly an admiring one. (Gag! I would have given the woman more credit. Of course, she didn't know the man quite like I did, so I cut her some slack.) "He tells me that you often ask for his expertise — his advice."

"Did he now?" I wanted to blast him for that, but we had a deal. I wouldn't blow his cover. Wouldn't give it away that *he* was the one who called *me* in, the one who'd been cuddling long before I darkened the doors of Gaetan Land. "Well, it's certainly true I've learned a lot from watching Detective Head."

Dickhead had the grace to blush at my veiled reference to busting him as a cheating spouse.

Yeah, we had a deal. But no one said I had to like it. And no one said I had to be nice about it either...

I smiled at Dickhead.

Dickhead smiled (a little sickly) at me.

I turned to Leola Pivans. "I cannot tell you how professional Richard's been through all this. And I must say, he blended in extremely well undercover. In fact, he was so concerned about maintaining that cover, he even agreed to take a turn on bringing in the treats!"

"Treats?" Pivans said. She was practically glowing with admiration for her senior officer now.

"Um, treats?" Dickhead's brown creased. "I don't —"

"I know — you left them at Gaetan Land. But I noticed them on the table and brought them along with me." I glanced at Constable Pivans again. "Can you believe it? I mean, with everything going on, I knew they wouldn't be serving the smoothies, but still our Richard thought to bring the snacks."

Dickhead cut in, "That's —"

"Right! I know." I retrieved the box from where I'd left it on the chair with my jacket and handed it to Dickhead. "So did you make cookies, like you said? You know, all frosted, with sprinkles? Oh, yum!"

His smile slowly returned. Yeah, the guy really thought I had brought him cookies. He winked, oh so subtly.

I gave him an equally subtle wink back. "They're homemade, aren't they?"

"Yeah, they are. My mother's special recipe." He started to open the box. And I put my hand on his to still that motion. "Why don't you take them to the staff room. Enjoy them with your coworkers." I left my hand right there on his until he chuckled, and agreed.

"The guys will love them, Detective," Pivans said.

Oh, I was guessing they would.

"Okay, I've gotta find Dylan and get out of here. Reports to write, you know."

"Of course," he said. "I'll be in touch."

Leola Pivans turned to walk away. Before Dickhead could walk away too, I did that pinkie/thumb phone thing and mouthed, "Call me."

He nodded.

Oh, I just bet he'd be calling... about ten seconds after his fellow officers poured their coffees and opened the package of penis-shaped cookies.

Epilogue

I T WAS MIDNIGHT by the time Dylan and I got back to the office. Yes, we could have gone to his place or mine or both (you know — him to his place, me to mine). Decisions, decisions. There were going to be awkward times ahead. Strange times. But, I wasn't running away from any of it.

And, hopefully, I was moving toward something else. That depended on Dylan. I was about to put forth what could very well be the best idea I'd ever had. Or the worst.

Time would definitely tell.

When I opened the office door, the red light was flashing on the phone. Without turning on the lights, I checked quickly, six messages — all from Dickhead. And I was betting each one was more creative and colorful than the last.

"What's that smile about?" Dylan closed the office door. There was just enough light from the hallway coming through the beveled glass window in the door for him to see my expression.

My smile faded. "Dylan, we need to talk. About us."

"Sure." He spoke without hesitation, but I could tell from his body language that he thought I meant our personal relationship, and that I was backing away from it.

Dylan tossed Blow-Up Betty behind the sofa and sat down beside me. "What's on your mind, Dix?"

"I . . . I'm your boss, Dylan. And well, this relationship we're having . . . this relationship we've started . . . There are all kinds of complications in this scenario. In this relationship. Well, the dynamics are . . . you know . . . wrong."

"Because you're the boss?"

"Exactly!"

"So you want to us to stop seeing each other, romantically. Even before we've really begun." He didn't raise his voice, but neither did he try to hide the frustration.

I didn't try to hide my grin. "Dylan, I want to propose —"

"Whoa, Dix! Isn't that a little extreme?"

I swatted him. "Let me finish. I want to *propose* that you stop working *for* me ... and start working *with* me. It would mean you'd effectively have to take a cut in pay. The hours ... man, they suck. Benefits? Well ... besides working with me, they're pretty much non-existent."

"So, what are you saying, Dix? My apprenticeship is complete?"

I nodded. "Yes. And I want you to be my partner."

Silence.

And the seconds ticked on.

Damn. He was going to say no. Going to say he had something else already lined up. Going to walk out that door.

"There's just one thing before I can accept," Dylan said.

Oh, thank God! He was going to accept. I released the pent up breath I hadn't even known I'd been holding. "What's your condition?"

"We have to be on a level field here if we're going to make this work. And I don't just mean the job, I mean the relationship."

He turned toward me on the couch, slid his hand into my hair until he was cupping my nape.

I shivered. My nipples hardened. "Of course."

His long, oh-so-talented fingers guided my head closer until the next words he spoke were almost against my lips. "We have to be equals in every way."

"I wouldn't have it any other way," I breathed.

He kissed me, long and dizzying.

"And we can have no debts between us," he said when he released me. The husky sound of his voice raised goose bumps on my skin. "Nothing ... owing."

Yeah, that wasn't just my intuition throbbing now as he urged me down on the couch. I knew what Dylan, my partner, my (oh boy!) boyfriend was referring to. Oh man, I knew what he was going to do.

"And right now, I owe you ... big time," he said.

"Can't have that," I said weakly, as his fingers undid my belt and worked the buttons and zipper on my pants.

Oh boy!

Thank you for investing the most valuable commodity you have — your time — in reading our book.
We hope we managed to make you laugh!

Word of mouth is the most powerful promotion any book can receive. If you enjoyed this book, please consider spreading the word. You can do this by recommending it to your friends, posting a review wherever you bought it, or reviewing it at Goodreads or other such places where readers gather, and mentioning it in social media.

Again, thank you!

N.L. Wilson
(aka Norah Wilson and Heather Doherty)

Other Dix Dodd Mysteries
The Case of the Flashing Fashion Queen (Book 1)
Family Jewels (Book 2)
Covering Her Assets (Book 4) — coming late 2013

Other books by the writing team of Wilson/Doherty
Young Adult/New Adult
The Summoning (Book 1 in the Gatekeepers Series)
Ashlyn's Radio
Comes the Night (Casters Series, Book 1)
Enter the Night (Casters Series, Book 2) — coming February 2013
Embrace the Night (Casters Series, Book 3) — coming Summer 2013
Forever the Night (Casters Series, Book 4) — coming Fall 2013
Read about the Casters series at http://castersthebooks.com

Available from Norah Wilson:
Romantic Suspense
Every Breath She Takes
Guarding Suzannah, *Book 1 in the Serve and Protect Series*
Saving Grace, *Book 2 in the Serve and Protect Series*
Protecting Paige, *Book 3 in the Serve and Protect Series*
Needing Nita, *a free novella in the Serve and Protect Series*
Paranormal Romance
The Merzetti Effect — A Vampire Romance (Book 1)
Nightfall — A Vampire Romance (Book 2)

About the Authors

NORAH WILSON is a Kindle best-selling author of romantic suspense and paranormal romance. She lives in Fredericton, New Brunswick, Canada, with her husband, two adult children, beloved Rotti-Lab mix Chloe, and kitty-come-lately Ruckus Virtute. (Yes, she has two names.)

HEATHER DOHERTY fell completely in love with writing while taking creative writing courses with Athabasca University. Motivated by her university success, and a life-long dream of becoming a novelist, she later enrolled in the Humber School for Writers. Her first literary novel was published in 2006. While still writing dark literary (as well as not-so-dark children's lit), she is beyond thrilled to be writing the Dix Dodd cozy mysteries and paranormal/horror with Norah. Heather lives in Fredericton, New Brunswick with her family.

Connect with Norah Online:
Twitter: http://twitter.com/norah_wilson
Facebook: http://www.facebook.com/NorahWilsonWrites
Goodreads: http://www.goodreads.com/
author/show/1361508.Norah_Wilson
Norah's Website: http://www.norahwilsonwrites.com
Email: norahwilsonwrites@gmail.com

Connect with Heather Online:
Facebook: http://www.facebook.com/heather.doherty.5
Email: heatherjaned@hotmail.com

www.ingramcontent.com/pod-product-compliance
Lightning Source LLC
Chambersburg PA
CBHW030251130626
46549CB00002B/485